# A STUDY IN SMOLDER

## FROST AND FIRE, BOOK TWO

Val Saintcrowe

Punk Rawk Books

**A STUDY IN SMOLDER**
© 2023 by Val Saintcrowe
www.vjchambers.com

Punk Rawk Books

All characters appearing in this work are fictitious. Any resemblance to real persons, living or dead, is purely coincidental.

All rights reserved. No part of this book may be used or reproduced in any manner whatsoever without written permission except in the case of brief quotations embodied in critical articles and reviews.

ISBN: 9798862454994
PRINTED IN THE UNITED STATES OF AMERICA

10 9 8 7 6 5 4 3 2 1

# A STUDY IN SMOLDER

FROST AND FIRE, BOOK TWO

Val Saintcrowe

# CHAPTER ONE

BANYAN THRICEBORN WAS in heat.

Or, not really.

Her *dragon* was in heat.

Actually, no. Her dragon was male, and he wasn't in heat, but when female dragons went into heat, it affected the male dragons—all of the male dragons—and it made them sexually excited. All of that traveled through the bond to the human riders who had bonded these dragons.

Which was why Banyan currently found herself in a room with two men who she was breathlessly begging to rip all her clothes off.

"Undo the *knot*," she said to Slate Nightwing, who was behind her, working the laces to her vest—she was bonded now; she should get a dragon-scale vest soon, shouldn't she? "Just get it off."

"Shh, you're all right," said Odion Naxim. He cupped her face with both of his hands and forced her to look into his yellow, reptilian eyes, which had elongated pupils. "We've got you. We're going to take care of you."

She tried to let her breathing regulate, but she was a bundle of need and desire. Her entire body felt like it was on fire. There was a rush of burning tingles around all of her sensitive areas. Her nipples, her mound, her entire pelvis. She needed relief, and she whimpered a plea to Odion, not words, just pathetic sounds.

Slate reached around her body, long fingers curling over her through her trousers. He splayed his palm out below her belly button and urged her backwards. Now, her ass was against him, and she could feel the pulsing hardness of his arousal there. He slid his fingers lower, deliberate, and then squeezed her entire mound, putting pressure everywhere.

She let out a mangled noise. *Perfect.* "Please," she cried out.

"That what you need?" whispered Slate in her ear.

"Yes, oh, yes," she said.

He squeezed and released and squeezed and released, and she writhed, mouth open in a silent scream. His movement made the burning better and worse all at the same time.

Suddenly, it concentrated, like a hole burning through her entire body, and her body exploded in a volley of clenches. She was having an orgasm, and no one had ever done that to her, no one except herself. Even when she was intimate with Odion, it always came down to her own fingers.

This...

It wasn't even... he wasn't touching her clitoris—well, he was, but it was through her clothes and her labia, and it was so indirect, and that shouldn't even *work*.

She sagged into Slate's chest, choking on air.

He gently patted her mound. "Shh. Better?"

She let out something like a sob. "Not really."

Odion kissed her mouth. "It's like that, yeah." He pulled away, smiling at her. "That was incredibly hot watching you fall apart like that."

Didn't he *mind* that it had been Slate to do that?

But, no, Odion and Slate had a history, and they'd had sex together without Banyan, and maybe she was intruding on them, not Slate intruding on her and Odion—and anyway, her dragon was bonded to Slate's dragon, and that was wrong. She was supposed to bond Odion's dragon. Everyone knew that she was supposed to do that. It was the plan. It was what the Quorum wanted for them.

Slate leaned over her shoulder and captured Odion's lips

with his own.

She sucked in breath, watching them kissing right next to her face. She should feel betrayed by that, right? Odion was hers, and she didn't want anyone else to have him. But... she... well, it must be the heat, because the kiss just made things inside her surge, pleasant things, overwhelming things...

Odion broke the kiss to look at her. "Sorry."

"N-no," she said. "I like it."

"You sure?" He brought his light lavender eyebrows together. They looked even lighter against his brown skin. "Because I know you didn't want this."

"None of us want this," countered Slate from behind her. "There." He'd undone the knot on her vest. "Lift your arms for me, Banyan."

She obeyed, liking this, being trapped between these two men—both very beautiful, admittedly. Slate was Aleenan, with light green skin, slanted eyes, slanted ears, and accents of deep red scales on his face to match his deep red hair. He had straight and pleasant features, broad shoulders, and strong hands. His voice was deep.

Odion was about the same height as Slate, and he was Hazain, thus the brown skin and purple hair, like all of his people. He was broader than Slate, and she was already in love with Odion. He was hers, and she was his, and she had never wanted to share him with anyone, but this—somehow—she didn't exactly mind.

Slate lifted her vest over her head. "None of us want any of this, really. Everything the heats do to us, it's a murky area of whether it's all against our will."

Odion raised his eyebrows. "What happened to, 'I chose you'?"

Slate shrugged. "You, I did choose. This? Her?"

Banyan turned to look at him.

Slate seized the hem of her shirt and tugged that up over her head too. Her breasts were bare now. Slate cupped one. His voice was gravelly. "I don't like you, Banyan, or did you forget that?"

She let out a little moan.

Odion tugged her away. "Don't be like that to her." He wrapped an arm around Banyan protectively.

Banyan pressed her bare breasts into Odion's clothes. Her breasts were tingling, and it was good and bad all at the same time. She rubbed herself into him.

"Hey," said Odion. "Your scales are coming in."

She drew back, horror splintering through her. She'd forgotten about that.

And when she drew back, she realized that was maybe why her nipples were tingling. Green scales — the same color as Erach, her dragon — were making little star patterns over her aureoles. She touched them, and a sizzle of goodness went through her.

It felt good, but… but… this was her *body*.

When a rider bonded a dragon, there were physical changes, like Odion's eyes, or Slate's scales. She knew it would happen to her, but she had never been exactly excited about it, and now, it was happening, and —

Odion rubbed his thumb over her cheekbone. "It's beautiful."

"It's on my face?" Her voice was squeak. She was still staring at her green-star covered nipples.

Odion chuckled gently, guiding her over to a mirror.

It wasn't much.

The scales went over her cheekbones, little bursts of green glitter there, shimmering in the lights. She had to admit that the color suited her coloring, that it matched the orangey-redness of her hair.

"Looks good," agreed Slate.

She glanced at him, unsure of what to do with him, how to take him. It was so confusing. Their dragons were mated, and she could feel him through the bond, was aware of him in a way that made her feel connected to him in a way she'd never felt connected to another human being.

But she felt his dislike through the bond too. Felt that, and felt that he wanted her, and felt that he was drawn to her, pulled to her like a magnet.

Her pussy let out a telltale tingle, and she let out a cry, fumbling with her trousers. She'd known it was likely that her genitals would get scaled. It was part of why the bond made the riders sterile, apparently.

But now, she pushed her trousers out of the way in a rush of awful dread.

At first, everything looked the same.

And then she realized her pubic hair—also orangey—was falling away.

She let out a groan.

She let her trousers fall and pool around her ankles and she brushed the hair away. Wisps of her hair detached and wafted slowly down to the floor.

She was all scaled there. Every bit of it. The green glimmering scales went up over her mound, coming together in a peak. And then they covered her labia and every aspect of her. She let out a funny noise, backing away to sit down on the bed and bend over to explore herself.

She wasn't sure how she felt about this. It was awful.

But...

Her fingers flicked through her scales—which were smooth and warm and much like skin, anyway, just green. And she was wet, lots of arousal seeping out of her scaled opening—Oh, Agnis and Ignia, did the scales go all the way *in?*—and everyplace she touched herself, it felt amazing.

Odion was on the floor, kneeling by the bed, eye level, grinning.

"You like it?" she said to him in a withering voice.

"*I* like it," said Slate thickly.

"You never saw it before it was like this," she said to him, glaring at him.

Slate sat down on the bed next to her. "Lie back?"

She started to protest, but the tingling seemed to rob her of her voice. So, she just did it. She lay back, letting her thighs fall open, displaying her body entirely to both of the men, who both moved in closer, heads crowding together.

Odion stroked her outer labia. "You're very glittery, Banyan."

She shivered. That felt amazing.

Slate's fingers traced little patterns over her mound. She tried not to make noise, but it came out anyway. "I think it's the most perfect little scaled pussy I've ever seen," he growled.

"Isn't it, though?" said Odion affectionately. His fingers found her clit.

She stiffened, letting out a mangled sound, shots of sweet goodness going all the way through her.

"Good girl," whispered Odion. He looked up at Slate. "She likes being called that."

*Not from Slate,* she wanted to say, but she couldn't say anything at all, because Odion's fingers were relentlessly petting her newly scaled clitoris, which seemed twenty times as sensitive as it had ever been before, and she was shooting off into pleasure, hitting the ceiling, bouncing around in the corners, panting, growing, bursting—

Fuck.

She jerked and spasmed against his fingers.

"Shit, Banyan," said Odion. "Look at you. You coming, pretty girl?"

She moaned.

"She's coming," said Slate softly. "Look how wet she's getting."

"Oh, good girl, Banyan, that's just what I like to see, my good girl getting so wet for me," said Odion. He yanked his shirt over his head. Now that she thought about it, why was she totally naked when both of them were clothed?

"Wet for *us*," said Slate darkly.

She turned to him.

He held her gaze, his dark reptilian eyes glittering and compelling. "Tell him, Banyan."

"Tell him what?" she breathed.

"Tell him you want me," said Slate.

"Good," said Odion, who was shedding his pants now. His own genitals were covered in scales—there were little ridges on the underside of his penis. "Because we're all going to have each other in a whole bunch of ways, and this is probably going to last *hours*."

"I..." She did want him. She just nodded, looking up at Slate and then at Odion. "Please?"

Odion spread her thighs and pushed his hardness into her, and she cried out. Odion gestured with his hands to Slate. "Show me," he said huskily. "I want to taste you."

Slate scooted up on the bed, so that his cock would be mouth level for Odion, and fumblingly undid his trousers.

Banyan was trying to deal with the way Odion's cock felt—better than it had ever felt before, and she didn't know *why* that was. Because of her new scales? The heat? Having had two orgasms already? He just seemed *right* there, a perfect fit, taking up all the space inside her in a very nice way, and she loved it.

But Banyan was also very interested in seeing Slate's cock, she found. She watched as it was revealed, a long, slender green cock, very curved, with a row of deep red scales running up from the based to the head and then bursting out from the tiny slit at the tip of it, like a little explosion of glittering red.

"Pretty," she couldn't help but whisper. She wanted to put it in her mouth too.

She'd still never put Odion's in her mouth. He wouldn't let her, for some stupid reason, even though he constantly put his mouth on her. He seemed to think that she would only be doing it out of obligation and he didn't seem to believe she wanted to do it.

Slate's hand was on her, reaching down, guiding her head towards him. "Go ahead."

"Wait, what are you doing?" protested Odion.

"She wants it." Slate's voice was husky.

She did want it, and she didn't need Slate to push her face down onto his pretty red-decorated cock. She took it eagerly into her mouth, gently swirling her tongue over the scales, and then sucking him deeper into her mouth.

Slate threw back his head, shutting his eyes. "Fuck, Banyan," he breathed. His hips canted upward, a half-thrust.

It gagged her.

She pulled off.

"Stop," said Odion darkly.

The gag had been overwhelming but not unpleasant. She remembered Odion explaining this to her, how you didn't mind pain and discomfort in heat, how it was good even when it was sort of bad.

Now, she put her mouth back, speaking around the hardness against her tongue. "Fuck me, Odion, please. Just fuck me?"

Odion gasped. He seized her hips, his cock snapping into her, deep inside her, piercing her.

She cried out.

And then she was lost to overwhelming sensation, two cocks taking up too much space in two places. She twisted to get a better angle on Slate's cock. He cupped her head, helping her, holding her in place, murmuring soft words of encouragement to her.

"You can't just use her like that," said Odion, who was out of breath, his cock slamming into her, harder with every thrust.

"She likes it," Slate said, his voice hoarse, his fingers gentle as he cupped her jaw. "Don't you, sweet Banyan, hmm? Just suck on that hard cock. It's got just what you need. That's it, take me nice and deep."

"Don't," whispered Odion, but his voice was affected. "Fuck, Banyan, *do* you like that?"

"Mmm," was all she could manage, her mouth too full, eagerly moving to take Slate down her throat. There was more gagging, and it was too much and just exactly right all at the same time, and her entire body was tingling, and Odion was big and huge and insistent as he pounded her pussy, and she was a rushing raging inferno, she was *molten*.

"She fucking loves it," said Slate in a ragged voice. "Great God Tan, through the *bond*, Odion…"

Odion made a wounded noise, fucking her harder. "Is that why, then? You want him because you're a mated fucking pair now? Slate, you know she's *mine*, don't you?"

"Shit, Odion, shit." Slate's eyes had rolled back in his

head.

"Mine." Odion's voice was even lower. "Banyan, look at me."

She did. She touched his chest, trying to tell him with her eyes that she agreed with him, that she was his, and that he was the one with his cock inside her pussy, and that he was the one she'd been destined for, and that this didn't mean anything…

But she didn't say any of that with her mouth, because she didn't want to spit out the frankly sort of *delicious* cock that was lodged in there, that was nudging itself down her throat, that was making her gag and every single gag made her whole body convulse and all of the convulsions made her already-stiff tipples twitch, made her very sensitive pussy clench. She gagged and then she clenched on Odion's cock. Didn't he like it, too?

"Yours, sure," said Slate in a low and lilting and ultimately *wicked* voice. "But she likes my cock a lot."

She moaned.

Slate pulled out of her mouth, running the tip of himself over her lips, over her chin. "Say it, Banyan, tell him."

"Give it back," she said, trying to recapture his cock, to get it back in her mouth.

"Fuck," moaned Odion. "Don't tease her, Slate, fuck her mouth just like she wants. Help her out."

Slate slipped back between her lips.

She moaned again, this time in pleasure.

"That good?" whispered Odion, finding an easier rhythm inside her, something less erratic. "You do like it?"

She moaned enthusiastically.

"Well… well…" Odion's strokes went deep and even. "I fucking love watching you suck him, Banyan. Fuck, you look beautiful like this, filled with both of us. You look *amazing*. I think it's going to make me come, actually. Can I come inside you?"

She moaned her assent.

"Will you take my come, like a good girl?" said Odion in a scratchy voice.

"Yes," she tried to say, but Slate's cock was choking her.

"Because you're mine," said Odion.

"She's yours, and she's got her mouth full of me," said Slate, who was gazing intently at Odion.

"Fuck you, Slate." Odion was grinning at the other man. "Fuck you, I'm going to make *your* mouth full of *me*, on your fucking knees, and make you beg for it."

"Promises, promises," crooned Slate.

"Shit," said Odion, and then he came.

Banyan had begun to feel as if she was just a toy they were using in some sort of tug-of-war, a sensation she did not find the least bit unpleasant, as disturbing as that was. She put her finger between her legs to stroke her own clit.

Slate fucked her mouth, and she felt her orgasm build up, and then it *burst*, sweet and wondrous. She clenched madly on Odion's softening cock, and only seconds later, Slate's salty semen filled her mouth.

They stayed connected for several moments before Slate extricated himself, flopping backwards on the bed.

Odion crawled over to him and kissed him.

Slate held the other man by the back of the neck. "I want you to watch me fuck her."

"Yes," said Odion.

They both turned to look at her.

She nodded, breath coming in gasps. "Yes, please."


ODION HAD HIS mouth on her nipple, and he liked the scales. He was rutting his hardness into her thigh, which was wrapped around Slate, who was buried inside her.

Again.

They'd done this very thing three or four times now.

They all liked it too much, and he wasn't sure where they were all going to be on the other side of it, especially because it was making him so hard to urge her to say things that he shouldn't be making her say.

"Tell me again how much you like his cock," he breathed into her skin.

She had her hand tangled Odion's hair, holding him against her breast. "It's so curved. It just rubs me right in this *spot*."

"You like it better than mine."

"Odion," she groaned.

"Say it," said Slate, his voice strained.

"Please, please, say it," said Odion. "Tell me you like him better, tell me his is bigger—"

"It's not," she moaned. "His is longer, yours is thicker, and I don't like—I want you again, and you—"

"Say it, just because it makes me fucking hot," said Odion in a grating voice. Because it did. He'd coaxed her into it at least twice now, and when she wouldn't say it, Slate obliged, assuring him he could tell through the bond that he satisfied her in a way that Odion never would, while Odion squeezed his own scaled and swollen dick while he spurted all over both of their skin.

"I do like it," said Banyan. "Just not better." She touched Slate's face. "Slate doesn't even like me."

"Yeah, I fucking hate you, clearly, and your sweet, tight, little green glittering pussy," Slate gasped. "I don't want to fuck this constantly, I don't feel like I'll never get *enough* of fucking you."

She threw back her head, grinding into the bed.

"Say it," urged Odion.

"His cock is bigger than yours," she whispered.

"Fuck," Odion muttered, jamming himself into her, poking her thigh with his erection, moving frantically against her.

"Better, Banyan," Slate said, staring at Odion, but snapping his hips hard against her. "My cock is *better* than his."

Banyan writhed. "What I'm going to need, boys, is more time to decide. More time with each of your cocks."

"Both of our cocks belong to you, Banyan," said Slate, turning to her, grinning. "But you like mine better."

Banyan just laughed.

"Say it," said Slate.

She gave him an impish grin. "No."

Slate grinned back, feral, and turned his attention entirely to her. "I'm going to fuck you so hard for that."

"No, not that," said Banyan in mock horror. "Anything but *that*."

Odion groaned, feeling his orgasm building inside him, his balls tightening. He rolled his head on his shoulders. "Fuck, you like fucking her, Slate?"

"You know I do," said Slate.

"You like fucking *my* girl."

"*Your* girl prefers my dick," said Slate.

"I don't," whispered Banyan.

"Yes, you do, pretty girl," soothed Slate. "Just lie there and take my cock, all right, Banyan? Take it and maybe touch your clit? You want to touch your clit?"

She put her fingers on herself. "You can't tell me what to do."

Slate grinned at her and then he grinned at Odion. "Both of you just begging for *someone* to tell you what to do, someone to take you over. Both of you so exhausted from being the best. But here, *I'm* the best, huh? I fuck her better than you. Odion Naxim, best at everything, but not here."

Odion shivered. Why was that so *good*? Why was it such a *relief*? "I'm going to come."

"No," said Slate. "Not allowed."

Odion let out a helpless laugh. As if there was any way that Slate could stop it.

Slate gave him a mischievous grin. "Beg."

Banyan let out a groan.

"You want him to beg, right?" Slate caressed her affectionately.

"Please, Slate, please," Odion said in a tattered voice.

"Fuck," moaned Banyan, licking her lips.

Odion's balls twitched. His ass clenched. He let out a keening cry and it burst out of him, and his cries were punctuated by Banyan, who was moaning about how good it was watching them touch each other, how much she liked it, and how much it was making her come, too.

"Kiss," whined Banyan. "Kiss each other again, please. I want to watch you kiss while I'm coming."

"Anything for you, Banyan," said Slate.

"Yes," Odion gasped.

So, they kissed for her.

And Slate came, filling Banyan's already full pussy of even more of his spend. And then they were all lying together on the bed, and there was more kissing. They were kissing Banyan and kissing each other and she was holding onto them and all of them were moaning, and it was *so* good.

Slate flung an arm over his face. "Might be wearing off?"

"Thank the elemental forces," Odion groaned.

"The heat?" said Banyan.

Odion kissed her lips. "Yes, sweet girl."

"Good," she breathed.

Fuck.

What had they done to her, including her in this perverse joining? What would she think of him on the other side of this? And why had he enjoyed watching her be taken by another man so very fucking much?

He clung to her. "You think you can sleep?"

"Mmm," she muttered.

Slate rested his head on one of her breasts.

She wound an arm around Slate, clutching him close as well. "My boys," she breathed, shutting her eyes.

# CHAPTER TWO

BANYAN WOKE UP to one of the bells ringing. She didn't know which bell it was. There were bells that rang all during the day at the Academy. The first one rang before the sun even came up, and they kept ringing until long after the sun had gone down.

She turned, her body aching, all of it aching, her nipples throbbing, sore and sticky between her legs—how many times had they mounted her, between the two of them? *So* many times.

They were both there, wrapped around her, warm and close and smelling of their co-mingled scents, all of them part of each other.

She let out a little sigh, because she wasn't actually displeased to be here like this with them both. Maybe she should be, because she was uncomfortable. She was aching and sore. She was—wow, she was covered in a lot of gross fluids...

She wanted a bath.

One long, long, very hot bath.

Maybe two, where she got out of one soiled tub of water and climbed into a clean one halfway through the experience.

She groaned.

But, no, she wasn't displeased at all. It all seemed worth it, *utterly* worth it, the most exciting and intense experience of her entire life.

Odion's hands roamed sleepily over her curves.

Slate pressed himself into her body.

They both hummed, sounding happy and pleased.

She sagged into them both, sighing again.

Time passed. She dozed in and out dreams that barely lasted any time and she forgot right away. But she woke now and then.

And then the door was opening, and there was a torch and someone was tossing a blanket over their bodies.

"Baths, soldiers. First level, waiting for all three of you. You have exactly one hour to be bathed and dressed and in my office." It was the voice of Colonel Rabi, who was one of the senior members of the Quorum. He was in charge of the Academy.

And he'd just seen her naked.

She should be outraged, really, but at this point... the entire experience had wrenched a great deal away from her. She didn't know if she'd ever be ashamed in the way she used to be.

"Good morning to you, too, sir," said Slate in an amused voice.

"I think I ordered you to leave the school, Rider Nightwing," said the colonel mildly. "If you had, things wouldn't be nearly as utterly fucked sideways as they are."

Slate huffed.

"*Baths,*" said the colonel. "You all smell disgusting."

The colonel and his torch retreated, and the door shut on them, closing them away in darkness.

For a moment, none of them moved or spoke.

"Well, maybe it's a mercy," said Slate, getting out of bed. "It was just going to be awkward, anyway. Now, we have to rush to get to his office and we don't have time to talk."

"Nothing to talk about," said Odion, crawling out of bed, too.

Nothing to talk about? She shook her head at both of them. On the other hand, what would she say, really?

"MUCH BETTER," SAID Colonel Rabi.
Banyan looked up at him, and his smile didn't meet his eyes. But then, maybe it never did. This man was never genuine. He was always playing some kind of head game or other. She didn't know what to make of him.
"Well, sit down." The colonel gestured to three seats that were set up facing his desk.
Banyan, Slate, and Odion shuffled in and sat down in them.
The colonel let out a heavy sigh. "I don't need to tell you what a disaster this is."
"I know male dragons sometimes leave their mates," said Slate.
"Rarely, very rarely," said the colonel.
"It happens, though," said Slate. "I know exactly what you're going to do. You're going to send her dragon off with Mirra and some other female dragon who's going into heat, and you're going to trigger Mirra's heat until Banyan's dragon—"
"Erach," supplied Banyan.
"You're not allowed to name the dragon yourself," said the colonel. "Because people tend to name the dragons names already in use, and that becomes confusing, and it's best if you let the Quorum look at the master list of dragon names and—"
"I didn't name him," said Banyan. "He told me his name."
They all looked at her now.
"What?" said Banyan.
"They can't do that," said Odion quietly. "They don't think in words."
"Erach does," said Banyan, looking back and forth between Odion and Slate and then to the colonel. "Well, not all words. He showed me a lot of images, but he definitely thought the word 'together,' as in, him and me, together. He

thinks we're going to defeat the Frost."

"We've never seen this dragon before, Banyan," said the colonel. "We keep tabs on dragons who we like to incorporate into the Academy, and this one is young and impetuous and unknown to us. Now, honestly, I was going to suggest he be killed."

"*What?*" This went through Banyan like a knife to her temple. She was on her feet. "You won't touch him." Her nostrils flared. Her hands were clenched in fists.

"Well, that bond is unfortunately more established than I'd hoped," sighed the colonel. "Sit down, Banyan, please."

"No," she snarled. "If you hurt Erach, I will *kill* you, sir."

"Noted, now sit," snapped the colonel.

She was shaking. She tried to gather herself. Felt confused. Eventually, she sat down. She was still shaking.

Odion took her hand and squeezed it.

"Well, that was too easy, anyway," said the colonel, rubbing his forehead. He nodded at Slate. "It's probably as you were saying, what we'll have to do, then. Send her dragon and Mirra off."

"Erach," she insisted.

"Dragons don't name themselves," said the colonel.

"Well, clearly my dragon is special," she said.

The colonel tilted his head to one side. Then he let out a helpless laugh. He slumped into his chair, looking up at the ceiling, laughing and laughing. "Yes," he managed finally. "Clearly. Your dragon is special."

"I'm sorry," she said. "Honestly, I'm confused. I'm confused about..." She glanced at Slate. "About so many things right now." She cast her gaze down at her hands, folding them together in her lap.

"Of course you are," said Odion, rubbing her shoulder. "Colonel, maybe she should just go on her break early. It's what? Next week? Send her home, let her have a little time to herself—"

"You want to send me away?" said Banyan to Odion.

He touched her face. "No, no, Banyan, no. I don't want to be separated from you at all, but you should probably have some space for a bit, after we… after there was so much invasive, er, penetration." He dropped his hand, looking off into the distance. "And this is to say nothing of what happened with Javor—"

"I thought you agreed never to mention him again!" she said.

"Javor?" said Slate.

"The man who tried to rape her," said Odion.

"Nothing happened," she snapped.

"Which isn't healthy, how you won't ever even *think* about it—"

"Why would I want to think about it?" she demanded.

"*Silence*," said the colonel in a low and lethal voice.

They all bowed their heads.

"You all sound like a pack of children," said the colonel. "And I know you're young, but you are all grown, you are all soldiers, and we are fighting a *war* here."

All three of them were quiet.

"We've always assumed it would be Odion and Banyan bonded to a mated alpha pair," said the colonel. "So, we need to try to rectify that. And as soon as possible. No trips home for anyone. Nothing is as important as this. While you're gone, Odion, you can be teaching her the basics of shooting bows and arrows. The minute we get this sorted, you two will be inserted back into the skirmishes here, but in the dragon corps."

"We're fighting skirmishes?" said Odion.

"Yes," said the colonel. "You're technically still a student, Odion, and you should be in the skirmishes. But we need to get your dragons mated first." He turned on Slate. "As for you, you have your orders, don't you, soldier?"

"Oh, yes, sir," said Slate. "Back to the watchtower for me with a new batch of body fodder, even though I told you that we are playing into the Frost's hands by staffing these watchtowers."

"We can't leave the villages unguarded."

"The villages don't have dragons," said Slate. "At least, if the Frost takes the villagers, it doesn't get new ice dragons."

"Well, don't let the Frost take the watchtower this time," said the colonel. "Fight it off, Major Nightwing."

Slate stiffened.

"Yes, you've just been promoted. You're in charge of the watchtower," said Colonel Rabi.

"In charge," said Slate. "My dragon isn't even mated. I'm not in a bask. You... you... *Major?*"

"Dismissed, major," said the colonel, sighing.

Slate's lips parted. His jaw worked for several minutes. Then he stood up, saluted, and walked stiffly out of the room.

Banyan wanted to reach for him. He couldn't just *go*. He was her... their dragons were... she could *feel him* through her bond. She let out a shaky breath.

"All right," said the colonel. "It'll take me some time to get things set up. For now, you may return to Odion's room if you wish. I'm sure you two have much to discuss. Been a lot of new experiences for you both. You're dismissed as well."

Out in the hallway, she wanted to go after Slate. She could feel him. She could tell he was going up the steps, climbing towards the top of the tower to the landing area where he would fly off with his dragon.

"We need to go to Slate," she breathed.

Odion's eyebrows raised.

She flinched. No, maybe not. Maybe she was hurting Odion saying that. "Or... no. We have our orders, I suppose."

"You sure?" said Odion.

She nodded. "Positive." She tried to smile. It didn't work.

They went back to Odion's room, which had been cleaned, though she didn't know by whom, because usually, it was the job of any student to clean their own rooms and sheets. She was glad of it, just the same. They both lay down on his bed, on top of the covers, right next to each other. They didn't touch. They stared at the ceiling.

It was quiet.

Odion eventually spoke. "H-how are you?"

"Fine," she said quickly.

"Sore?"

"A little."

"That's normal," he said.

"Are you sore?"

"Sure."

More silence.

"I'm sorry," he said finally. "I'm sorry I just… gave you to him like that."

"Is that how it happened?" she breathed.

"You did like it," he muttered. "But in heat… you… you like things."

"Yeah," she said. "I'm understanding that now, I think."

"I'm sorry," he said again.

"It's not your fault," she said. *What happens to Slate now? Will we see him again? Will we fuck him again?*

She couldn't ask those questions. She didn't even know why she wanted to. Shouldn't she want things perfectly settled between her and Odion? Slate was a problem, an obstacle. She and Odion were endgame. This…

"Maybe when it's just us," he said, "it won't be like that, anyway."

"I'm sure it won't," she said. It would be entirely different.

"You always like me to be… in charge," he said. "And that's how I… What *he* does to me, I'm not into that, not really. It's just him. Slate. I'd never ask you to…"

"To what?"

"Nothing."

She rolled over on her side. "I could take charge of you sometimes, if you want. We could switch off. If it's good for you, I want—"

"No, that's not what I'm saying."

She blinked at him. "It's because he's a man and I'm not? Because he can fuck you?" Not that they'd done that, which she'd found kind of disappointing, to be very honest. She'd wanted to watch them put their cocks in each other's asses, but then she'd wanted every perversity she could think of when the heat had been riding her. She would have let one of them put it in *her* ass. She'd thought about that, being sandwiched between them, full of them both like that.

"I don't..." Odion shook his head.

"Well, maybe in heat," she said.

"Let's just... we don't have to talk about..."

"Yeah, I guess it is embarrassing," she said in a low voice, turning away from him.

"I don't want you to see me differently," he said.

"I don't," she lied. Because of course she saw him differently. They'd all been stripped entirely bare to each other. Each of them had shamelessly begged the other two to please them, revealing shameful fantasies and desires, and they'd all been very vulnerable with each other. At the time, it had seemed heady and good, pulling them all together, but now it only seemed sordid and horrid. "It's like you said, we don't have to talk about it."

# CHAPTER THREE

LATER, BANYAN WENT back to her room to gather her things, but they weren't there, of course. Someone had already packed everything up. Raini told her that two men had come in and chucked everything into a bag. It wasn't as if Banyan had a lot of possessions. They didn't allow such things here at the Academy. They were soldiers. They had three changes of uniform and she'd had a whistle as a capitan of her bask, but that was around Raini's neck now.

"They promoted you?" said Banyan to Raini.

Raini nodded. "And they sent Gelso off to bond a dragon. He's moving up to dragon corps. I heard it happened to ten others from various basks."

"But that's ahead of schedule, moving people up. Six months earlier than it should happen."

"Right," said Raini. "And I guess, since you're Banyan Thriceborn, you know why all this is happening."

"We don't know. We're guessing," said Banyan. "Odion says that he thinks the Frost is coming here. That we students are going to be the last hope of defeating it."

Raini drew back. "But that would mean…? Where would the army be? All of the graduates of the school who are out there? Dead?"

Banyan nodded.

"What did you see out there? Is it bad?"

"It turns us," said Banyan. This was some sort of secret,

and she knew she was probably supposed to keep the secret, but she was done keeping secrets for the Quorum, especially when the Quorum wouldn't explain to her why the secrets needed to be kept. "It infects us and makes us into monsters. That's what the ice monsters are. People—riders—who are nothing but rage and fight and who try to bite and infect and spread the Frost. And it can get dragons too, and they breathe this icy wall of air that freezes everything and makes clouds of..." Banyan gestured, trying to explain this.

Raini's eyes were the size of tea cup saucers.

"Should I not have told you?" Banyan whispered.

"I don't think I'll tell anyone else," said Raini. "If cadets knew this, they'd leave. It's too dangerous, Banyan."

"Maybe they wouldn't. You're not leaving."

"I don't know," said Raini quietly.

"Raini, you're not. We need you. You're good. You can fight, and—"

"How do we fight against something that takes us over?" said Raini.

"I don't know," Banyan had to admit.

"I volunteered for this because I knew I could never be a farmer's wife," said Raini. "Or a blacksmith's wife or a tavern owner's wife or—I don't like men, so I thought this was perfect for me. But I was hoping to live to see thirty years old, you know?"

Banyan gave her a wry smile. "I do know." She reached out and took Raini's hand in hers.

The other woman jerked. It was rare for the soldiers to touch each other in that way.

"If we don't do this, no one sees thirty," said Banyan. "The Frost will turn every man, woman, child, and creature, and we'll cease to exist."

Raini let out a shaky breath. "Puts it in perspective."

Banyan squeezed the other woman's hand.

Raini squeezed back.

And then Banyan left her, wandering aimlessly through the school, and she felt angry, because this was the way, always the way. She connected with people, she found a place in the school, and then the Quorum ripped it away. She never got to be comfortable or really form connections.

Just with Odion, that was.

It would be handy if she could feel him through her bond, but she couldn't.

She could feel Erach, who was evading men in Academy uniforms who were trying to get an iron shackle around one of his legs. He found that amusing.

She could feel Slate, too, but he was distant now, too distant for her to quite make out where he was or what he was doing. She could feel a hint of his emotions—he was feeling determined and a little frustrated. She could feel his dragon, Yilia, who was with him.

She went to the library.

Dove was there. She was what was called a scholar, which meant that she worked in both the library with the books, the healing wing, and with writing down the events of what was happening for records. Scholars would specialize upon graduation, but Dove was still training so she did rotations in each of the disciplines.

"You look amazing," said Dove, coming over to touch Banyan's green scales. Then, seemingly realizing what she was doing, Dove pulled back. "Oh, apologies, I shouldn't have touched you without asking."

Banyan hadn't minded. "It's all right."

"I wanted to be a dragon rider, but I didn't qualify," said Dove. She was Hazain. The Academy was in Hazai, and it was only recently, when the threat of the Frost had intensified with the appearance of the ice monsters, that the Academy had included others from other Trinal Kingdoms—Noch and Aleen. In Hazai, every third-born child was sent to riders. Many were rejected, but if you were a third-born child, you had no choice but to give yourself to the Quorum.

"You were the third child in your family?" said Banyan.

Dove nodded. "I got absorbed into the scholars instead of the dragon side of the school. I'm good at being a scholar, but I'm sad never to bond a dragon, never to fly."

"I'll take you flying sometime," said Banyan.

Dove grinned. "Really?"

Banyan nodded.

Then Dove's grin faded. "There's no time for things like that."

"Don't you get to go home for the midterm break?" said Banyan.

Dove shrugged. "I suppose. It's not really my home. I never grew up there. I visit twice a year, and I always feel like a stranger. They're proud of me, but they also see me as evidence of the oppression of the Quorum. They resent the fact the Quorum takes their children and they have no recourse. My presence opens up this smoldering resentment in them."

"I guess I understand that," said Banyan. "But it would be a time you could ride. Except I'm not going to be on break. I have to go off with Odion and try to get our dragons mated."

"Yeah, I heard something about that," said Dove. "And your dragon is some new dragon no one's ever seen before?"

"My dragon is special," said Banyan, sure this was true. "Actually, that's why I'm here. I was wondering if there were books about the dragons? My dragon thinks in words."

"What? Dragons are animals. They don't talk."

"All right, well, mine does, and I was hoping there might be something about dragon communication?"

Dove tapped her lower lip. "There are dragon books. Not on communication, really, I guess, but everything else. Reproduction, basks, flight patterns—"

"All things I've studied, in other words," said Banyan. "Well, show me where they are. Let's see what I can find out."

Dove did, and Banyan spent the next several hours pouring over books, paging through them, looking for information.

But—as Dove had said—there wasn't much of anything about dragon communication. There were discussions of the bond altering rider's temperaments, though, as if they were taking on a disposition that mirrored their dragon's, and she found that fascinating. At first, she thought that this tended to fly in the face of the idea that dragons were animals, but then she realized that animals did have dispositions.

Growing up on a farm, there were a number of cats that settled in the area to eat rodents and spend lazy afternoons curled up either in the sun or on one of the Thriceborn children's laps. She had noted that some cats would hide at the approach of any human and some were curious. Some were imperious and some were lovable. Cats had dispositions, it was quite true.

The same could be said for the dogs that helped to herd the sheep and cows on the farms. Some were friendlier than others. Some were lazier than others.

Erach's mind caressed hers, from afar, affectionate.

It went through her like an embrace. She felt a rush of pleasure and happiness at his closeness and connection.

*My dragon*, she thought.

Suddenly, she wanted to go to him.

She shut the book and stood up.

Then she opened the book back up and sat down again. She reread what she'd just read, trying to process it. Really? That was what it said? She read it again.

Yes, apparently, a male dragon had mated to more than one female. She hadn't known that was possible.

*That's not what you want,* she scolded herself. She took a deep breath. *I want Odion and only Odion.*

Whatever connection that Odion and Slate had, it was clearly strained anyway. They were competitive with each other. Slate was dismissive toward Odion, and she didn't even understand that bit he did where he taunted the size of Odion's cock, because, well, it was ridiculous.

She had seen exactly three erect cocks in her life, but they'd all been roughly about the same size. Certainly none of the men she'd been intimate with had a penis big enough to warrant the idea it was abnormally large. Of course, she knew this was a thing that men cared about.

To her thinking, it couldn't really be about female

pleasure, however.

Odion's cock was rather nicely thick, had a bit of girth to it, which she thought contributed to pleasure. But there was Slate, with that wicked little curve to his cock, which meant that when he was inside her, he was dragging against that sensitive place inside her, right behind her belly button, and it was very, very good.

But men never much talked about girth or curvature.

This was probably because they had never asked women what sort of cocks were superior. And women probably didn't volunteer this information to the men they loved, because, well, when you loved a man, things like that mattered less. You didn't fall in love with a man because of the shape of his cock. If it was nice, that was a bonus, but it wasn't that important in the grand scheme of things.

And mostly it wasn't important, Banyan thought, because they were all basically about the same size.

Men.

On the other hand, she couldn't say she was entirely displeased by the competitive aspect either. It seemed to stir her in some way she couldn't quite explain, two men wanting her, two men competing to please her? There were things about that she couldn't help but like.

She sighed and closed the book again. She put the books back on the cart to be reshelved (she'd tried to reshelve the books herself once and gotten a stern talking-to from Dove about how it was best to leave such things to the librarians, because it was more complicated than Banyan could *understand*) and then she climbed up the stairs all the way to the top of the landing tower, where Erach was circling above, waiting for her.

She grinned up at him, her heart surging with the feeling of connection to him.

"Good," came the voice of Colonel Rabi, who was coming up the stairs onto the landing area. "He comes to you, anyway."

Banyan turned to look at him. "Sir?"

The colonel dropped a bag on the ground at her feet.

"You fly your dragon and follow Odion and Mirra, and we'll have this cleared up in no time, hopefully. We're sending you out somewhere that you can be alone, which we hope the two of you appreciate. And the minute the mating is accomplished, you're expected to report back here."

"Yes, sir." A pause. "What happens to Yilia?"

"Yilia? Oh, Major Nightwing's dragon," said the colonel. "Well, she'll be mated soon, we hope."

A surge came through the bond at the mention of Yilia, from Erach. It was a mixture of adoration and sexual attraction and possessiveness. It was intense. Banyan swallowed. "What if, um, what if Erach doesn't want to give her up?"

"Ah, Erach," said the colonel. "We know why your dragon has a name. He's the only surviving member of a bask that was guarding the south quadrant of Noch. He hadn't yet bonded to a rider, but he was born there, and he was coddled and loved by the riders, and they named him. He can't talk, but he probably heard the name. Dragons learn their names. Elemental forces, *dogs* know their names. Your dragon is not special."

She bristled at this. *Is too,* she thought. But maybe she was simply vain and used to being special and different. It was strange, because she resented it and craved it all at the same time. She longed to be just like everyone else, but she probably wouldn't give this up if given the chance.

She was so consumed with these thoughts that she didn't realize that the colonel had not answered her question.

What happened if Erach would not give up Yilia?

Dragons might be animals, but it would be foolish to think that dragons had no choice when it came to mating, wouldn't it?

On the other hand, maybe that was exactly what the heat was, the eradication of choice.

She hadn't *chosen* to be with two men.

However, the comparison that Odion had tried to draw, to Javor's attempt to force her, it wasn't even remotely the same.

And she thought, even if she'd been in heat, even if she'd had that agonizing desire writhing under her skin, making her burn from the inside out, and there had only been Javor, she thought...

She'd still have fought him off.

Never with Javor.

So, it wasn't choice, and yet it wasn't refusal, either. She hadn't been violated, not exactly. She felt confused, but not as if violence had been done to her.

At that moment, Odion appeared on the top of the landing tower. He grinned at her, and she found herself smiling back. He closed the distance between them, addressing the colonel. "Sir, where are we headed?"

"Fort Tillian," replied Colonel Rabi.

Odion stiffened. "Fort Tillian," he repeated in a wooden voice.

The colonel's mouth curved—almost a smile, but a cruel one. "Problem, soldier?"

"No, sir."

"See to your dragons, if you don't mind," said the colonel. "Get them to mate."

"We'll do everything we can," said Odion.

"Do not come back here until it's done," said the colonel. "Understood?"

"Yes, sir," said Odion.

"Yes, sir," said Banyan.


ODION CIRCLED THE watchtower on Mirra's back, stroking her flank, shaking his head. It had taken everything within him not to react when the colonel had told him where he was sending them. What was wrong with that man? Why had he done this?

He probably had some reason for it, and it probably was because he thought it would make Mirra more emotional, more likely to go into heat, more likely to be taken, Odion didn't know.

When they landed on the landing tower, Mirra was antsy, and she took off again. The other female dragon who'd come along, the one who wasn't bonded and who was due for her heat imminently, flew off as well, following behind Mirra.

Banyan was stroking her dragon, the green shimmering Erach, looking deeply into his eyes as if she and the dragon were having some kind of conversation. Odion wondered if she did have a special dragon, one that was smarter than the others. He supposed that it would make sense, if so. Banyan was next-level good at everything she put her mind to.

Mostly, he enjoyed it, but sometimes, he couldn't help but feel threatened, just a little. He was only human, in the end.

He had sworn to himself he would never be resentful about it and that he would never ask her not to threaten him. He would embrace the challenge of the threat—let it make him better. Either because he learned the grace of defeat or because it helped him rise to the challenge and improve.

The way of it was this: only one person could ever be the best.

That was how the definition of best worked, after all.

He wanted it to be Banyan, not him, anyway. She deserved it.

He waited, watching her with Erach, and then eventually, the dragon flew off. Banyan shrugged at him. "He doesn't want to do it."

"He told you that?" said Odion.

"He says… it was hard to understand," she said, "because it was all kind of pictures and ideas and a swirl of emotions, but I think the gist of it is that Mirra is too young, and he feels wrong about taking her before she's mature."

Odion nodded. "She is young. I bonded an established bask." This was typical, after all, to bond young riders to the young offspring of older alphas. The young dragons were able to stay at the school, out of relative danger, and they could train. Both their dragon parents and the Academy benefited from the arrangement. "She was very young, though, and I think they did that to me because they wanted to give me a challenge. They were always trying to stack the odds against me, just like they're always doing that to you."

"I've noticed," said Banyan.

"Besides," said Odion. "This is where it happened."

"Where what happened?"

"Where her family died," said Odion. "Where the riders all bonded to her mother and father and brothers all died."

Banyan's eyes widened. "But why would the colonel send us here?"

Odion ran a hand through his hair, looking off into the distance, remembering the ice clouds on the horizon, the ice dragons flapping through the white sky, the way it had all gone so quickly, the way he and Mirra had barely even escaped.

"He's horrible," said Banyan. "I hate him."

"Me too," said Odion. "But I think he does that by design. It's all part of their plan, their games, all of it."

She shook her head. She was furious, and he could see the way the fury made her jaw clench, made her body stiff. "Doesn't make any sense. It's almost as if he's working against us. Doesn't he want us to be mated?"

Odion turned to look at her, furrowing his brow. Hmm. That was definitely something to be considered. He shook his head. "You think... he's using the Slate thing against us?"

"Could it be another challenge?" she said. "Some other way to make us stronger in whatever disturbed way the Quorum thinks to hone us?"

"He said not to come back until it was done," said Odion. "So, if he really doesn't want us to do it, he's playing a very strange game with both of us."

"Yeah, why would he say that?" She crossed her arms over her chest, staring off into the distance, shaking her head.

"What should we do? Waste time trying to understand Colonel Rabi or try to figure out what we should do here?" muttered Odion.

She turned on him. "Are they dead or changed?"

Odion's face fell. "I don't know. We didn't stay to watch and see if they got back up. But the Frost…"

"It's likely, then," she said. "That they'll come back, that we'll have to fight them. That's why we're here, Odion, and it has nothing to do with the mating situation. It's about the Frost, about us fighting the Frost." She looked off in the direction of where her dragon had flown off. "Are they safe out there? Our dragons?"

"Safer than we are. They can breathe fire."

"But the Frost turns dragons."

"I don't think I've ever seen an ice dragon I didn't recognize," said Odion. "It seems to only turn dragon with riders, not wild dragons, and maybe that happens because the dragons are distracted by their bonded humans. Maybe they're safer on their own."

She nodded once, a harsh nod. "Good. Then they stay away from us. Tell Mirra that, and I'll tell Erach the same."

Odion reached out through his bond to Mirra.

She reached back with a tendril of fear. He realized she was afraid of the mating from the pictures she was suddenly sending. She really was only about four years old. Dragons were sexually mature at the age of one, but they usually didn't mate until they were at least ten years old.

Dragons' lifespan tended to be fifty to sixty years, just a bit shorter than a human lifespan. It was common for riders to spend the last twenty or thirty years of their lives alone after their dragons passed on. Riders who lost dragons young to violent deaths would often bond again, but a rider whose dragon died of old age almost never did.

So, the Quorum wanted his very young dragon to mate. Luckily, she wouldn't become pregnant. That sort of thing was controlled by an injection given by the scholars at the Academy. A female dragon had to go off the injection to conceive. This was done strategically, not left to chance.

Of course, the Quorum would want Odion and Banyan to head up a bask, so that would mean offspring, and then mating riders to their dragons' children.

Except there would be no time for that. The Frost was

coming imminently. It would take many years before their dragons could have a bask with children old enough to fight.

So, the Quorum must have some other idea.

Banyan was touching him.

He turned to her. "Hey," he murmured. Things were strained between them, now, and he wasn't sure why exactly. It might be what had passed between them in the heat, or it might simply be that she was mated to another man.

"Will you be all right going inside?"

"I'll have to be."

"Fuck the Quorum," she snapped. She entwined her fingers with his. "We'll go together."

He swallowed hard. No one did this for him, ever, maybe his whole life. He had a vague memory of his mother when he was very young, gathering him into her arms when he had fallen and skinned up his knee and he was sobbing about it. But... when he saw his mother now, there was distance. She looked at him like a stranger, a grown man, a tool of the Quorum. She would never comfort him now, and he would never show her his weakness.

He didn't show anyone his weakness, in fact, but Banyan seemed to see it anyway, and she was kind to him, and it made him feel like sobbing.

He didn't sob, of course.

She led him down the stairs into the watchtower, holding his hand. At the top of the stairs, she turned to him. "All right? Or should we pause for a bit?"

"I'm fine," he said.

"You're not," she said. "That's all right, though."

He tilted his head to one side and the words came out for the first time, even though he'd felt it for a long time. "I love you."

Her face blossomed into a happy smile. "Oh, Odion, I love you, too."

They just stared into each other's eyes for long moments more, and he felt a bit drunk on her gaze, on her smile, on *her*.

Then they went further in. He showed her where the oil was for the torches. He showed her where the blankets were stored and they made up a bed to sleep in.

Someone had been here since the Frost had toppled the place. It had been cleaned and put in order in the meantime. It helped, not seeing any of the things that had been here when he'd been here before.

"Do you want to talk about it?" she asked him.

"No," he said, which was a lie. But it was better not to.

"All right," she said.

So, they didn't talk about it. Not about the people who'd been in his bask, not about the dragons, not about the attack, nothing.

Instead, they went into the kitchen and found flour, and Banyan knew how to make a quick unleavened bread, though she set out some flour and water to form a yeast culture for the future.

They ate bread and some of the store of salted meat they'd brought from the school. The school had food from the Hazain farms, fresh vegetables and meats. Here, they had to make do with preserved fare.

He was intrigued by the yeast, checking it over the next few days, finding the way it changed to be fascinating. "Where does it come from?"

"The air," she told him. "I suppose." Then she told him about something that a scholar had told her, that there was a theory about illnesses that could travel in the air. "But it doesn't seem the Frost is that kind of illness."

Odion had thought about this, too, but he couldn't make sense of it. The standard sort of understanding was that the Frost had once only been a strange illness that appeared from time to time amongst people.

People would catch it when they went high into the frozen peaks of the mountains in Hazai. They would come down and they would grow ill, and they would eventually die. All of their organs would freeze—not of cold necessarily, because they'd be warm—but they would stop moving, and then—without a heartbeat, without lungs to breathe—they died.

But then recently, the ice monsters had appeared.

Well, there was some confusion about this, however, because the truth of the ice monsters was hidden from most people. The Quorum didn't want anyone to know that people *turned into* ice monsters.

"This is what I think," Odion said to Banyan. "I think that when people were getting the Frost sickness, they were always getting the same thing that turns people into ice monsters. But I think if you come back down the mountain before the transformation is complete, if you're in the warmth, you just die, you don't turn into a monster. And if you stay in the cold, you do."

"Could be," said Banyan quietly. "It doesn't make sense for the monsters to have spontaneously appeared, like they say. On the other hand, if the monsters were always infecting people, with *bites*, wouldn't we have known about that?"

"It does seem like a thing you'd say if you came down with the sickness. 'Oh, maybe I got this from that rabid ice creature that *bit* me.'"

"There's more to it," Banyan decided.

"There is," said Odion. "Because once you're turned, it's like your essence or something gets absorbed into the Frost. It gets your memories or something?"

"The colonel was telling me this."

"When they came here, they flew in a skirmish configuration," said Odion. "The ice dragons used strategies I've seen used in the dragon arena at school."

"Right," she said. "Right, so that's why the Quorum is messing up the current skirmishes, changing all the rules. So, this way, when the Frost arrives, if everything we've been taught is different, it can't use our strategies against us."

"Exactly what I thought," he said, nodding at her.

"But none of that really helps us," she said. "Because we don't understand what the Frost wants."

He nodded slowly, as if he understood. But he didn't get

it. "What do you mean?"

"Last year, when I was given a bask, I started studying the Dragon War, trying to figure out strategies, how to win battles, just anything I could."

"That's smart," said Odion. "Why didn't I think of doing that? I never went to the library, and it was all right there."

"You didn't have chaos to fight either," she said. The skirmishes during Odion's time had been more ordered than they were in Banyan's. "Anyway, the point is, each of the countries in the Dragon War wanted something. Noch wanted to control land that Hazai controlled and Aleen wanted to get Hazai out of the harbors on the southern edge of their land, because they wanted to dominate the spice trade."

"Right," said Odion, nodding, though his schooling on history hadn't been thorough. Growing up marked as a dragon rider, it hadn't been thought important to teach him all about the reasons behind the Dragon War.

"But the Frost? What does it want? If it advances and kills everyone, there will be nothing left, just like the Dragon War. It ended because they realized if they kept fighting, everyone would die. And that's why dragons are never used against each other in warfare anymore. It's also why no one from the countries we trade with ever encroaches our borders. They don't have dragons."

"Yeah, I never thought about that." He furrowed his brow. "Well… the Frost is hungry."

She let out a breath, slowly, thinking about that. "Maybe."

"It's always hungry and never sated," said Odion. "It just wants to eat and eat and eat until…"

"But it can't eat *everything*," said Banyan. "What kind of creature eats so much that it destroys its food source?"

"A diseased one," said Odion. "Maybe the Frost infected itself with the sickness."

She barked out a laugh.

"I don't know," said Odion, shaking his head. "I don't understand it at all."

"That's exactly the problem," she said.

Later, they lay in bed together, but they didn't touch. She tried at one point, but he stopped her, saying that they should rest. They needed to heal after the insatiable heat they'd been through. They were both sore. And if Mirra did go into heat again, it would start all over again.

She accepted this, but she seemed disappointed.

He kept thinking about reaching for her, kissing her, soothing her, having her the way they used to, which was gentle and sweet and affirming of their love for each other.

Well, *had* it been that way?

Certainly, gentler than heat, though. Certainly, less troublesome.

They slept.

And then the days passed.

The yeast culture grew. They made bread. They spent the afternoons playing rousing games of throwing stones and using a set of fraying playing cards to pit themselves against each other.

They cooked together and went walking in the woods around the watchtower.

At night, they didn't touch.

A week went by.

Then one morning, a dragon approached. They went up top to the landing tower to watch it alight.

It was Deke Midgurd, the man Banyan used to be entangled with, climbing off a purple dragon. Deke, bonded and scaled, a spray of ugly, bumpy scales across his face (encompassing one eye, which had turned reptilian, then across his nose, and down his cheek, like he'd been clawed there, and it had revealed scales beneath). He still couldn't grow a beard.

He wasn't pleased to be there.

"Sorry to interrupt your love nest," he said.

## CHAPTER FOUR

BANYAN DIDN'T KNOW how to be around Deke anymore.

He'd been home for the midterm break, he said, and he'd seen her mother and his mother, and everyone. And a dragon had been out in the woods, a dragon that had followed him from the school, a dragon that had bonded him accidentally. He'd flown back on the dragon's back, directly to the South Ridge Academy, and the colonel had said that even the dragons were getting worried about the Frost, and they were bonding early.

"Then," Deke said, spreading nut butter on a slice of bread that Banyan had given him, "he sent me out here to you."

"But why?" said Banyan. "If he wants to know if we've made progress…" They hadn't. She and Odion had discussed it, and they didn't feel it was right to force Mirra to mate when she was young and frightened. Erach certainly wasn't inclined. They wanted to be mated as much as anyone but not at the cost of terrorizing a young dragon.

She had wanted to say something to Odion about the thing she'd read in the book, about a male dragon mating more than one female. She knew this wasn't actually unheard of in the animal kingdom. After all, a bull usually had a number of female cows that were all essentially mated to him. A rooster and his hens was quite the same way.

But she didn't say it because she didn't want to admit she wanted them both.

She didn't want to tell Odion that, and she didn't want to say it to herself.

She couldn't really want two men, anyway. That wouldn't work. It would be exhausting. They'd be jealous of each other. Ignia's teats, they'd been jealous during the heat. True, she'd found that arousing, and they'd seemed to find that arousing, and the jealousy and rivalry had been part of it, but…

It would hurt them.

How could anyone wish to be in a romantic relationship in which they were competing for someone else's affections? It *couldn't* work.

Of course, it seemed to work fine for the chickens.

"He said that he was afraid that you two were having fun 'playing house' out here," said Deke. "That my presence would serve to convince you to get on with it. That I wasn't to leave until you were, well, mated to each other." He made a face. "He also seemed to take special joy in telling me that you'd been in ménage à trois with two men. He's a horrible man, Colonel Rabi."

Banyan nodded. "In that, we agree."

"So, I'm here because you don't like me," muttered Deke.

"We don't," said Odion.

Banyan glanced at him.

Odion raised his eyebrows at her. "We don't, right? Are you going to have sex with all the men eventually? Is he part of it? Is Colonel Rabi part of it? Are we going to—"

"No," said Banyan, glaring at him.

"I don't share," said Deke stonily.

"If you want that, just tell me," said Odion.

Her eyes widened. "You'd be all right with that?"

"Well…" Odion looked Deke over. "I've never found him attractive, I admit, but maybe I'd get some kind of perverse pleasure in fucking him. Bending him over, filling him up, dominating him."

Deke's face turned purple.

Odion laughed, enjoying his discomfort.

"Your sexual attraction to men is disturbing to me," muttered Banyan.

"Because it's unnatural," said Deke.

"*No*," said Banyan. "Because it's all… about aggression and submission and… and…" She coughed. "All right, maybe sex is always about that."

Odion laughed.

Deke made a face. "No, it's not."

"Wait until your dragon goes into heat," Banyan sighed. "Or, if your dragon isn't female—*is* your dragon female?"

"Male," said Deke.

"Oh, Agnis and Ignia," said Banyan. She glanced at Odion. "You don't think the colonel is trying to make *his* dragon mate Mirra."

"I'll hang myself if that happens," muttered Deke.

Odion dragged a hand over his face. "All right, well, Deke, you get your dragon clear of ours, all right?"

"I'll tell Erach to protect Mirra if it's necessary," said Banyan.

"But she'll be in heat," said Odion. "So, if he's protecting her, maybe he's… mounting her. Maybe he can't resist."

Banyan knew the dragons didn't have a lot of control when it came to the heats either. They passed the madness of their sexual abandon onto their bonded riders. "This is a mess, is what it is."

"Agreed," said Deke.


THE HEAT CAME in the middle of the night. Odion woke sweaty and tangled in the sheets of the bed and he pulled Banyan into his arms.

She snuggled into him, letting out sleepy sighs, but she didn't wake up.

Odion reached out to Mirra—not too much, because being too merged with his dragon when she was in heat was always disturbing—and found that she and the female dragon were together but that neither Erach nor Deke's dragon (Flach) were nearby.

*Just me, then,* he thought.

He passed the night wide awake and alone, trying to be quiet as he stroked himself off again and again. Heat usually only lasted four or five hours. Well, as long as there weren't male dragons nearby triggering the symptoms and elongating it. Apparently, Slate had once been in a heat that went on for days because a male dragon kept coming in and setting off Yilia with his scent. The dragon hadn't been one the Academy approved of, so the male dragon was shooed off again and again. But his scent kept the heat going on an excruciating amount of time. Hopefully, that wouldn't happen. Hopefully, it would be over by morning.

Two hours into it, he got up to go seek some extra towels to clean himself up, and he ran into Deke coming up the stairs with a torch in his hand.

Odion eyed the other man. He really didn't have any desire to have any intimacy with him, not a bit. But Deke noticed his erection making a bulge in his pants. And Odion wasn't wearing a shirt—he'd shed his sleeping tunic when the rush of heat had come for him.

Deke was clearly threatened by Odion's lack of clothing, by his arousal. He backed away, hands up.

And Odion didn't know what possessed him to pursue the other man, because he knew he wouldn't have done anything to *anyone* against their will. He just... he hated Deke, and it was funny.

So he chased him down the stairs and out of the front door and Deke was swearing at him and brandishing a knife.

And then, outside in the darkness, Deke's dragon swooped down and landed. Deke climbed onto the dragon's back, panting.

Odion held up his hands. "I was just messing around. It's a bad joke, but come on—don't fly your dragon around Mirra, all right?"

"You stay away from me," said Deke hoarsely, clearly terrified.

Odion backed away, still holding up his palms. "I swear, I won't touch you. Come inside. Send your dragon off. It's all right, I swear."

But Deke and his dragon were taking to the air, flying off into the distance.

And Odion didn't make it all the way up the stairs before he had to stop and reach into his pants to relieve the pressure there.

Banyan found him like that, in the stairwell, leaning his head back against the wall, rubbing his own cock and groaning softly.

"What's going on?" she said.

"Heat," he said.

"Not me," she said.

"Well, no, Mirra's isolated," he said. "Hopefully, Deke stays clear."

"Deke?" she said.

"Yeah, he ran off when he realized I was affected by the heat." He beckoned to her. "Come here?"

She put both of her hands on her hips. "What did you do to him?"

"Nothing. Nothing, really. It was just a joke. I wasn't going to touch him at all, but he…" He shut his eyes. "I probably pushed it too far."

"So, now he's out there with his dragon? What if they close in on Mirra? What if his dragon mates Mirra, Odion? I don't care what's going on with you. I know you don't want that."

His eyes opened in slits. "Definitely don't want that."

"I'm going to get Erach to follow Deek," she said, turning and stalking up the steps.

"Hey, seriously? You're just leaving me here like this? Can you at least flash me one of your tits or something?"

She made a rude gesture over her shoulder and continued her ascent up the steps.

Fuck.

He let go of his erection and went after her.


DEKE CLUTCHED THE neck of Flach, trying to calm himself down. He could tell that his sheer terror was affecting the dragon, and that his own emotions were bleeding into the dragon's own. It wasn't safe for either of them to be flying when they were this distracted.

Not that he knew much about having a dragon.

They had classes in the Academy about care and feeding. What dragons ate, when they slept, why they were called a bask (it was because they all liked to bask together in the sun, lying out in the afternoon on flat rocks in the mountains or by streams), when they moulted, that sort of thing.

But actually riding a dragon?

He'd had no training in that.

Thankfully, it was fairly self-explanatory. You climbed on, you held on, and that was all there was to it. The little spot between the dragon's legs and its wings seemed perfectly designed to secure two human legs. As if it had been destined or something.

He and Flach seemed to work quite well together, as if it had always been meant to be. He was glad of that.

He hated this assignment.

He hated Banyan Thriceborn.

Once, he'd loved her. He'd adored her. He'd sacrificed everything for her, gone off to that stupid Academy, and now it was done.

Here was the incredibly fucked-up thing: he had decided he wouldn't go back to the Academy.

Yeah, he'd left the Academy for break, and the whole journey back (which had been taken in a sidecar on a dragon, and he'd thankfully not vomited this time — apparently the glider training was good for something and he was no longer afraid to fly) he'd thought to himself that he was done. There was no reason to go back to the

Academy, no reason at all. He would ask his father if he could help on the farm. His family would be glad to have him back. He'd find a nice Nochan girl who'd find his time at the Academy exotic and exciting. She wouldn't excite him, of course, not like Banyan had, but excitement was overrated when it came to women.

He didn't want an exciting woman anymore.

No, he just wanted one who would actually love him.

Banyan had never felt anything for him.

It turned his stomach when he saw her look at Odion. Why couldn't she have looked at *him* that way?

But, of course, he knew the answer to that. She didn't look at Deke that way, because Deke was nothing to look at. He had some talent, of course, enough to distinguish himself and to make it into the Academy. He'd been accelerated ahead of schedule, becoming a cadet sooner than he should have been. But none of that was enough.

Why should Banyan want him when she had Odion Naxim?

No, she never would.

She never had, not even before Odion had come into her life. She had never felt anything for Deke at all, as was evidenced by the way she behaved when they made love. She was still and mostly silent and kept her eyes closed and if she said anything, it was only to criticize his skills at attempting to pleasure her.

He'd been convinced he was appalling at it, utterly clumsy, that it was all his fault.

And then he'd bedded Atohi once, and she'd climbed astride him and worked her hips against his hardness and told him when to move and when to stay still and used his body to bring about her own pleasure, and he'd realized that Banyan was just missing that. Missing warmth, missing interest, missing exuberance.

Odion seemed pleased enough.

Maybe she was different with him.

That made Deke feel angry.

Suddenly, however, his thoughts were interrupted by a

sensation. The anger within him was melting away, melting into... arousal.

And that was when he realized that he hadn't been paying any attention to where Flach was going.

He burrowed into the dragon's mind, but the dragon was now thinking nothing but singleminded images of the hindquarters of female dragons. He was triggered by the heat of the female dragons.

Deke would not let Flach mate Mirra. He'd kill the dragon first, even though he didn't know if he'd survive the murder through the bond. It'd probably kill him too. Just as well.

He could not be mated to Odion Naxim.

Not because Odion was a man, not exactly, though Deke was none too keen on the idea of sodomy.

Because Odion was Odion.

Because it was unthinkable.

No.

Deke could not get control of the dragon, however.

And then, miraculously, from above, in came Banyan's dragon, flapping its wings into Flach's face, scratching at the other dragon with long talons.

It was just enough for Deke to get into the other dragon's mind and pull him up out of the influence of the heat. He forced Flach to gain altitude, taking his dragon higher and higher.

They climbed, high above the clouds, in the thin, frigid air.

There, everything seemed pristine and safe.

Deke sighed in pleasure, clutching his dragon, and they flew and flew.

Eventually, Flach began to flag, and Deke knew the dragon wished to touch down. But when they came down out of the darkness to alight on the side of the mountain they'd been circling, they went down into snow.

Deke had heard of it, but he'd never seen it. It glowed in the scant light that still emanated from the moon—heavy on the horizon, almost ready to set as morning came.

It couldn't be safe here, of course.
The Frost lived in the snow.
But it was wondrous. He'd never seen something so very beautiful. It covered all of the surfaces of the trees and it blanketed everything in a glittering white powder.
He got down off the dragon to traipse through it. It was quite cold, but it was delightful. He tossed it in the air. He packed it up into a ball and tossed it. He fell backwards and ran his arms and legs through it.
He found himself giggling like a little child.
Snow.
Who knew it was like this?
And then he heard a voice.
"Hello?"
He straightened up. "Hello?"
A figure approached. The figure waved. "Ho there! My name is Genevieve."
He wasn't sure what to think.
She got closer. She was wrapped up in furs, only a bit of her skin poked out. It was dark, but she seemed just like, well, a woman. She didn't seem to be threatening.
Except, of course, he felt something else, a little shiver at the back of his neck, something that warned him. He had the urge to jump on the back of Flach and take back to the air, not to speak to this woman.
But she was closer now, smiling. "Are you cold? Are you hungry? We never get any visitors all the way up here. If you'd like, you can come back to our house."
"Our house? Who do you live with?"
"Others," she said. "Other souls who lost their way in the snow and cold. It's cozy there. Come, there's food." She was smiling, and now she was close enough that he could see that she was pretty.
He let out a breath. "I shouldn't. I should get back to…"
Well, really, did he want to go back there?
Truth was, he'd rather never go back to the watchtower, never spend another day watching Banyan look adoringly at Odion or him slip his arm around her and kiss her temple.

"Are you sure? Don't you want to warm up for just a bit?"

"You know what?" He nodded. "I do."

Her smile got very, very wide, showing off all of her very white teeth.

That alarm shot through him again.

But then she had her hand on his, her gloved hand, and she was tugging him through the snow. "What's your name?"

"Deke," he said.

"Deke," she breathed. "Deke's a good name. I like Deke."

# CHAPTER FIVE

BANYAN TOOK ODION to bed at first out of pity, because he was in such a bad way with the heat. But somewhere in the middle of it, she felt Erach become engaged by Mirra's heat. She was on her hands and knees, Odion behind her, driving himself in and out of her. She liked this position because the little nubs on the underside of his cock rubbed all the way up and down the front of her, stimulating her clitoris from the inside.

She'd never come this way, not just from his cock, but as the heat began to ride her, it became more and more intense, and she began to suspect it might happen.

She threw herself into it with abandon, thinking about Odion and Slate rubbing each other's cocks and feeling guilty about it because she didn't think she should be fantasizing about another man when she was with Odion, even if Odion was involved in the fantasy.

The truth was, often, to come with him, she had to employ a little bit of fantasy. It wouldn't be a real fantasy, because it would be about Odion. She'd just make him a tad more naughty or forceful than real-life Odion would be. She'd make him call her a naughty name or order her to bend over for him or imagine him pulling her hair.

None of these things made her actually orgasmic in reality. They weren't things she even actually liked, she didn't think.

It was only the *idea* of them that turned her on, and mostly when it was in her own head and she could control the idea. It would get her right into the place where she could finally fall over into an orgasm. Without the fantasy, she didn't think she could come.

At least... she'd never come without a fantasy, anyway.

Well, that wasn't strictly true. The first time with Odion, there hadn't been one, she thought, but she'd never been quite able to duplicate that. She kept trying, but then it would go on and on, and she'd just call something up because she was getting frustrated and she wanted to come.

Now, she thought about the way that Slate had taunted Odion and the way that Odion had let out little sighs of deep pleasure with each bit of degradation, the way his voice had broken when he'd said Slate's name. *Fuck, Slate,* he'd said, so turned on, so affected.

Her body clenched, her pleasure gathering like a storm cloud.

"Odion," she breathed. "I'm close."

Odion's finger wormed its way down to her clit. "You need this?" he panted.

She groaned, surging against the pressure there, still picturing the two men touching each other.

Her orgasm seemed to shatter her, it was so intense.

She let out little sobbing cries, clenching against him, moaning his name again and again.

And then—in that moment—it happened.

Odion's fingers dug into her hips and he let out a garbled cry.

Her knees gave out and she fell right onto the bed.

He slammed into her.

And she was—they were—the dragons—she could see it through Erach's eyes—and then Mirra's and then—

*Mated.*

## CHAPTER SIX

ERACH WAS A mass of guilt the next morning, but Banyan could feel through the new bond that Mirra was pleased to be with him, pleased to be mated, and very much admired the green dragon. Mirra had fallen for him.

Erach felt manipulated and confused, having been too separated from his first mate for their bond to have kept him from straying. He was not pleased at being mated to a dragon so young. He was anxious at the idea he could have impregnated her.

And then alternately anxious at the idea of having impregnated Yilia, feeling as if he'd abandoned her.

Erach went off flying that morning and stayed gone.

Odion toasted bread over the fire and gave her shy smiles now and then.

She smiled back.

It felt good to be mated to him. Right. Just exactly right.

But if she'd hoped that the mating would eradicate any residual feelings she had about Slate, it hadn't. Instead, she felt strange about it all. *What was that for?* she thought.

Why had it all happened?

Why had she mated Slate? Why had she fucked him? Why had she been so very, very aroused by the two of them together?

She took the toast Odion gave her and didn't say any of this aloud. She didn't want to hurt him.

"Well, I guess we go back now," Odion said.

"I guess so," she said. "Are they going to make Mirra and Erach have babies to bond others so that we can have a bask for fighting?"

"I don't know," he said. "Doesn't seem like there's time, does there?"

She shook her head. "It doesn't."

"Well, I know Mirra's been given something from the healers that keep her from conceiving. They give it to the female dragons. Having fighters out of commission because they're about to give birth or have helpless young to tend to — it's not really conducive to war."

"Good," she said, passing this along to Erach. She hoped it would reassure him.

It wasn't until noon that either of them thought of Deke.

Then Erach sent her images of chasing Deke off. She realized that the reason that Erach had been under Mirra's thrall was because he'd been protecting the young female dragon. Where had Deke gone?

She and Odion climbed aboard their dragons and flew all over, looking, but they didn't see him or Flach. If the two were injured somewhere, it wasn't anywhere obvious.

She had a feeling that Colonel Rabi would say to leave Deke behind. They'd completed their mission, after all, and they needed to get back to the Academy. Deke wasn't important, not in the end.

But she thought of explaining that to Deke's mother when she got home for a visit, how she'd just left him here to die in the wilderness. She couldn't. They would go out tomorrow. They'd look for him.

In bed that night, Odion held her against his chest. "We can't stay here for too long. I know you want to. I know you feel guilty about him, I know you're thinking about his mother, but — "

"You can read my mind?"

"No," he said.

"I can't read yours."

"I just... when you're really upset, I get things," said

Odion. "I think it's just strong emotions."

"Well, I'm not getting anything from you." She tilted back her head to look up at him.

He smiled down at her.

Her brain exploded with the jarring, *Banyan Thriceborn is mine.*

It was so loud it made her head throb.

She gasped.

And then she kissed him as hard as she could, and he kissed her back, and rolled her under him and they were distracted by that, which was why they didn't hear him come in.

He still had a key for the lock, so he just let himself in.

And then he stumbled up the stairs and to their room and threw open the door.

And there, in the doorway, face pale, hair stringy and white, eyes colorless and unseeing, stood what remained of Deke Midgurd.

He was an ice monster.

# CHAPTER SEVEN

ODION SCRAMBLED OFF Banyan and got off the bed, looking around frantically for whatever he could use as a weapon. Why didn't they have anything in here, after all? There were actually bows and arrows down in storage, and he should have been teaching Banyan that, should have been following his orders, but he hadn't done that.

After all, when was the last time he'd had any real leave? When was the last time he'd been allowed to do nothing at all? He'd only wanted to enjoy it, as long as it might last.

They had knives. They strapped knives on when they went out riding their dragons, but they took them off and hung them on the wall right by the stairs, which meant they weren't here, and they were no good to them.

And while he was thinking all this, Deke was barreling toward him, letting out some kind of strange inhuman keening noise.

Odion thrust his body between Deke and his mate. He could not let Deke *touch* her.

Deke tackled Odion into the bed. He lowered his face to Odion's shoulder, opening his jaw wide.

*He's going to bite me,* Odion thought, feeling a strange and awful calmness radiate through him at the thought of it.

Banyan's foot shot out and slammed into Deke's forehead.

Deke's head went back and he staggered backwards,

letting out another cry.

Banyan leaped off the bed and snatched up one of her shirts where it was draped over a chair. They were both enjoying small rebellions out there, like not hanging up their clothes in the wardrobes. Not doing so at the Academy resulted in focus trainings and being put on emptying-chamberpot duty. Here, no one could stop them.

She balled the shirt up and stuffed it into Deke's mouth. Then she propelled Deke—face first—into the wall and held him there, shoulder at the back of his neck, pinning his face to to the wall.

Deke moaned and slobbered around the fabric in his mouth.

"Odion, get something to tie him with," she said.

"Tie him?" said Odion. "We have to… he's changed."

"Just… *please*." Her voice was a screech.

He went out and found some twine and came back to her.

She snatched it from him and tied Deke's hands and tied Deek's feet. She used the twine to tie his jaw closed by securing the knot on the top of his head, with the twine wrapping under his chin. Then she let go of him.

Deke turned around and tried to come for them, growling, trying to move his jaw, which he couldn't do. He flopped onto his belly and tried to get forward, but he didn't make much progress.

"We have to put him out of his misery, Banyan," said Odion tightly.

She bit down on her bottom lip. Her eyes were shining.

"You'll tell his mother he died bravely fighting the Frost. You'll tell her he was a hero. You'll—"

"Fire," said Banyan. "We'll get the dragons to do it."

Odion licked his lips. "Banyan."

"I know," she said. "But I can't do it. And I can't let you do it. So…"

"If one of us orders our dragons to burn him, it's the same thing."

"No, it's not. It's the best way to eradicate the Frost anyway, right?" said Banyan. "If this is infectious, how do we know that leaving his lifeless body won't make it spread to animals or the ground or…" She trailed off.

It was quiet.

Finally, Odion nodded. "Fire," he agreed. Privately, he thought that this was an agonizing thing to do to Deke, but he wasn't sure if he should say that aloud.

"They don't feel pain," Banyan was telling him.

"Sure about that?" said Odion.

"When I was fighting the one at the other watchtower, when your arm was broken, it didn't react no matter what I did to it." She let out a moan. "That one was an 'it,' but Deke…"

Odion bent over and hauled Deke upright, holding him by his bound arms, so that the man faced away.

Deke tried to turn and get his mouth on Odion, but it was useless.

"We have to get him outside," said Odion. "The dragons can't burn him in here."

"No, I guess not," said Banyan.

"So, you need to cut his legs free to make him walk."

Banyan did it.

It was not easy getting Deke down the stairs. More than once, Odion thought about just grabbing a knife and plunging it into the man's head. But he could feel Banyan through the bond, and hurting her would be untenable. He loved her, and they were closer now than ever. No, he wouldn't do that.

Eventually, they deposited him on the ground outside the watchtower and Banyan called in Erach, who stalked around the area, looking at her from time to time, as if the two of them were having a legitimate conversation.

Odion could feel Erach through the bond, but it was through Mirra, and it was sort of tinged with his dragon's admiration for him, with lust, with attachment. If Erach was thinking in words, Odion certainly couldn't tell.

But finally, Erach squared off and opened his jaws, and smoke trickled out of his nostrils, and Banyan hid her face against Odion's chest, letting out little whimpers.

Odion steeled himself for the blast of fire.
Deke spit the fabric out of his mouth. "Please don't, Banyan, please."

## CHAPTER EIGHT

BANYAN WHIRLED, LETTING go of Odion, turning on Deke.

He didn't even look like himself now that he'd been leached of all color. His freckles were still there, but they were whiter than his pale skin. His hair was entirely white. His lack of a beard was white too. His eyes were colorless. His lips were colorless. His teeth gleamed.

"Please," he said and he sounded just like Deke.

"They talk?" said Banyan to Odion. "They *talk?*"

"No," said Odion. "No, they don't talk. I mean... I don't know. This is the closest I've ever been to one."

She whipped her head around to look at Odion. "What do you mean? They killed your bask. Here, you said."

"Yes, but that was dragons—ice dragons. None of the people. Well, maybe one was riding on the back of one of the dragons, but he stayed back, out of sight, and I couldn't really make him out. I guess I kind of thought that maybe they got changed together and they were just—I don't know—frozen together."

"I can talk," said Deke.

"Yes, I hear you talking," said Banyan. "But *shut up.*"

Odion rubbed his forehead. "I guess I saw Genevieve after she changed."

"Genevieve," said Deke. "She's the one who gave me the gift."

"Shut *up*." Banyan screamed it. Deke cringed.

"But she didn't talk. She came at me, like this, all ragey," said Odion. "I thought they just turned into rage-filled beasts."

"Well," said Banyan, "think about it. Can rage-filled beasts conduct a war? If it was just that, we'd have won already, right? I mean, there's got to be some reason we haven't rooted the Frost out and gone into the mountains with our armies of dragons and melted it out of existence. And that's because... because it talks. It's intelligent. It's... *what* is it?"

"It's nice," Deke said to her with a little shrug. "It feels good. No more pain. And you know how there's always this hole in you? This feeling of, 'Why?' and 'What does it all mean?' That feeling? It goes away. I came to give you the gift, both of you. We would welcome you into the open icy arms of the Family."

"Seriously, shut your *mouth*," said Banyan, sinking both of her hands into her hair. She paced.

Odion made a tent with his fingers and rested it against his lower lip. "Well, we can't kill him now."

"Obviously we can't kill him." Banyan was still pacing. "But I can't send him home to his mother either. I get the strong feeling he'd bite her."

"I mean, we'll have to kill him eventually," said Odion. "But he has information, Banyan, things we need to know."

Banyan stopped pacing, looking up at him. "You're right."


"I'M HUNGRY," DEKE was saying through the door.

They had him locked away in one of the empty bedrooms. He kept pounding on the door and rattling the knob and begging to be let out.

"I told you," Banyan said, "we'll feed you after you tell us what we want to know."

"Just give me something now," whined Deke. "Please?"

Banyan wasn't sure what to do. None of this made sense. If Deke could talk, why attack them when he came in? Why not stand in the doorway, or in the dark, and pretend to be normal Deke? If the one who'd attacked her at the other watchtower could talk, why hadn't it talked then?

Maybe... maybe the talking came in waves or something? Maybe sometimes they could talk, and sometimes they were mindless beasts? Surely, if Deke could talk, the time to have done it was while she was tying him up.

"All right," she said, "I'll give you some bread."

"Thank you," said Deke. "I'm really starving here."

She opened the door a bit.

Deke's arm thrust out and he seized her. He pulled her arm closer, opening his jaws—

She wrenched it back and slammed the door shut. "Never mind," she snarled. "You tricked me."

"No," said Deke pitifully. "I'm just not hungry for bread." He sounded a little terrified about this, actually. From through the door came the sounds of loud and broken sobbing.

Banyan rolled her eyes.

"Let's kill him." Odion was lounging on the other side of the room, his expression hard.

"No," she said to her mate. She turned back to the door and forced her voice to be soft. "It's all right, Deke. It must be scary not to understand all these changes you're going through."

"They didn't tell me," he wailed. "They didn't tell me anything. They just sent me to you. They said if I could bring you into the Family, too, it would be a boon to the purpose."

"The purpose?" she said. "What's the purpose?"

"I don't know," he said. "I don't know. But I think it's... it feels like it's... biting."

Banyan groaned.

"You're not going to feed me, are you?" said Deke.

"If you want me to feed you myself, no," snapped

Banyan. "You can't bite me. I'm sorry."

"But please?" said Deke. "You'll like it, I swear. I was afraid, too, but it's nice. It's *so* nice. And *I'll* like it, and we'll both—"

"Stop," she growled.

"Kill him," said Odion.

She glared at him. "Interrogating him was your idea."

"Yes, and we tried, and we're getting nothing from him, and he doesn't know anything, and now we have to kill him."

"Don't kill me," said Deke. "I don't want to die. I'm not ready to die." More sobbing.

"All right, we're not going to kill you," said Banyan. She was lying to him. They were going to have to kill him, weren't they? Agnis and Ignia, but she felt in over her head here. "Don't cry. Take deep breaths, all right?"

"All right," said Deke thickly. The noisy sounds of his breathing came through the door.

"There, is that better?"

"Yes," said Deke softly. He sounded like a little boy.

She hated how vulnerable he sounded. She hated that she was lying to him. Something inside her twisted. She let out a breath of her own, equally noisy. "Look, Deke, you need to help us by telling us the things you know. The more you can tell us, the more useful you are, do you understand?"

"I could be your spy," said Deke. "You could send me back, and I could infiltrate the Frost, and then I could report to the Academy and—"

"Let's start with what happened. How the bite happened?" She didn't think they could trust him to be a spy, not if he wanted to bite people that badly.

"She just did it," said Deke.

"That was this Genevieve person?"

"Not Genevieve," spoke up Odion. "She would never have bitten anyone. She could be fierce, of course. She was a rider. But she wouldn't have—"

"Odion," admonished Banyan. She could feel from the bond that Odion had unresolved issues about all of this. He hadn't wanted to talk about it before, but maybe she should have pressed him to talk about it. Locking it away wasn't helping him. She sent as much reassurance as she could through the bond to him, but she couldn't concentrate on him right now.

She turned back to Deke, well, to the door that Deke was behind. "Sorry, Deke. Let's go back before the bite, then. How did you, erm, meet Genevieve? *Did* you meet her?" He must have, if he got her name. He hadn't simply been attacked. Or had he? "Maybe she just jumped on you and bit you. Is that what happened?"

"No." Deke was offended. "Of course not."

"All right, then, what happened?"

"Well, she approached me. She said there was food and warmth and shelter. She was all wrapped in furs, and I couldn't see that she was… that her hair… that everything was white. It would have bothered me, I think, if I had, but now I like it better. The way you two look, it's not pure."

"So, she's an ice monster."

"We're not monsters!" Deke was adamant about this.

"Well, you're… you're sick, at least. You have the Frost sickness in some way."

"No, I'm not sick. I'm transformed. It's better this way."

"Let's not argue about this. Continue with your story. You went with Genevieve?"

"Yes, and we went into a cavern, and it was dark, and it was cold, but she started taking off her clothes, and I couldn't see her, but I could feel her, and then—"

"All right, well, maybe skip over some of this part," said Banyan, who was thinking about a conversation she'd had with Dove once about a man with the Frost sickness who said a woman had approached him and solicited his sexual attentions before, well, biting him. "You got closer to Genevieve, then, *that* sort of closer? And then she bit you?"

"Actually, yes," said Deke.

"Genevieve doesn't even like men!" said Odion, sounding sulky.

Banyan shot him a look over her shoulder.

"Sorry," said Odion with a sigh. "I don't mean to—"

"You're upset because they were your bask, and you saw them die, and now they're not dead, but they're out there doing the bidding of the Frost," said Banyan. "I understand."

Odion sighed. "You're right, of course. I shouldn't be interrupting, however. It's not as if I think he's lying or anything. I suppose I *wish* he was lying." His face fell.

"Later," she whispered to him.

He nodded. He raised his voice. "So, what happened after the bite, Deke?"

"It hurt," said Deke. "It hurt for a long time, but I was frozen and I couldn't move, and I couldn't make any noise, and I just had to endure it. More of them came during that time, and they bathed my body in icy water and whispered to me, welcoming me to the Family, and telling me that we must spread the Frost far and wide, that it is all that matters anymore, that it is everything. And at first I resisted, but then the pain began to fade, and I began to see."

"Was there a leader?" said Banyan. "Someone in charge? Someone giving orders?"

"We don't need that," said Deke. "We all want the same thing."

"What do you want?"

"Just… to bite, I suppose."

"But why?"

"Because that's how we spread."

Banyan glanced at Odion, thinking of their conversation, of how the Frost was simply hungry.

"If we don't spread, we die. It's like…" Deke thought about it. "It's like sex, I suppose, except better, because when you have sex you can't be assured of doing any sort of reproducing, but when we bite, we spread and we make our offspring. In a way, Genevieve is my mother and I her son, but we are so much more than that. We are the Family and we are all things to each other."

Reproduction. Of course. Every creature had an undeniable urge for that, to continue on the next generation.

So, that was it, then.
That was all the Frost wanted.
To spread.
She walked off.

"Banyan?" called Odion.

"Stay there," she said, going past him, going down the stairs, through the door at the foot of them, outside, into the late afternoon air. She looked up at the peak of the snowy mountain that rose overhead, stark and white against the blue sky.

She wanted to scream.

No treaties, then.

No peace.

Nothing like that.

And they couldn't simply let the Frost have its territories either, expect it to stay in the frozen peaks of the mountains. Because all it wanted was to spread.

*But why? Why now? If it's been there in the snow and ice all along, why is it expanding now?*

Maybe it couldn't before, she thought.

Maybe it was stuck there, and any time the Frost came down into the warmth in the form of the sickness, it just killed its host, because it couldn't survive in the warmth.

But then maybe, it infected a dragon once, and it could breathe out icy clouds and then, suddenly, for the first time, it could travel.

She grimaced, looking up at that peak.

Well, she'd wanted to understand, hadn't she?

But now she did, and it was all hopeless.

ODION HAD HIS head in her lap and she was stroking his hair, and he couldn't remember ever being this vulnerable with another person. It felt insane, actually, positively idiotic. But it felt *good*. He didn't want to stop. "It was my fault, really."

"How could it have been your fault?" Banyan's voice was low and comforting, her fingers rhythmic in his hair.

"Because everything was confused. The Quorum sent me out here and they told them—the alphas of the bask, Jem and Marti—to listen to me, because I was some sort of savant, because I was going to fix everything."

"And what did you tell them?"

"Actually, nothing. They wouldn't listen to me. Not that I had any ideas at that point. I didn't know anything about it. I'd never seen the ice dragons. I didn't *know* about the ice dragons, because the Quorum sent me out here blind. The alphas ignored me and ridiculed me and put me on kitchen duty and made me wash the dirty dishes and then—then the Frost came—"

"So how was it your fault again?"

He was quiet. He let out a little whimper. "Elemental forces, Banyan, it's always my fault."

She stroked his hair. "That doesn't help us, that guilt. It makes us more cautious, and if we're too cautious, we don't attack boldly enough and we lose."

"You know, I've thought this," he muttered, shutting his eyes, burrowing into her. "I've thought that it broke me. Now I don't trust myself anymore. Being back in the glider arena with you, it felt like coming back alive. Because nothing bad can happen there. No one can die."

"Well, someone could fall," she said.

"You know what I mean."

She stroked his hair. "It's not our fault. It's the Quorum's fault."

And suddenly, he understood. "Oh," he breathed.

She'd gotten it, too. "Yes."

"That's why they do it," he said. "The focus training, taking away all our choices, molding us into soldiers with no other attachments, all of it. They don't want us to feel guilt."

"They take all the guilt and all the responsibility, and then we'll do whatever they need, commit any atrocity, take any risk, and when the other soldiers die, it's not because of us, it's because of them."

He rolled his forehead into her thigh, groaning.

She stroked his hair.

For some time, neither of them spoke.

Then, from across the room, the door where Deke was trapped rattled again.

Deke had stopped speaking again recently. For a time, he hadn't shut up. He'd answered all their questions, and then—when there weren't any more—he'd resorted to begging for his life. He'd been pitiable, and Banyan had cried, and Odion had felt revulsion crawl up his arms, thinking of Elm, thinking of the man who'd helped Javor attempt to rape Banyan, thinking about how he hadn't been *able* to kill that man.

But then Deke had shut his mouth, and Odion had been flooded with relief. He'd said to Banyan, "Now, I'll do it now, and it'll be done. You don't have to watch."

But she wouldn't let him.

He could feel her reticence through the bond. Disturbingly, he felt the remnants of the way she had once loved the other man, the way she had been connected to him.

Odion had only ever been sexually intimate with Banyan and Slate.

He tried to think about killing Slate, even if Slate were an ice monster.

Maybe he understood. Maybe.

It was only… Banyan and Deke hadn't even had good sex, so, surely, it was different.

He was jealous of Deke, he guessed.

Interesting that the quality of that jealousy was so different than the quality of his jealousy for Slate and Banyan. It wasn't that he wasn't jealous of Slate. He was. But it was different somehow. He also cared about Slate. He couldn't help but worry, of course, that Banyan might end up wanting Slate more than she wanted him. Or that Slate might find Banyan to be more appealing than Slate found him.

Fuck it all.

Why was he thinking about this right now?

He lifted his head. "You have to let me do it, Banyan."

She shook her head. "No. It has to be me."

"That's insane. Absolutely not. I wouldn't ask that of you."

"For him," she said, her voice breaking. "It'll be easier for him if it's me." Tears started to leak out of his eyes.

"Well, I don't care about him."

"I know!" Her voice cracked.

"Banyan—"

"But I do care," she whispered. "I do, and he's not actually a bad man. He t-tried. He… didn't deserve this. If it was me, and I had a choice between him or you, I'd want you to do it."

His eyes widened in horror. "Never."

"Promise me," she said, nostrils flaring. "Promise me, if I get bitten, you'll do it."

He shook his head. "No."

"Odion, I don't want to be some slave to spreading the fucking Frost all over the Trinal Kingdoms. If it gets me, you will save me from that."

"If it gets you, I will let you bite me," he said. "And we'll just… together."

She got up, dislodging his head from her lap.

He caught himself on his hands and pushed himself into a sitting position. "Come on, Banyan, there's no way I could ever—"

"It's what I want," she said to him, walking toward the door where Deke was kept. "But if you get bitten, I'll let you go, then. I won't kill you."

"That's—" He groaned. Was that what he wanted? "Banyan, don't go in there."

She snatched one of the knives off the wall, drawing it out of its scabbard. Brandishing it, she unlocked the door.

"Banyan."

She went inside.

Odion sat there for a moment.

Then there was the sound of a scuffle and Odion hurried

over.

He stood in the doorway.

Banyan was up against the wall, her arm wrapped around the back of Deke's neck, her legs around his waist. He was facing away from her, struggling even as she held him fast.

"I'm very sorry, Deke," she was whispering in a broken voice. "I'm so, so sorry. But I want you to know that I'm going to be here with you through all of it, all right? I'm here, and I won't leave you. I'll be *right here*."

Deke went limp. "Banyan?" His voice seemed to surface. "What are you doing?"

Banyan showed him the knife. "You know what I'm doing. You know I have to."

"No, you don't."

"Deke, I can't let you spread the Frost. I know you think you want to do that, but you're just sick, that's all. And I have to stop that."

"But it's nice, Banyan, and if you let me bite you, you'd see that."

"It would kill all the humans," said Banyan. "If you spread to all of us, none of us can reproduce, right? So, what would be left?"

"I don't know," Deke said quietly. "It's not... we haven't really..."

"Just instinct," said Banyan. "Blind instinct, like heat. Makes you act in ways that don't even make sense."

"Please, Banyan, I don't want to die."

"I know," she said. "I'm sorry. But I have to."

"You don't!"

"Stop wasting what time you have left trying to convince me otherwise," said Banyan. "Do you have anything you want me to do? Anyone I should talk to? Messages you want relayed? Unfinished business?"

"Shit," said Deke. He let out a sob.

"Deke, do you?"

"Are you going to tell my mother what you did?"

"No," said Banyan. "I'm going to tell her you died a

hero's death, and that you were instrumental in helping us understand how to defeat the Frost. Because it's true. What you told us is going to be very helpful. We're all grateful. The Quorum is, too. Thank you for your service, Deke."

Deke sniffled. But no tears appeared in his colorless eyes. His lower lip trembled. "Just, um, tell her I love her, I guess? And my father, too, and my sisters and brothers. And, uh, Atohi, she and I had, um, it was basically just physical, I guess, but—"

"You were fucking Atohi? What about Tendai? I thought she liked Tendai?"

"I... don't know." Deke was miserable. "She wouldn't care, I guess."

"I'll tell her you mentioned her as you were dying," said Banyan, relenting, her voice thick. "I'll tell her that, and she's not made of stone, it'll mean something to her."

Now, Deke and Banyan were both sobbing.

"I'm so sorry, Deke," whispered Banyan. "If there was any other way, if I knew another way—"

"But there is," said Deke. "You don't have to do this."

"I do."

A pause.

"I'm scared, Banyan," said Deke in a very small voice.

"I'm here with you," she whispered. "I'll be here with you until it's done." And the knife was in his temple, so quick, a glint in the air as it moved.

Deke's eyes widened in surprise, and he choked.

And then, just as quick, he went lifeless.

She pulled the knife out.

Blue-black blood rushed out of the wound.

She held him, tears falling onto his color-leached skin. "Shh, Deke, I'm here, I'm still here with you. I won't let go."

Odion felt a lump rising in his own throat. This was the worst thing he thought he'd ever seen. He wanted to leave. He wanted to run from it, lest it crawl down his throat and take him over and ruin him.

But if Banyan had to stay for Deke, he had to stay for Banyan. And Deke was gone, but she knew that, and wasn't ready to let go of him, so Odion would stay until she was.

He stayed.

She held the lifeless body of Deke and whispered to it, and dark blood flowed over them both, and time slowed to a crawl.

## CHAPTER NINE

THEY BURNED HIS body.

Banyan realized afterward that maybe letting Deke bleed all over her was a really stupid idea, because if the disease was blood borne, like Dove had said, then maybe she could catch it from Deke's blood.

But she washed and washed and washed it away.

She didn't catch it.

They went back to the Academy the next day. She and Odion decided that they weren't going to share what they knew with the Quorum. Probably, the Quorum already knew. The Quorum might be trying to give them the gift of guiltlessness by taking away all their choice, but they didn't want it.

They'd find a way to be brash in the face of the truth of it.

War was always this way.

War was always murdering people who cried and begged and were scared.

That was what made it ugly.

It was a nice idea to pretend they were killing monsters, of course, but there weren't any real monsters. There were just beings who wanted things. Sometimes those beings' wants collided with other beings' wants. That was all there was.

It wasn't noble.

It wasn't good.

It wasn't even really justifiable.

Except, well, she wasn't going to let the Frost kill them all, was she? Of course not.

Even so, there was nothing decreeing that humans had a better right to exist than the Frost did. The Frost was the same as they were in some ways. It just wanted to live and reproduce and eat and spread.

Was that so much different than humans in the end?

Even so, she would still stop the Frost.

And why?

Because she *was* human. She was *not* the Frost. So, her allegiance would always lie with her own species. Some things could not be changed.

Colonel Rabi took the news about Deke with no expression on his face. Then he asked a lot of questions which seemed to imply that Deke may have been killed for some petty reason by one of the two of them—either because he was her former lover and there was apparently always some reason to kill your former lover—or because Odion saw him as a rival or because they'd both simply been annoyed with him.

Banyan said tersely to the colonel, "He died a hero, fighting the Frost, sir."

The colonel just shrugged. "Well, we'll be sure to tell his family that."

By the evening, she and Odion were in the dragon arena.

They'd been inserted into the dragon corps, but they hadn't been given a bask, as such. Most dragon corps were organized much like the glider corps, in basks—small groups of soldiers numbering between four to eight. Most of the basks were riders who were bonded to actual dragon family groups, though it was rare of the alphas to be part of the training corps. Most of the alphas were out in the field fighting the actual Frost while their children were here, safe, playing war games in the arena.

However, there were sometimes basks of dragons who weren't affiliated, because occasionally, riders bonded lone dragons, and occasionally, things happened like what had happened to Odion, where a whole bask was killed except one survivor, and occasionally, dragons left their basks because they were old enough and wanted to seek their own mates and form their own basks. So the lone-dragon basks were rare, but they were not unheard of.

But not for her and Odion, no. Just the two of them, then. They'd fight other basks, grossly outnumbered, and Banyan shouldn't have expected anything different.

Their first skirmish was that afternoon.

While the glider corps tended to have their skirmishes in the morning, the dragon corps fought in the afternoon.

And the dragon arena was nothing like the glider arena.

The glider arena resembled a big wind tunnel. It was a vast circle, many stories high, with no ceiling, open to the air above. It was a long cylinder. Riders launched from the top on gliders and glided all the way to the bottom.

By contrast, the dragon arena was shaped like an oval, ringed with seating, and with two entrances on either side for the two basks to enter from. The dragon arena did have a ceiling, though it was also several stories high.

There were other walls and constructions built throughout the arena, but these were manipulatable, using a mechanism built into their foundations. They could also be jacked up so that they rested on wheels and wheeled about the arena, then lowered so that they were stationary and sturdy. These were called "movables" by the students. In this way, the arena was always changing. It would be set up in a different configuration of movables every day.

The goal of the dragon arena games was to "kill" the other team by ridding them of their flags. Like the glider arena, each of the baskmembers had a flag. In the glider arena, it was on top of your glider. In the dragon arena, it attached to your shoulder.

Usually, flags were shot off with arrows. The arrows bounced off a body, but they were smeared with a substance made specially by the scholars that only stuck to the flags.

Games went on until every member of one team was flagless or until an hour and a half had passed, whichever was sooner. If the skirmish ran out of time, the team with the most players left standing at the hour-and-a-half mark won. This was true even if the numbers of the basks weren't even to begin with — which they usually weren't.

So, their first skirmish, the opposing bask, Bask Seven, simply decided that their best strategy was to wait it out. Bask Seven kept all of the bask hiding behind a movable shaped like a pyramid, and left two dragon riders to hover over the pyramid and defend them. They didn't even care about getting Banyan's and Odion's flags.

It didn't matter.

There were six members of Bask Seven, and there were only two members of their bask (which had been called Bask Thirty-two, as they were the last bask assigned). Bask Seven didn't have to take either of them out. All they had to do was bide their time.

Banyan and Odion spent a bit of time trying to engage with the hovering riders, which was awkward considering Banyan had never shot a bow and arrows before.

"Sorry," Odion said, "I was supposed to be teaching you out at the watchtower."

"You *could* have taught me," she said.

"Sorry," he said again.

She was pretty terrible at it, considering she'd had no practice whatsoever. And their engagement didn't do anything at all. Odion nearly got one of their flags, but then they moved into a defensive position wherein all that could be seen were their dragons' legs and below their wings.

So, Odion and Banyan regrouped to try to think of a strategy against them.

"We can't sneak up on them," said Banyan. "They're going to see us coming."

"No," said Odion. "I suppose we can't."

"But they're all just huddled behind that pyramid, probably playing cards," she fumed. "It makes me—" She stopped suddenly. "Wait."

"What?"

"Is there a rule we have to stay on our dragons?"

"No?" said Odion. "I guess not?"

"Right, then, you and Mirra and Erach go and distract them, and I'll sneak up behind them on foot and shoot all their flags off," she said.

"That's brilliant," said Odion. "But, um, I think you should let me be the one shooting, love? Because, uh, you're kind of awful with a bow and arrows."

She huffed. "That is only because you didn't teach me."

"Noted," he said. "It really is my fault."

"It is," she said. "But all right, fine, you can sneak up on them."

He grinned at her. "This is going to be fun," he said. "You and me playing games in the dragon arena."

She grinned back. "It will be."

It would be nice to have a distraction from all of the ugliness out there, actually. Games, not war.


BASK SEVEN WASN'T even surprised that Odion and Banyan beat them. The lieutenant who headed up the bask grinningly shook both of their hands, saying it was fun to see what the two of them came up with and he knew his little idea wasn't going to work in the end.

When they left the arena, they went back to Odion's old room, but it was stripped.

"This is starting to wear on my nerves," said Banyan, looking around the room. "Would it kill someone to tell me when I'm moving, or where I'm moving? Just once?"

"Well," said Odion, "you have to admit that it's nice not to have to pack your own shit."

She laughed, shaking her head at him.

They both knew the Quorum did it to knock their feet out from under them from time to time. As long as the ground was constantly shifting, they never felt safe, and they always had to be ready to react. It was a tactic, another head game. Everything was games here.

They went to the end of the hallway to talk to the dorm mammi there.

His name was Cris. Even though mammi was the diminutive for mother that children used in the Trinal Kingdoms, not all the dorm mammis were female.

Banyan had met Cris before. He had explained to them that he wasn't actually officially titled "mammi" that he actually had a rank in the army. He was an honorary Rider First Class, even though he didn't have a dragon, and this position was called Dorm Wing Coordinator.

"You two are back," he said to them.

"Do we still live here?" said Odion. "Or did they move us to an entirely different wing?"

They were still senior officers in the south corps, a division of the dragon corps, which was divided in four — north, east, west, and south. The divisions correlated with the towers of the school. Anyway, they should be in this wing, still, which was designated for senior officers.

"You guys get a double," said Cris. "You're a mated pair, right?"

"Right," said Odion, grinning. "I forgot about that." He turned to her. "We might get a bath."

"A bath?" said Banyan.

"Did we get one with a bath?" said Odion to Cris.

Cris was running his fingers over the ledger in front of him. "Room W12. It has a bath."

Odion punched the air in a sign of victory.

"What do you mean, a bath?" said Banyan. Usually, baths were taken in the basement of the school, near both the well and the kitchens. Students had to haul and heat their own buckets of water and they put them into wooden tubs which sat in long lines in the bathing rooms (there were two; one for female students and one for male).

She soon saw.

Their room was spacious, with a large bed, a massive window that overlooked the woods behind the school, and an attached bathing room. It had a huge bath that had been built in. It was large enough for two. It was made of smooth polished wood and beaten copper. It was gorgeous. There was even a hole in the floor with a pulley system so that hot buckets of water could be pulled up into the bath from the basement.

"Of course, it helps to have subordinates in your bask to order to heat the water for you," said Odion, peering down into the hole. "It's just you and me."

"We'll switch off," she said. "Take turns. One of us can heat water, one of us can have a bath." She ran her fingers over the lip of the pretty tub.

"The point of a bath this big is to share." Odion waggled his lavender eyebrows at her.

She felt herself blushing as she smiled. She let the blush happen. Usually, she tried to get those under control by imagining flicks all over her face. It was the way she'd learned to control her emotions in focus training.

"We should also break in the bed, of course," said Odion, going back out into the bedroom.

She stayed in the bathroom. "We can keep the chamberpot in here instead of behind a screen." Privacy for such things! She hadn't had that in… far too long.

"Get out here, Rider Thriceborn," called Odion.

"Shouldn't I have a better rank?" she said, coming to the doorway of the bathroom. "What are you? A capitan?"

"I feel like I should be getting a promotion, too," he said. "We should all be majors, like Slate."

She stiffened at the mention of him.

"Shit," said Odion. "Are we not supposed to ever talk about him?"

"We can talk about him," she said, too quickly.

But then they were both quiet and neither of them said anything.

Odion lay back on the bed, letting out a long, low sigh. "I hate that I let that happen to you. I know it messed you up. And with us, it messed us up too. Everything's been sort of awkward since."

She had an urge to go to him, to sit down and touch him, run her hands all over him comfortingly. Maybe it was his desire for that, coming through the bond. Maybe it was something she wanted. She didn't move, however. "It's not awkward."

He let out a long, low laugh.

"I mean..." She fingered the edge of her vest. "When do I get a dragon scale vest? Do I have to wait until Erach moults?"

"Changing the subject," said Odion, turning to look at her. "It's not the same when we make love."

"It is, though," she said. "It is exactly the same."

"No, it's not."

"It is," she insisted. "Because, before, we were both holding back. The heat made us wide open, and we showed each other all our secret and shameful hidden desires. And now... we're trying to go back to holding back, and..."

He sat up on the bed, nodding. "You're right, actually. You're exactly right." He tilted his head to one side. "Except if you're ashamed of your desires, then maybe you don't really want them."

"Maybe I don't," she said, because it was confusing. It was like the little fantasies she used to have an orgasm, wherein she imagined Odion doing things Odion didn't do. The intensity made it arousing, pushing the limit, just a little, here and there. That was powerful. But did she *really* want that?

"I mean, I'm ashamed, too," he said with a little shrug. "You saw what Slate does to me, and it's, uh, it's shameful."

She came over and sat down next to him, but she still didn't touch him. She wanted to say that she didn't understand it, but the truth was, she did understand, because she knew what it was to desire that kind of dominance sexually. She knew how it set her free. But she wasn't sure how it made her feel to see him cast in a subservient role. "It's shameful," she agreed. "But that's why it's arousing."

He nodded, hanging his head. "I don't need you to—"

"I love you," she interrupted. "I want to make you feel good. If you need that—"

"I just got done saying I didn't," he said sharply.

"But if it's just us," she said. "If it's only ever you and me, then you need to get it from somewhere, and I'm your only option."

"It *is* just us," he said, nodding. "Yeah, I promised you, and I meant to keep that promise, and I know the heat blindsided us, and maybe you don't even forgive me for that, in the end. In a way, I lied to you, Banyan."

She had never looked at it that way, but she supposed, from a certain point of view, it was true. "No, you didn't," she said anyway.

He eyed her. "You know he could never be to me what you are to me."

She could feel that through the bond, of course. And having been bonded to Slate, she knew that her bond with Odion was a thousand times stronger than that bond had been. This bond was a final layer on an established relationship, while whatever she'd had with Slate had been only a physical connection. "I'm not jealous of him."

"No?"

That was a lie. She was jealous, and she knew that Slate could never be to Odion what she was, but at the same time, she could never be to Odion what Slate was. "Not at all." She crawled into his lap, lowering her voice suggestively. "Let's break in the bed."

He grinned up at her, a wicked and pleased grin. "Let's."

She pushed him back on the bed and straddled him, working at his trousers.

"What are you doing?" He was smiling.

"It occurs to me that I've never put my mouth here," she said.

"Yeah, but you don't have to—"

"I want to, and shut up with that."

"But it's all… the scales." He was trying to stop her hands on the buttons.

"Odion, I am covered in scales." Now that she thought about it, though, he hadn't put his mouth on her there since. She rocked back. "Aren't you going to lick me now that I have a scaled pussy?"

"Of course I will," he said. "You're gorgeous there. I *like* it."

"Well, I like it too."

He hesitated.

She furrowed her brow. "*You* don't like it. Your own genitals, I mean. You don't like the scales."

He shrugged. "It doesn't matter." His voice was dull.

"Was it so different before?" she whispered, and now he wasn't stopping her, so she finished unbuttoning him. He was there, soft and encased in his scaled foreskin, and his penis looked almost adorable that way. She couldn't stop herself from running a finger over it.

It jumped against her, as if it was preening into her touch.

Odion let out a little laugh.

She moved her finger back. "Sorry. Is that all right?"

"Uh, definitely," he said.

"Why don't you like it?"

"It's, uh, it's ugly," he muttered. "Most people, their scales match their dragons, but mine don't."

"You'd rather your penis was pink?" Mirra was a very pink dragon.

He laughed again, shrugging. "I don't know. *You're* kinda pink, there, Nochan."

She looked down at her pale, freckled arm. "Pink?"

"It's a normal skin tone," he said.

"So, it's the color?"

"No, I don't know, it's just ugly."

"I don't think it is," she said, and she stroked him again, stroked his black, gleaming scales and the brown-purple head of him peeked out of his foreskin. She bent to kiss that.

He sighed.

"I like it very much, you know." She took the head of him into her mouth and gently sucked.

He groaned. "Banyan," he managed. His cock expanded in her mouth, growing very, very stiff.

This delighted her. She opened her mouth and tucked him all the way down her throat, running her tongue over the little nubs on the underside of him.

He grunted, letting out barely intelligible swear words.

She came off of his cock. "I wonder if you could see it the way I see it? See that it's beautiful, not even a little ugly?"

He caressed her face. "That sounds nice, but I don't know, love. I think it *is* just ugly."

"Well, all right then." She licked a long line up over those nubs of his.

He moaned.

"Maybe that's part of it, then," she whispered. "Maybe you think of it as if you're just subjecting me to this ugly, scaled, very intense cock of yours, and I just have to take it?"

His breath was ragged. "Go on," he murmured, touching her face.

"It's so much cock, Odion, so much."

He thrust himself into her mouth.

She moaned, but then his cock took up too much space back there, cutting off her air supply, stopping her noise.

He pulled out, cringing. "Shit, that was fucked up. I didn't mean—"

"Do it again," she said throatily.

"Fuck," he said and did thrust again. He thrust three times, but gently, fucking her mouth with each languid movement of her hips. And then he came, filling her mouth with his salty spend.

She swallowed it and giggled.

"You're laughing at me?"

"No." She wiped her lower lip. "No, just... that really turned you on, huh?"

He pulled her up to kiss her mouth hard. "Maybe," he said in a voice with no bottom.

She was still giggling.

He touched her lower lip, smiling at her. "I feel like you're laughing at me, and if I wasn't right on the aftermath of an orgasm, I think I would even care."

"I'm not laughing at you," she said. "I'm just... I like it, I think. Making you lose control? It makes me feel good."

He rolled them over. "I like it, too, love." He was pulling

aside her clothing, undoing her trousers. "In fact, it's your turn now."

She surrendered to his hot mouth on her body. He hadn't licked her like this since the scales had come in. She was somehow more sensitive and less, if that made any sense. She'd always felt as if there was too much pressure when people touched her, that it hurt, but now, she could stand the push of his tongue, and it just felt good.

She rolled her hips into his mouth, letting out a series of deeply satisfied moans that seemed to bubble up out of the center of her and overtake them both.

She tried to hold onto the sensation, let it take her, let it overwhelm her.

But eventually, she succumbed, thinking instead about Slate, holding her face, smiling at her indulgently, saying, *You like that, don't you, sweet Banyan? Suck nice and hard on my cock, just like that. Good girl.*

And then she came against Odion's tongue, guiltily, thinking that next time she needed to think about sucking Odion, not Slate, never Slate, *no more* Slate.

Fuck.

# CHAPTER TEN

THERE WAS ONE person Banyan did share the information about the Frost that they'd learned with and that was Dove.

Dove listened quietly to the entire explanation, shaking her head at intervals, making little noises of shock and interest.

Eventually, when Banyan was done, the scholar said, "It doesn't make any sense."

"I know," said Banyan. Then, "Wait, which part?"

"Just, if it's all the same, why is the sickness so different?"

"I don't know," said Banyan. "Maybe because of heat somehow?"

"They can survive in heat," said Dove. "Deke could. He was an ice monster, and he was fine in the heat. His organs weren't shutting down."

"Right," said Banyan. "But… well, I don't know. Doesn't it take weeks for a person to succumb to the Frost sickness?"

"True," said Dove, tapping her lower lip. "True. It could be the same thing."

"You're saying it's not the same thing."

"Well, look, there's only one person I know of who had a bite," said Dove.

"Yes, but didn't the stories sound similar to you?" said Banyan. "Some infected woman biting a man, luring him in with sex?"

"It did, but there are key differences," said Dove. "For

one thing, the man who told me about that bite certainly didn't mention this woman having white hair and white skin and colorless eyes. She wasn't an ice monster."

"He did say she was strange, though, didn't he?"

Dove considered. "I suppose. I'd ask him more questions, but he's unfortunately dead."

"If it's not the same thing, then... what?"

"Well, then *what* is the sickness?" said Dove. "We've always called it the Frost sickness, but maybe this — with the ice monsters — is something entirely new. Maybe it's not connected at all. Why would they think it was connected, you know? They don't even seem to have anything to do with each other except that they both originated in the ice peaks."

"But why conflate them if they don't have anything to do with each other?"

"I don't know," said Dove. She gave Banyan an ironic smile. "The Quorum works in mysterious ways."

Banyan scoffed. "I'm about over all of their mysterious ways, to tell you the truth." She sighed. "Well, I could defeat the Frost and we'd still be left with this illness is what you're telling me."

"We don't know how that sickness is spread. We don't know anything about it," said Dove.

"It seems to me that the things we don't know would fill up the whole library," said Banyan.

"That's the unfortunate truth," said Dove.

The two women parted ways, both frustrated.

Banyan returned to her double room with her built-in bath and her beautiful mate, and every day, she and Odion fought skirmishes in the dragon arena. When they weren't fighting skirmishes, she was practicing with a bow and arrows in the practice area.

She found that it was much easier to aim the thing when she was on the ground than when she was on the back of a dragon.

Odion's idea of teaching was vastly undeveloped. He mostly criticized her, never offering much in the way of suggestions on how to improve.

She knew that was because this was the way he had been taught, and she didn't hold it against him.

Still, most of her education fell to herself.

She observed other riders in the arena, and she saw various techniques. Some of them reached for one arrow at a time. Others would seize three or four at a time, and pulled the bow back in rapid succession, one after the other. This increased the number of times one could fire, but seemed to decrease accuracy.

She sought to determine why and to figure out how to have both speed and accuracy.

She was a fast learner.

Within a week, she and Odion were regularly defeating everyone they were pitted against in the arena, though they did sustain two defeats—both by basks with eight members, who easily outnumbered and overwhelmed them.

So, of course, the Quorum decided that they must make things more interesting.

She and Odion were already hopelessly outnumbered and they had to fight against the odds, but the Quorum needed to handicap them worse.

Over the coming weeks, they had skirmishes that involved their being given short notice, with the other team already in place when they arrived (this was a favorite of the Quorum, having been employed in the glider arena), being forced to fight skirmishes with less arrows than the other bask, being forced to share a dragon, and being forced to fight without dragons, just to name a few.

It could have frustrated them, but it didn't.

Sometimes, Banyan would look back on this phase of their lives as the last time she was really and truly happy in an easy way.

Nothing mattered. Nothing was at risk.

It was all games, just games, and she and Odion were excited and electrified by the challenges.

The only thing that happened that shocked her was her first quake. She had heard of them, and she even knew that the ground where the Academy was built was unsteady and that—from time to time—it shook and everything built on it shook too. But experiencing it was something quite different. She was very alarmed when it happened, letting out a series of squeaks.

Odion had laughed at her, folding her into his arms. "Just one of the quakes. Last year, we had two of them. Surely, you've heard of them?"

"Yes, yes," she had said, laughing, too.

They laughed a lot, those days. They took baths in their built-in bath, one of them down in the basement, heating the water for it to be hauled up, one standing up in their room and calling down playfully to the other.

They made love, and she tried not to think about Slate and tried not to fantasize—and sometimes she didn't. Sometimes she did. Odion didn't know, but she didn't think a relationship had to be one where there were no secrets. Maybe it did. If so, hers was a failure. She couldn't bring herself to change it, though, and she couldn't tell him.

Surely, it would crush him to think that she was attracted to another man.

She didn't want him to not be satisfied with her, after all, did she? She wanted to be enough for him.

Sometimes, she woke in the middle of the night, his body pressed into hers, the hot pulse of him throbbing against her skin, and he'd breathe urgently in her ear that she needed to take him now. "Can you take me, Banyan?"

She liked that, was excited by his demand, his need. She liked being wanted in that way.

It cemented to her that she was enough for him, and that felt good.

One night, she and Odion were just getting out of one of their dual baths. The water was cold and neither wanted to get dressed and go down to the basement to heat more water.

There was a knock on their door.

Odion went to open it, wrapped in a towel. She stayed in the bathroom, hiding behind the door. It wasn't common for them to get visitors to their rooms. People were not friendly with them, as a general rule. They were isolated and strange and too good at the skirmishes and people either admired them or hated them.

It was Rils Markir, who had been accelerated out of the glider corps early along with a number of other students at mid-term. It had coincided with graduating a number of students ahead of schedule also.

Banyan knew it was because the Quorum was churning out riders—body fodder for the Frost—but she didn't entirely understand why.

Slate's point, that giving the Frost more bodies was foolish, was a good one.

On the other hand, the Quorum had recruited more riders to the Academy so that they would have more fighters. They couldn't simply stand by and allow the Frost to attack. They had to resist somehow.

Banyan didn't like thinking about the Frost. She wanted to think of nothing but skirmishes and the school and baths and how to have orgasms without fantasizing. These were the problems she wanted to solve, nothing more.

"Naxim," said Rils. "Look at you."

"Something I can help you with?" said Odion.

"Well, everyone else said you were too stuck up the ass of Colonel Rabi to ever help out, but I said you've got a bit of a rebellious streak," said Rils. "And I know Thriceborn does. I still remember the way she beat me in the glider arena." He pitched his voice louder, because he knew she was listening.

She came out of the bathroom, also wrapped in a towel. "Hello, Rils."

"Senior prank," said Rils.

"Are we seniors?" said Banyan. This was her first year at the school, technically.

"I think I am," said Odion. "You're definitely not."

"Well, at the rate we're all being accelerated, we don't even know if we'll ever get to be seniors, so we decided anyone who wants in can help," said Rils. "Do you? Want in?"

"Is this a thing?" said Banyan. "Is there usually a prank?"

"Oh, it's a thing," said Odion. "And it's usually around this time of the year, I guess. Beginning of the fourth quarter. One year, I remember they stole all of Rabi's uniforms and he had nothing but underwear. He didn't come out in them, though, more's the pity. And another year, they arranged all the movables in the dragon arena into a big sculpture that blocked the doorway."

"What was it a sculpture of?" said Banyan.

"A cock and balls, obviously," said Odion.

She snorted. "So mature."

"It's a prank, Banyan," said Odion, grinning at her. "Let's do it. I could stand something fun."

She nodded. "We're in."

"Knew it," said Rils. "Meet us in the basement at the midnight bell for a planning meeting."

At the midnight bell, they were both wide awake.

Banyan was beginning to feel nervous. Maybe this was a prank on them, not on the school. Maybe they were going to be set up for something. Maybe they'd get in trouble themselves.

Odion shrugged. "Who cares? What could Rabi even do to us?"

"Don't say that." She pointed at him. "You'll jinx us. The colonel has left us alone, too alone. It's actually making me nervous."

"Maybe," admitted Odion. "I still say we risk it."

She had to agree. It was too much fun not to attempt it.

So, they carefully and quietly sneaked out of their room and made their way all the way to the basement.

They found Rils and the others in the mens' bathing room, all standing in amongst the empty tubs, holding torches.

"You're here," said Gelso Raxx, waving to her. Gelso had been a member of her glider bask who'd been accelerated as well.

She waved back, grinning at him.

"Well," said Carn Milx, the lieutenant of Bask Seven

who'd shaken hands with them after their first win in the arena, "here you two are. Now we can begin."

Odion smirked at him. "Are we going to have to do everything? You lot don't even have an idea for the prank, do you?"

"Oh, we have an idea," said Rils. "You know that shipwreck in the mouth of the moat under the castle?"

"No?" said Banyan.

"You've never seen that?" said Odion. "I have to take you out and show you. It's this ancient thing, stuck right there. I never understood why a ship of that size was sailing in the moat anyway. Obviously, it was going to get moored."

Banyan shrugged. She wasn't always so very observant about her surroundings, it was true. Sometimes, she was consumed with her own inner thoughts, and didn't notice anything else.

"Well," said Odion, "what about it?"

"We want to put it in the dining hall," said Rils.

"What?" said Banyan. "How big is this thing?"

"It's possible," said Rils. "There's that big window in the dining hall. It can be opened. If all of our dragons fly this thing up there, we can get it inside."

Banyan thought about everyone coming into the dining hall and seeing a ship sitting there, and it made her laugh. "That's ridiculous."

"Entirely the point," said Rils.

"I like it," said Odion. "It's bold."

"We're going to be the last class of this Academy," said Carn. "We might as well go out with something big."

"Right, who knows, but next year, we're just overwhelmed with ice monsters," said Rils with a shrug.

Banyan and Odion looked around at all of them. They didn't know about the ice monsters, because the Quorum didn't tell them.

Banyan wondered if she should say something, if it would help or hinder them. These students were already bonded to dragons. There was no backing out at this point. The reason the Quorum gave was that they didn't want to scare the prospective riders away, and yet, they still hadn't told them.

Carn tilted his chin back. "Nothing to say to that, you two?"

"What do you want us to say?" said Odion. "That you're right, that the threat is imminent, that we think the Quorum is preparing for a final battle that's going to take place here, at the school? Well, guess we've said it."

Everyone was quiet, then.

A solemnity descended onto them all, robbing the fun outing of its youthful joy.

"All right," Banyan said eventually, "how do we do this?"

"I think the first step is to figure out how intact that ship is," said Rils. "Someone needs to go down there and inspect it. We also need to see how difficult it's going to be to get it unstuck from the mud."

"Well, I haven't seen it, so I'd like to go down there," said Banyan.

"We'll do it," said Odion.

"I'm in, also," said Gelso.

"Report back tomorrow evening?" said Rils. "Same time, same place?"

"Absolutely," said Banyan.

They dismissed and all tiptoed through the darkness back to their relative beds.

The morning brought their classes. They were on a unit about edible plants in their field survival survey and learning about moulting in their dragon studies course.

The afternoon was a skirmish.

They fought Bask Twenty, who had four members, and they were obliged to wear blindfolds.

Banyan found the blindfold terrifying at first, but Erach wasn't blindfolded, so she simply had to allow him to be her eyes. Through the bond, she could see whatever she needed to see.

At first, her aim was off, but then she adjusted for the difference in height between her and the dragon. And then, she and Odion made quick work of the other bask.

Before dinner, then, she found herself trekking down the muddy banks of the moat to find the shipwreck.

It was, indeed, a huge ship, half sunk in the mud, its sails long rotted away, otherwise very much intact, though it hadn't been moved in some time.

She found it hilarious—both that it was here and that she'd never seen it. It was the sort of thing she wouldn't have believed if someone had told her. Too incongruous to be real.

"Maybe it's a pirate ship," she said as she climbed onto its tilting deck and wandered around on it. "Someone tried to pirate the school and got stuck."

"Yes," said Gelso, coming in after her, chuckling, "here we are in a huge pirate ship, just sneaking up on this stationary school."

She snorted. "All right, you don't have to make fun."

"Well, I don't think it's a pirate ship is all," said Gelso.

"We wouldn't know, though, would we?" said Odion as he climbed aboard also. "The only way to tell is if the ship is flying a pirate flag, and all the flags have rotted away."

Banyan opened the door to the cabin at the back. There was nothing much inside, just darkness, but there were ladders descending into the depths of the ship below. "Should we go down?"

"Why not?" said Gelso.

"Maybe there's treasure," said Odion.

"Yes, well, what would we do with that?" said Banyan, swinging herself round on the ladder.

"Buy ourselves a nice farm and grow nothing but radishes," said Odion.

Banyan's laughter echoed into the belly of the ship. "Radishes?"

"Don't you like radishes?" said Odion. "Here we are mated for life, and we're not even a good match."

She snickered, reaching her foot down for another rung on the ladder. "I came to the Academy to escape being a farmer's wife, don't you know? I wouldn't—"

Something grabbed her foot.

She kicked at it, looking down, and she saw only a flash of white.

Her foot collided with something, which went off into the darkness. She was free. "Up," she shrieked at Gelso, who had been coming after her. "Something's down here."

Gelso took a moment to switch directions, but then he was scrambling up the ladder, and she came after him.

Odion's eyes were wide. "What?"

"Ice monster," she said. "Human. It had hands."

"Wait," said Gelso. "Wait, what?"

"Just stay back," said Odion.

And then, from below, it appeared, climbing up the ladder. It was awful. Half of its face was gone, but it wasn't rotted, just gone. Inside, the meat of it was gray and dead, and its bone gleamed through, a hard and white cheekbone there. It had no eye on one side, but on the other side the eye was blank and colorless.

Gelso let out a guttural sound, backing away, shaking his head. "What is that?"

"We don't have weapons?" muttered Odion.

The thing crawled up onto the deck, getting to its shaky feet, gurgling as it ran for them.

Banyan moved out of the way.

Odion seized part of the railing on the side of the deck and it came away with a splintering crack.

Gelso just stood there, mouth open, and the thing fell on Gelso and dug its teeth right into Gelso's cheek.

Gelso shrieked.

Odion drove the splintered piece of the railing into the back of the thing's neck. It came out through its lack of an eye. It went still, collapsing on Gelso, who was still screaming.

# CHAPTER ELEVEN

BANYAN SPRINTED INTO the library. Where was Dove?
Dove had to be in here.
There in the back of the stacks. Banyan rushed over to her. She took the other woman by the arm. "Come with me."
Dove had a stack of books in her hands. "Come with you where?"
"I can't tell you, just come," said Banyan.
"I can't leave the library. I'm the only person here."
"Dove, would I come and get you if it wasn't important?"
Dove regarded her for a moment. Then, she nodded, set down the stack of books, and followed Banyan out of the library.
They had Gelso in a room in the top of the north tower which was abandoned. There were a number of these rooms scattered about, rooms that the undercadets used as places to meet up and have sex.
It may or may not have been a good place to keep him. Banyan wasn't sure. She and Odion were immediately in agreement that they wanted to hide the bite, that they wanted to keep Gelso from the Quorum, and that this was the thing to do.
Dove saw him, lying on the bed in there—which was stripped of sheets—with his face wrapped in strips from his shirt, and she was utterly confused.
Banyan and Odion began explaining what had happened,

tripping over their words to get it all out. As they spoke, Dove began to shake. Finally, she held up both of her hands. "He needs to go to the healing wing."

"Does he?" said Banyan. "What's going to happen to him there?"

"Near as we know, the existence of the ice monsters as turned riders isn't acknowledged," said Odion quietly.

"You said you didn't know if this was the same as the Frost sickness," said Banyan. "But if it is, if it behaves like the Frost sickness, that will tell us something. Now, after Deke was bitten, his transformation was complete in what?" She looked at Odion. "Twelve hours? Sixteen hours?"

"It was quick," said Odion. "But the Frost sickness usually takes weeks to kill someone, right? So, if he doesn't transform, we're going to know something."

Gelso sat up in the bed. "I'm an experiment?"

Banyan went to him and took his hand. She squeezed it as hard as she could. "I'm so sorry, Gelso, but there's nothing they can do for you in the healing wing, anyway." She looked at Dove. "Right?"

Dove nodded. "It's true. We just try to keep people comfortable."

"Hey," said Odion. "Banyan mentioned something you said to me, and it's been bothering me. She said that with the patients with the Frost sickness, you have a drug you give them to make them fall asleep?"

Dove nodded. "Yes."

"Why don't you give that out to patients when, you know, you're forcing us to go through getting our bones healed, because that's excruciating."

Dove's eyes widened. "I don't *know*."

"That's never come up?" said Odion. "You were there when my arm was broken. Five people were holding me down."

"No, I know," said Dove. "It's definitely never come up. We never use that drug, except with the Frost sickness, and not until the end. Usually, to be honest, after we give it to them, they don't wake up again. They get taken away."

"Taken away where?" said Banyan.

"I assumed to be buried," said Dove.

"So, they're dead?" said Banyan.

"No," said Dove. "No, they're usually still… well, the sickness stops breath and it stops the heartbeat. It stops everything, but… they're still alive, because they're warm and because, when you touch them, they react in their sleep, so…"

Gelso extricated his hand from Banyan's. "I want to go. I want to go home. I want to go see my family, and I want—if this is it, if this is all I have, let me take my dragon, and—"

"No, because you might bite them," said Banyan.

Gelso looked at her with welling eyes. "Fuck." He flopped back on the bed. He looked at the ceiling and began muttering a litany of swear words under his breath.

Banyan tried to take his hand again, but he wouldn't let her.

She got up from the bed. "I-if you make it through sixteen hours, and you're not transformed, maybe. Maybe one of us can take you to see your family."

"No," said Odion. "No, Banyan, that's insane. We can't risk—"

"He's a person, Odion," said Banyan. "And we didn't turn him over to the Quorum, because the Quorum thinks of us like soldiers first and people last."

"It's hard enough to hide him at all. If we leave the school, we can't hide that. If we don't show up for skirmishes—"

"Let's fake a heat," said Banyan. "Can we do that?"

"It's too soon!" said Odion. Then he thought about it. "Maybe we can. Sometimes, after a mating, dragon's mating schedules can be erratic. Could work." He nodded slowly. "But only if we need to leave the school."

"All right," said Banyan, taking a breath. They had a plan, then. She turned to Dove. "Can you get us supplies? Bandages, ointments, things he might need?"

Dove chewed on her bottom lip. "I think so. But I'll need to be careful, because if anyone sees me taking things, there will be questions."

Gelso groaned. "Does it hurt?"

Banyan remembered Deke talking about the agonizing pain, even though he was entirely frozen and couldn't move. She was torn. Should she tell him the truth or reassure him? If it was her, she decided, she'd want to know. "I think it might," she whispered.

Gelso rolled over into the bed, hiding his face. "Can you... leave me alone?" he bit out.

"Sorry, I don't think that's a good idea," whispered Banyan.

"But outside the door, I think," said Odion. "We can wait out there. If anything happens, we'll hear you."

"*Fuck.*"


BANYAN AND ODION passed the night together outside Gelso's room. Both kept telling the other to go and get some rest, but neither of them could have possibly slept. They stayed there, together, like sentries, until morning came.

Gelso was not transformed, not after twelve hours, not after sixteen.

They skipped their morning classes. Students didn't show up sometimes, and there usually wasn't punishment until it became habitual. The skirmishes were deemed more important.

By lunchtime, Dove was back, and she checked his bandage and looked him over and told them all that he seemed to be presenting entirely like the patients with the Frost sickness. His only current symptom was numbness in his hands and feet, which was fairly typical. Furthermore, she'd discovered something.

She didn't want to talk about it in front of Gelso.

The three went into the hallway, where they spoke in hushed whispers.

"I got one of my superiors drunk last night," said Dove.

"Her name is Micha, and she's only a few years older than me. We were students together. She graduated only last year. Anyway, I knew she was helping with the bodies of the patients who've succumbed to the Frost illness, and I got her talking about it. It wasn't easy. I could tell when I brought it up that she'd been told not to talk about it. She made me swear that I would never let on I heard it from her."

"What did you find out?" said Banyan.

"They're not dead," said Dove.

"You said that before," said Banyan.

"She says that usually, they don't come out of the drug that we give them, the one that puts them to sleep," said Dove. "Except it doesn't put them to sleep, not exactly. It… it's a poison. It would kill a normal person."

"Wait, that drug kills them?" said Odion.

"Well, no, because they don't die," said Dove.

"Unless you get their brain," supplied Banyan in a dull voice. "It *is* the same thing."

"If they come out of it, they're aggressive," said Dove. "She says they try to grab onto the scholars, that they try to bite them."

"It's the same," said Banyan.

"Yes," said Dove. "And so, what they do, is to stab all of them in the back of their skulls, subdue them, kill them, and then… then we burn the bodies."

"What is the difference?" said Banyan. "Why does it take them so long to transform, when it only took Deke a few hours? And why do they go into those rages? Why do they come out of them? I don't understand any of it."

"It's got to be the cold," said Dove. "I think being in freezing temperatures probably speeds up the transition."

"So, then, Gelso has weeks," said Banyan. "We can take him home."

"I think so," said Dove.

Banyan put her hand to her chest. Good. That was at least one relief in this awful mess of things. She was glad he'd have his chance to say goodbye.

## CHAPTER TWELVE

THEY HAD A skirmish that afternoon.

Banyan and Odion talked to Gelso, and they locked and barricaded him in the room and hoped their theory was right. They left him there.

Afterward, they hurried back to find him all right in the room. He was eager to leave, and they told him they were putting that into place with the colonel. They'd announce the heat and then go and take him with them.

There was a knock at the door.

They all went quiet.

"Hello?" called Odion finally.

"It's Rils," came the voice through the door. "I followed you. You guys never showed last night for the meeting about the ship."

The prank. The stupid, stupid prank. If they'd never gone out there, this never would have happened.

Banyan flung open the door without thinking. She was angry, and she wanted to blame Rils. She wanted to scream at him that this was his fault.

Belatedly, she realized she didn't want anyone to know about Gelso, and she wasn't sure how much she could trust Rils.

But Rils had seen into the room now, and he was gaping at Gelso. "What happened?" said Rils.

Banyan tried to shut the door on him.

He caught it and stopped her.

"Just go away, Rils. Go away and pretend you didn't see anything."

Rils pulled a handkerchief out of his pocket and wiped at his nose. "Sorry, I'm a little under the weather," he said. "Not sick enough to get out of the skirmishes, more's the pity."

"Rils," said Gelso, grinning at him weakly. "You need to know about this. Everyone needs to know."

"No," said Banyan.

"No," said Odion.

Gelso sat up in bed, glaring at the both of them. "You two spend all this time trashing the Quorum, complaining about how they keep secrets, but in the end, you just do their work for them."

Banyan bowed her head. She stepped away from the door and motioned for Rils to come inside.

Rils stepped over the threshold. "What is going on?"

"What do you know about ice monsters, Rils?" said Gelso in a strangled voice. "Because you're looking at one."

Rils's eyes widened. "What?"

"It's an infection," said Banyan. "The Frost sickness, it infects riders and changes them, and it infects dragons and changes them, and the Frost's army is... us. It's riders and their dragons."

Rils staggered over to sit down on the bed next to Gelso. He looked him over. "*What?*" he said again.

"We're taking him home," said Banyan. "We think he has a few weeks. We're going to take him to see his family, and then we'll be there with him at the end, and we'll—"

"What are you even saying?" Rils said, shaking his head again and again.

It took a long time to explain.

And then, that night, Gelso seemed to come down with Rils's runny nose. Except it was worse, possibly because his body was weakened by the Frost sickness already. His body temperature raised, and he got a fever, and he shivered and shook through the night.

They didn't take him home.

They talked about it; but he was too ill to be put on the back of a dragon. They didn't know what might happen to him in that time. Dove came to look him over, and she wasn't sure what to do. His fever was so high that she said they might treat him with an ice bath—but she didn't know if they should cool his body down with the Frost illness.

So, they waited.

The fever raged through Gelso.

And news spread like wildfire through the entire Academy about the ice monsters.

So, the next morning, Colonel Rabi was at the door with an army of scholars from the healing wing, and they took Gelso away, and Banyan tried to protest, but she couldn't stop it and neither could Odion.

Gelso was borne off, and the colonel ordered them to go to his office and wait for him there.

On the way through the hallways, they debated leaving.

"We could just get on our dragons and go," said Odion. "He's angry. He's not going to take this well. On top of all of that, he's going to find out that we hid things about Deke. We could go."

"Where does that leave us?" she said. "We need to be here. If this is where the Frost is attacking, this is where we belong, isn't it?"

He stopped walking. "Is it, though? We could escape all of it, Banyan. Just you and me. We'll defect and go live on our own."

"As defectors, if we're ever discovered, we'll be executed. We'd spend all our lives in hiding. What punishment could he possibly give us that we can't handle?" she said.

He nodded once. "Besides, we wouldn't like it. We'd… this is what we do, isn't it? We're soldiers, and this is all we're good at."

She was glad he understood.

They waited in the colonel's office for nearly three quarters of an hour.

When he arrived, they both stood up straight, at attention.

He did not tell them to relax their poses. He walked in front of them, arms clasped behind his back, quiet, seemingly thinking.

Banyan didn't like this. She wished he'd just get it over with.

Finally, the colonel stopped. He faced them both. "I wish you'd come to me with your questions about the ice monsters. I wish you wouldn't have used a sick student to conduct some kind of science experiment. Gelso Raxx deserves better than that. But, I don't know, I suppose that's what you did to Deke Midgurd. And I suppose I'm to blame. I have personally made it my mission to burn out bits of both of your humanity, after all. I need you to fight. I need you to be efficient. I need you to save the Trinal Kingdoms. It's amazing the things a person can justify in pursuit of that goal."

Banyan wanted to protest. She didn't.

"Permission to speak, sir," growled out Odion.

"Have a seat, both of you," said the colonel.

Warily, they both sat down.

The colonel sat down, too.

"That is not what he was!" Banyan burst out with. "He was *not* an experiment. We were trying to give him dignity, which is something that the Quorum doesn't even seem to understand."

The colonel eyed her and then he barked out a laugh. "Dignity. Hiding him up there in that dirty room without any care. You got him sick on top of the Frost sickness. He'll probably die from that fever before it even has a chance to transform him."

"Well, that was Rils," muttered Banyan. "I didn't... neither Odion nor I caught his sickness." Her shoulders slumped. "We should have thought about how weak Gelso was. But, colonel, we were going to take him home so that he had the chance to say goodbye to his family, and—"

"No," said the colonel. "No, out of the question."

"But we—"

"Ask me your questions," said the colonel.

Banyan glanced at Odion.

He was glowering at the colonel.

"What did you want to know?" said the colonel.

"They're the same thing—the Frost sickness and the ice monsters?"

"Not exactly," said the colonel. "The Frost sickness can infect anyone, yes, but it behaves differently when it infects a rider, someone who's already been transformed by a dragon bond—or when it infects a dragon. And we don't entirely know how it's different, only that the Frost sickness eradicates the mind of a normal person and it *absorbs* the mind of a dragon rider."

"Absorbs?" said Odion. "What do you mean by that?"

"We don't know exactly. We've never seen the transformation happen to a rider. We didn't even know it was happening at first. Some riders and dragons went missing when they were doing routine patrols on the icy peaks. Then they reappeared, transformed, and attacked the watchtower they'd come from. One soldier escaped. He said that the ice monsters knew all of the routines of the watchtower, knew when to attack and how to get inside. They fought like riders, using our techniques and training. They…" The colonel threw up his hands. "And so, this is why we proposed the treaty. This is why we decided we needed to fight. But frankly, everything we have done has only served to strengthen the Frost. It grows, and as it grows, it absorbs all of our best and brightest. Once they are transformed, they fight with single-minded focus to advance the Frost. We don't even know what it wants."

"It wants to spread," said Odion.

"How do you know this?" said the colonel. "From Deke Midgurd, I suspect. He was your first experiment."

"We didn't experiment on him," said Banyan.

"He attacked us," said Odion. "He was transformed. We—I wanted to kill him, but Banyan couldn't, so we waited, and then he… started talking."

The colonel sat up straight in his chair, his face ashen. "No. They don't talk."

"They do," said Banyan. "He was still Deke."

"Except he wasn't," said Odion, looking at her, his voice going gentle. "He wasn't Deke anymore."

Banyan's face crumpled.

Odion pointed at the colonel. "You never insult her for what she had to do out there. Never say that Banyan doesn't have humanity. You… despite everything you have done to us, she remains the most caring and… and *good* person I've ever met. I wanted to kill him, and she gave him a death that…" Odion was overcome.

Banyan felt tears forming in her eyes and she was terrified she'd cry in front of the colonel.

The colonel was on his feet. His hands were shaking. He held up a finger. "Wait. Let's… I need to gather the highest ranking officers in the Quorum. You'll tell us all."

Banyan felt her stomach sink. She looked at Odion.

He wasn't looking at her. He was fuming, clenching his hand into a fist and releasing it.

The colonel left the office, door banging on his way out.

Odion sprang up out of his seat. "*This* is what he thinks of us, Banyan. That we're not human."

"Well," said Banyan quietly. "It's what we think of him, too."

Odion let out a funny laugh and collapsed into his chair.

It was quiet.

"No," said Odion. "That's not fair. He has the power and he manipulates us. He's the broken one, and he's trying to break us into his image and—"

"Do we tell them?" She swallowed. "They didn't keep this from us, after all. We found out things they didn't know. Do we tell them?"

"They don't deserve to know," said Odion. "What are they doing with this knowledge, Banyan? You're the one who pointed out to me how they benefit from this entire situation, amassing this army that they can use—"

"They're not the ones amassing an army," she said to him. "The Frost is."

Odion sighed.

"The Frost is real. It's coming for us. The Quorum is the best equipped to stop it. It's... lesser of two evils."

Odion sighed again.

"So," she said softly. "We tell them."

The colonel was back in five minutes, and he ushered them out of his office and up a set of stairs and into a different room, which had a round semi circle of a desk, fitted with ten chairs. Some were filled, and others came in, taking their seats.

Banyan had seen these men and a few women, in the hallways of the school, or looking down on the dining hall from time to time. She knew many of their names, but she had never spoken to most of them. A few were teachers, but most were distant figures.

They all took their seats and they stared at Banyan and Odion, who were standing in the middle with Colonel Rabi.

"Well, then Matthew," said the woman seated in the middle. General Frax, Banyan knew. "What is all this?" The general was Colonel Rabi's mate. Well, their dragons were mated, anyway.

"Tell them," said the colonel to Odion. "Tell them what you told me."

Odion let out a breath. "We, um, we were sent on a mission to mate our dragons, and the colonel sent Banyan's ex-lover out there for some reason."

"Odion," snapped the colonel.

"Well, what was the purpose of that?" said Odion. "Why did you think that would encourage the mating?"

The colonel folded his arms over his chest. He addressed General Frax. "Sir, when Deke Midgurd transformed, they say he talked."

The general furrowed her brow. "What did he say?"

"We didn't get to that," said the colonel. He turned back to the both of them.

"Mostly he begged for his life and cried a lot," said Odion.

Banyan spoke up. "He told us how the transformation happened. He was seduced by a transformed rider, someone named Genevieve, who used to be in Odion's bask. She bit him during the course of the, erm, interlude."

"Seduced how?" said the general.

"Well, I asked him to skip over that part, actually," said Banyan. "I don't know. He said she told him there was food and warmth and shelter somewhere."

"She talked, too?" said the general.

"All of them talked," said Banyan. "But Deke went in and out of it. Sometimes, he was pure rage, just trying to bite us, and then he would sort of, I don't know, surface, and then he was just himself."

"He was *not*," said Odion firmly. "You said it yourself. He said he wanted to go home to his mother, and you said he couldn't, because he would bite her, and he didn't even deny it. He just tried to convince you to let him bite *you*."

"Well, that's true," said Banyan.

"Go back," said the general. "All of them? How many did you see?"

"Only Deke," said Banyan. "But he said there were a number of them that were there during his transition."

"How did the transition work?" The general leaned forward, very interested.

"He said that he was in a great deal of pain, but frozen," said Banyan. "As in, he couldn't move."

"That's the final stage of the Frost sickness," said the general, leaning back in her chair. "Very interesting."

The colonel addressed her. "He tried to convince you to allow him to bite you?"

"He said it would be nice," said Banyan. "That he'd like it and I'd like it. He said that I'd be part of some family, and that… how did he put it?" She turned to Odion for help.

"I don't know," said Odion. "He said that it gave meaning to his life, wanting to spread the Frost. He called it… the purpose or something?"

"Yes, I remember that," said Banyan. "The purpose."

"And what is the purpose?" said General Frax.

"Biting," said Banyan. "Spreading."

"Why does it want to spread?"

"That's how it reproduces," said Banyan.

"Yeah, and that's why they're a family," said Odion. "He said Genevieve was like his mother or something. It's all extremely weird."

"But intriguing," said the general, shaking her head slowly. She eyed them. "So, what happened after that?"

"Well, we had to kill him," said Odion. "He had told us that all he wanted to do was bite people. He couldn't be trusted. And he didn't want to die. He cried and begged. He volunteered to be a spy for us into the Frost."

"But we couldn't trust that," said Banyan. "And we knew, if we let him go, he would bite someone straightaway, as soon as he got the chance. So, we had to."

"We did."

"You didn't even consider bringing him back here to the Academy," General Frax said.

"Well, how?" said Odion. "On a dragon with one of us? He would have bitten whoever he was close to. Maybe there would have been some way to try to bind his jaw, but nothing foolproof."

"We were operating under the assumption you didn't want to lose us to the Frost," said Banyan, leveling her gaze at the general.

The general's mouth curved a little, a ghost of a smile. "You're not joking about the younger generation's lack of respect for their superiors, are you, Matthew?"

"Let me handle the punishments for all of this, if you don't mind, Marigold?" said Colonel Rabi. "I am the one in charge of the Academy, last I checked."

"And I am the one in charge of the *army*," said the general.

"Yes, sir," said the colonel.

"Oh, take them away," said the general. "We have much to discuss."

# CHAPTER THIRTEEN

ODION STOOD IN the doorway to their room, shaking his head. He should have figured. "Well, they did it again."

"Moved us?" she said. "We lost the room? That's part of the punishment?"

"Looks like," said Odion. He leaned into the door frame, sighing heavily.

Banyan rubbed her forehead, her cheekbones sparkling, and she was beautiful, even when she was worried. "Well, at least we kept Dove out of it."

"Yeah, one good thing," he said, reaching for her. He couldn't help it. He wanted to touch her all the time.

She let herself be pulled into his arms, resting her forehead on his shoulder. "Odion," she breathed. "Odion, how bad is it going to be?"

"Bad, probably," said Odion. "Worse than what we can imagine. It's best not to try to imagine. You know how they treat us when we do well, after all."

She laughed helplessly, clutching him. "I do."

"When we do well, they promote us and give us really hard challenges," he said. "When we do badly, they…"

"What do they do?"

"They're creative." He tightened his arms around her. "What do you fear the most? It'll be that."

She shuddered, grabbing a fistful of his vest. "I still don't have a dragon-scale vest, you know, and no one talks to me about that."

He chuckled. "You do have to wait for the first moult. But when that happens, we'll get you something, don't you worry."

"You know what I fear the most?" She looked up at him. "Being alone again."

He touched her face. "They won't separate us, surely. Aren't we supposed to be the thing that finally stops the Frost? You and me, and our mated dragons, and whatever bask they're going to give us. I wish they'd share their plans, don't you?"

"I'm beginning to think one of the reasons they don't share is because they don't know nearly as much as we think they do," said Banyan.

He grimaced. He was frightened she was right. It was terrifying thinking of an all-powerful Quorum withholding information as it ruled absolutely. But it was somehow more terrifying to think of it all being chaos, and the Quorum trying to retain whatever power it could against some unseen and unknowable force that sought to destroy them all. He was beginning to see that was the way of it, however.

They wandered out to find Cris, who told them neither of them were assigned on this wing anymore. "Sorry, I don't know where they've put you. I did see them carting out your belongings, though. And I was told, if you came to see me, to send you to Colonel Rabi's office."

"We just came from there," muttered Odion.

He and Banyan went through the halls, clutching each other, his arm around her shoulders, hers around his waist. The colonel wasn't in his office, so they waited outside for nearly an hour, touching the entire time.

He leaned against the wall and she leaned against him. He held her close and she burrowed into him.

But when the colonel appeared, Banyan extricated herself and stood up straight. "Sir, may we please see Gelso?" she called.

"Permission to speak, sir," said the colonel blandly.

"Permission to speak, sir," repeated Banyan, frustrated.

"Not granted, soldier," said the colonel, going into his office.

Banyan made a face at the back of his head.

"Inside, both of you," said the colonel.

They went inside.

This time, the colonel did not tell them to take a seat, so they stood at attention behind the chairs and watched as the colonel sat himself down at his desk, getting comfortable. "Rider First Class Raxx is in a restricted area of the healing wing due to his fever. It is very high, and he is very ill. He's apparently delirious, at any rate, and would not recognize you. He's a dead man walking, and there's debate that we would be kinder to kill him now. I, however, have come out on the side of continuing your experiment. Gelso is a casualty, after all, that's inevitable. We must learn as much as we can from him. But you two have done enough damage, and you will stay out of it."

"Not even to say goodbye?" said Banyan.

"You were not granted permission to speak, Rider First Class Thriceborn."

Banyan stiffened at the title.

"Yes," said the colonel. "You've been demoted. Both of you. Lieutenant Naxim."

Odion shrugged. He didn't care what they decided they wanted to call him.

"Rider Thriceborn, you will report to your new bask in the dragon corps."

"We're getting a bask?" said Banyan. "Because—"

"No," said the colonel, "and that's going to be one hour of focus training for you, Rider First Class Thriceborn."

Banyan rolled her eyes.

"You are assigned to Bask Thirty-three, a new bask that is headed up by Lieutenant Atohi Axin."

Banyan blinked. "Atohi is higher ranked than me?"

The colonel turned to Odion. "We're sending you to the field."

Odion's lips parted. "Oh."

"You're direct superior will be Major Nightwing," said

the colonel.

"You're sending me to Slate?" said Odion.

"It was thought," said the colonel, "that since you stole his dragon's mate from him, he wouldn't look too kindly on that. I argued against it, if you want to know. I..." He looked back and forth between the two of them. "I realize that's very complicated, isn't it? It seems to me to be rather a punishment for Banyan, leaving her alone while wondering what is happening between the two of you. And because of that, I'm going to give you exactly fifteen minutes to have a discussion amongst yourselves alone. I don't have to do that, you realize. My orders are simply to separate you and send you off."

"But, sir," said Banyan. "Why are we being separated? Is that really the best thing we should be doing against the Frost? Maybe you should send both Odion and I out into the field, and maybe—"

"Two hours of focus training, soldier."

Banyan bowed her head, silent.

"I'll be back quite soon," said the colonel, and got up from his desk. He left the room, closing the door behind him.

Odion furrowed his brow, shaking his head. "Slate probably *is* angry."

"After the way it all went down, how could he not be?" Banyan murmured.

"And there's no way he'll want anything from me," said Odion. "It was only ever when our dragons were in heat, and Mirra won't go into heat for months. And Yilia's on the same schedule, so..."

"What if some other dragon out there is on a different schedule? What if that triggers a heat?" Banyan touched his arm. "I'd rather it be with him, all right? I don't *mind* if the two of you—"

"Yes, you do. You definitely mind. You were very worried about the idea that we couldn't be faithful to each other—"

"That was before the heat, though. I understand it differently now."

He sighed. "What if some dragon *here* goes into heat?"

"Erach and I will leave," she said. "He's mated, so he'll be stronger, and he'll want to leave."

"It's all right," he said. "I don't care if you have to fuck someone else, all right? I get it. And if you're giving me permission to get relief, then I'm giving it to you, too."

She grimaced. "This is horrible, to separate us like this. They never separate mated pairs."

"They're just angry," said Odion. "It won't last."

"I hope not," she said.

"It won't." But he wasn't really sure about that, in the end.

And then the colonel was back, before they could even touch each other or kiss goodbye, and there was no time for it. She was sent off to her new quarters, demoted into a rider in one of the basks, and he was climbing up the landing tower to climb aboard Mirra.

He took to the air and he had a vague thought of defecting again.

But what was the point without Banyan?

He flew to Slate's watchtower. It sat at the base of a snow-capped peak, surrounded by stately fir trees, barely visible until you got on top of it. He and Mirra landed on the top of the tower, and he was relieved when there was someone there straightaway to take his scroll containing his orders.

The rider escorted him to Slate, who was in the bottom of the watchtower, in the weapons room.

Odion felt his heart start to beat faster and faster as they approached the other man. He wasn't sure what he was supposed to say to him. He had tried not to think about Slate since Slate had gone.

It had been easy. Banyan had been there, and Banyan was everything.

Right?

Wasn't she?

Why was his heart pounding like this?

ATOHI AXIN HAD shaved the sides of her purple hair but left it long and curly on the top. It tumbled down over the dark skin of her forehead, over her purple eyebrows. She looked Banyan over, walking around her as Banyan stood at attention in the middle of the common room in her bask.

In the dragon corps, the riders and riders first class of a bask lived together in rooms off a common area, while the lieutenant or capitan who headed up the bask lived in senior officer rooms a floor down.

Banyan had not been able to go into her room yet, though, because Lieutenant Axin had been waiting for her here. Once, Banyan and Atohi had been roommates. Back when Banyan was an undercadet, back before everything got insane. It hadn't even been a year ago, and here they were now, both of them promoted to the dragon corps already.

The Quorum was definitely panicked.

Atohi hadn't yet spoken.

Banyan realized she had not told Atohi that Deke had mentioned her before he died. *Broken promise,* she thought guiltily. How could she have forgotten that? She'd sent letters to Deke's family, and she'd done the best she could else, but she'd never spoken to Atohi, even though they were both students here in the same school.

Should Banyan bring that up now? She wasn't sure it would endear her to Atohi.

And after all, Banyan couldn't help but be a bit rankled at being put beneath Atohi Axin, at being demoted, at being under someone. She'd never served under anyone except Javor Derowen and that had turned out pretty badly.

"Well," said Atohi, "I think I'm supposed to be grateful to have been given the great and mighty Banyan Thriceborn as part of my bask. But you realize it's highly irregular for you to be put in here mated to an alpha? That I know this isn't about me at all, but is some sort of humiliation for you. How am I supposed to deal with that? Being put under me humiliates you?" Atohi tilted her head to one side.

Banyan didn't say anything. She knew better than to speak out of turn when a superior officer was speaking. She'd wait until she was ordered to speak.

Atohi shook her head. "Do you hate me, Banyan? I never hated you, you know. I never felt much of anything for you except bewilderment. I know everyone thinks you're amazing, but I don't really see it. I think you just luck out and end up with other people who are brilliant."

Banyan schooled her expression as best she could.

Not well enough because Atohi laughed. "You have my permission to speak freely, soldier."

Banyan licked her lips. What could she say? "I don't hate you, of course."

"Of course." Atohi laughed again, shaking her head.

Banyan lifted a shoulder. "What I'm good at, actually, is seeing other people's brilliance. Maybe even at pulling it out of them. But I've never much had a chance to do that. I was working on it, in the skirmishes with Odion in the glider arena, but ever since we've been here, in the dragon arena, it's just been me and him. I haven't had anyone else to work with."

"Seeing other people's brilliance," said Atohi, bringing her eyebrows together. "Hmm. How does that work?"

"Let me just watch," said Banyan. "Would you do that? Watch your practices, watch the skirmishes, that kind of thing. And then, if I can give you some suggestions on how to improve—"

"I'm not giving you my bask," said Atohi.

"I don't want your bask." She didn't. Banyan wanted *all* the basks. She had looked at General Frax and realized that was where she needed to be, in the middle of everything, orchestrating it all.

"So, you don't hate me. I don't hate you. And you're not humiliated to be here?"

"I…" Banyan bowed her head. "Maybe I could stand to learn some humility, sir."

Atohi laughed. "Fine. You watch. We'll see what comes of

that." She pointed. "That's your room."

Banyan swallowed. "He, um, he mentioned you at the end."

Atohi froze. "Who?"

"Deke."

It was quiet.

Atohi drew in a breath and moved in closer. "You couldn't blame me for that, I suppose. Not after you just left him behind, broken-hearted. He adored you."

"He had a funny way of showing that," said Banyan, thinking of the way he'd insulted her, saying that having sex with her was like having sex with a stone wall.

"He was never the same after you were gone. He didn't even fly as well."

"Because he relied on me to see his brilliance," said Banyan.

Atohi considered this. Another long silence passed. Then Atohi said, "If you tell me that Deke Midgurd said he loved me—"

"He didn't," said Banyan. "He said he thought you would think it was only physical, but I think he... well, it was the end. He wanted you to know he was thinking about you, that's all. I should have told you before. I don't know why I didn't—"

"Because you do hate me."

"I *don't* hate you."

"Well," said Atohi in a low and liquid voice, "I don't hate you either. Dismissed, Rider First Class Thriceborn."

## CHAPTER FOURTEEN

ODION HELD OUT the scroll.

But Slate simply stood there, gaping at him, lips parted, in shock.

Finally, the other man looked down to see the scroll Odion was proffering, and he reached out and snatched it away.

Odion's heart was still pounding.

Slate unrolled it and read. He rolled it back up, his movements careful. He tucked it away, and only then did his gaze meet Odion's again.

Odion found himself flinching as he looked into the man's reptilian eyes. Not everyone changed that way during the bonding, but he'd always felt kinship with Slate because they both did.

"What the fuck did you do?" said Slate.

Odion shrugged. "It's so much to get into, I don't even know where to start."

Slate dug the scroll out and handed it to Odion. "Here, you read it."

Odion shrugged. "I mean, I did. They gave it to me, and I had a long flight." It didn't say much, other than that Odion had been demoted and that this assignment was to teach him to obey orders and that any measures Slate wished to take would be at his own discretion. He tried to give the scroll back.

Slate shook his head. He folded his arms over his chest. "She's all right?"

Odion wasn't sure he'd been expecting that. "I didn't think you liked her."

Slate laughed softly, looking up at the ceiling. Then he stepped around Odion and headed out of the weapons room.

Odion stayed there, looking down at the scroll for a while, figuring someone would tell him what to do. When no one did, he eventually went up the stairs. This was set up like all the watchtowers, with a common room and a kitchen and bedrooms opening onto the common room for all of the riders.

The common room was full of the other riders, most of whom he knew as former students. There were six of them, besides Slate. They'd been talking, but at the sight of Odion, they all quieted.

Odion wished that surprised him, but he was used to this, used to being an oddity, being someone who everyone stared at, someone who everyone resented. *I'm not here to show off for you this time,* he wanted to say. *I don't know what's going on anymore.*

"Odion," called Slate from the kitchen.

Odion made his way in there.

Slowly, the conversation began again in the common room.

Slate nudged him toward the fire pit in the corner, where a spitted bird was roasting. "Turn that a quarter-turn every fifteen minutes or so, huh?"

"Sure," said Odion, sitting himself on the stool next to the fire pit. It was hot, but the windows were open and it was late in the day. The fire wasn't unpleasant.

Slate was kneading bread dough on a floured counter across the room. His back was to Odion. "For a while, I thought maybe they weren't going to manage it. Then one day, Yilia was beside herself when the mating bond broke. That was bad for both of us. I did the best I could for her, but there was only so much I could send through the bond back to her. Then he showed up."

"Who did?"

"Erach," said Slate. "They talked."

Odion turned to him, but all he could see was Slate's back as he kneaded the bread. "What?"

"I mean, they don't talk, not like we do, not with words, but they communicate," said Slate. "I think the mates, the basks, they can communicate like they communicate to us through the bonds, sharing pictures and emotions, and sending things to each other, mind to mind. Our way of communicating, it must seem so primitive to them."

"Yeah, I think you're right about that," said Odion, turning back to the roasting bird, wondering if he should attempt to turn it yet.

"Anyway, he made her promises."

"What kind of promises?"

"Banyan's dragon promised my dragon that as soon as the Frost is eradicated, he'll mate her again, and leave your dragon in the lurch."

Odion winced. Mirra would be devastated. But then, she hadn't wanted to be mated at all. Maybe she'd get over it. She was young.

"Erach the dragon seems to think that we're going to be Frost free this time next year," said Slate. "What do you think about that?"

"I don't think anything," said Odion.

"So, he doesn't talk to Banyan about these theories of his?" said Slate. "Or, is he just blowing smoke up my dragon's ass? By the way, Yilia doesn't want anything to do with him. She's never going to forgive him for breaking their bond."

"Banyan hasn't told me anything about Erach, really," said Odion. "But if Erach thinks that, it's probably simply because it seems as though the Quorum is trying to graduate everyone in the school this year. We think the Frost is going to attack the school."

"How soon?"

"Don't know."

"Why'd they send you out here, then?"
"Don't know that either."
It was quiet.
Slate turned around.
Odion was staring at him.
"No extra rooms, you know. No extra beds either. But I have a double bed because usually there's a mated pair heading up a bask out here. You'll have to bunk with me."
"Oh," said Odion, surprised at this.
"That a problem, lieutenant?" Slate raised his dark red eyebrows.
"No, sir," said Odion.
Slate smirked. "Oh, you *like* me outranking you, don't you? Makes you all hot and bothered."
"No," said Odion, going back to the meat to turn it.
Slate laughed and laughed.

BANYAN DIDN'T HAVE the same kind of free time now that she was part of a bask. Furthermore, she was forced into doing focus training during her free time because of the orders of the colonel. So, it wasn't until later the following day that she was able to get down to the library.

There, Dove looked up at her, but only shook her head, as if to say that she couldn't speak to her.

Banyan lingered anyway, so that it wouldn't look suspicious, getting a few books off the shelves and sitting herself down at a table to page through them.

At some point, Dove appeared next to her, kneeling to run her fingers over the spines of the books, as if she was looking for a place to reshelve a book. She had several in her arms. However, as she did this, she spoke quietly to Banyan. "Midnight bell. Meet me in the healing wing."

Banyan nodded at her book, but didn't look at Dove.

Then she had to report to the dragon arena for a skirmish. Atohi ordered her to stay to the back and observe, as had been part of their agreement, but Atohi made it sound as if it had been all her idea.

"Since you're the great and talented Banyan Thriceborn," sneered Atohi, "you see if you can't come up with some winning strategies for us, hmm?"

"Yes, sir," Banyan said, hanging her head in obedience.

Then they all climbed onto their dragons and lined up at the entrance.

In the dragon arena, dragons entered from the ground, through rounded doorways that were wide enough to fit their wings. They were only wide enough for them to come out one at a time, though, so it was customary for the basks to send out their riders from best to worst, putting their best on the front lines.

Banyan noticed that Atohi went first. This might have been an act of false arrogance, or it might be because Atohi genuinely thought she was the best. Banyan also couldn't discount that Atohi had some other kind of strategy altogether.

She came in last, and the bask was already in the air. They were all amateurs and this was their first skirmish. None of them seemed to know how to fly or how use their bows and arrows. They were fresh from the chaos of the glider arena, however, and it didn't serve them badly.

Most of the riders in the dragon corps had come up from the strict configurations of the former glider corps, where capitan cadets signaled their basks to do pre-practiced moves with various whistle patterns.

Odion had changed all this, eschewing the whistle, signaling his bask with organic movements like spreading his glider wings or diving.

But when Banyan had come into the glider corps, they had been nothing like that, due to an experiment the Quorum was running. So, she'd come up in an era of chaos and no planning whatsoever. So had Atohi's bask.

Atohi didn't let out a whistle, but she did yell, "Let's fuck shit up!" at the top of her lungs.

And then her new dragon riders flew facefirst into the

other team, who'd never seen such a disorganized and insane attack before. It came from all sides, and it wasn't the least bit practiced, and it shook them.

If Atohi's riders had known anything about how to shoot arrows, they could have used that surprise to shoot the flags off the other team. But as it was, they only knocked one off—purely by chance, since their arrows weren't sailing anywhere near the direction they wanted them to.

And then the other bask, Bask Seven, rallied, and the leader, Kibler Reece, called out the name of a configuration, and his bask moved together like a swarm, and they made quick work of Atohi's people. All of them were out in a few moments, including Banyan, even though she could have defended herself. She didn't, however. It would have gone against orders, and she didn't want to make an enemy of Atohi—assuming she hadn't already done that from the first day she'd arrived at South Ridge Academy.

That evening, Bask Thirty-two had the dragon arena for the extra practice session that was open to the lottery.

Banyan stood in the stands with Atohi as they watched the rest of the bask fly overhead.

"We're all lone dragons," said Atohi. "They bonded us all to dragons without basks. Why do you think they did that?"

"I have no idea," said Banyan. Privately, she wondered if it was an attempt to fight the Frost. Was a bask more likely all to fall to the Frost because they were all so loyal to each other? Maybe if the basks were more loosely organized, they had a better chance of getting away.

"And I can't believe they made us fight a skirmish without even having had one practice." Atohi's lip curled. "They're fucking bastards, aren't they?"

"They sure are," said Banyan tightly.

"Well," said Atohi, "what did you see that I didn't see?"

"I guess I don't know what you saw," said Banyan.

Atohi drew in a breath, looking over the riders. "We need to work on the fundamentals. How to fly. How to shoot bows and arrows."

"Yes," said Banyan.

"They fly differently than we do," said Atohi. "They seem like an army, and we seem like a ragtag batch of guerilla fighters."

"That's on purpose," Banyan said. "The Quorum is trying something out, I think, trying to see if a chaotic style is more effective than an organized one."

"Is it?"

"Not quite," said Banyan. "But anticipating chaos and mimicking certain aspects of it may give us an edge."

Atohi considered. "All right. Anything else?"

"I like to specialize," said Banyan. "Figure out what each of the members of my team does best, and have them work only on that. We'll have designated shooters—maybe short-range and long-range? And we'll see which dragon-rider pairs are the fastest and which have the most endurance. If certain dragons work better with other dragons, we'll always pair them together. We need to be looking for our strengths and figuring out ways to improve them."

"Should we learn those configurations?" said Atohi.

"No," said Banyan. "We're already behind on that. They have years of experience with that. We'll never beat them that way. We beat them at what we already know how to do. We get better at what we're already good at. We don't have a lot of time, Atohi. You must realize there's a reason they're accelerating us."

"The Frost is coming," said Atohi darkly.

"Here, I think," said Banyan. "To the school."

Atohi nodded. "I see."

They were both grim after that. Atohi split everyone up and sent half of them to run speed drills and left the other half to be taught how to shoot bows and arrows with Banyan.

Practice was over too quickly, before they'd accomplished much.

They had a skirmish the next day.

At the midnight bell, Banyan carefully got up and eased open the door to her room. The common area was dark and empty. She tiptoed through it and out the door without incident.

It took her ten minutes to end up in the healing wing, and when she did, she didn't see anyone.

Then, from one of the dark corners, Dove appeared, grabbing her by the arm. She led her down a narrow corridor and into a small room.

There, lying on the bed, was Gelso. He was quiet and sleeping, his face flushed, his hair sticking to his head with sweat.

"His fever's breaking," said Dove. "And... something is strange, I think. I can't be sure, of course, but I think something's happened to the Frost sickness. Look." She carefully lifted one of Gelso's hands and extended one of his fingers. "Usually, at this stage in the Frost sickness, if you do this, the finger stiffens, but see?" Dove bent the finger at all of its joints.

Gelso murmured in his sleep, tugging his hand back, curling it under his face.

"What do you mean, something's happened to the Frost sickness?" said Banyan.

"I'm going to keep my eye on him," said Dove. "But I wonder if the fever burnt it out of him. Think about it, Banyan, the disease needs to be in the cold. If it's cold, it seems to be accelerated, and if it's not, it takes longer. So, maybe, if you raise the patient's temperature enough, you burn it right out of him."

Banyan's eyes widened. "A cure?"

Dove nodded, smiling. "I mean, I can't be sure. We'll keep our eye on him, though."

Banyan backed out of the room, shaking her head. "A cure?" she whispered, her voice full of tears, her entire body full of shame.

"Hey." Dove followed her, closing the door behind her, closing Gelso away. "What's wrong? This is good news."

"If there's a cure, Dove, I killed Deke for nothing."

"No, I don't think so," said Dove. "Once the transition is complete, I'm not sure if it's possible to undo it. This worked because Gelso was still in the early stages."

Banyan chewed on her lip. "Oh. So, then, we can't cure the ice monsters."

"Probably not," said Dove. "I don't know. We could try, of course."

"How?" said Banyan.

"Expose them to the fever, I suppose."

"How do we do that?"

Dove tapped her lower lip. "Well, there are small vials of various illnesses kept in stasis in the basement of the healing wing of the Academy. They are various ways that we can keep them stable, mostly through temperature and certain other rituals."

"Magic?"

"Healers don't like to think of it that way," said Dove. "But what else are the elemental forces than magic, really?" She shrugged. "We are scholars, not magicians, according to the Quorum, but I am not always sure what the difference is, I have to admit."

"We'll try it at some point, then," said Banyan. "But we'd need an ice monster and one of the vials, and a controlled environment to test it. It would be complicated. At this point, we need to lie low."

"Yes," said Dove. "For now, we just watch Gelso. I'll let you know if it turns out I'm wrong."

"Good," said Banyan.

On the way back to her room, after she and Dove had parted ways, Banyan rounded a bend and came face-to-face with Colonel Rabi.

"Sneaking around in the middle of the night, Rider First Class Thriceborn?"

"Just working on the senior prank, sir," she said.

"Senior prank," said the colonel. "You have to be joking."

"I figure I have nothing to lose in terms of punishment," said Banyan. "Maybe the prank's going to be a little less lighthearted this year, sir." She didn't want him to know about Dove. She didn't want to get Dove in trouble, and she also could not risk Dove's access being revoked. They needed Dove to help them find things out. It was important.

"Oh?" The colonel laughed softly. "You're going to get me back with a senior prank, Banyan? Truly?"

"Get you back, sir?" She glared at him. "So, you admit my treatment has been mean-spirited and personal?"

"I admit nothing of the kind. You're not even a senior," said the colonel.

"It seems everyone's a senior this year, sir."

His lips thinned. He gave her a nod. "Very well. Carry on, soldier. But you might spare me the brunt of the prank, remembering that I just let you go with no punishment this evening?"

Banyan gave him a cryptic smile. "I'll do what I can, sir."

He chuckled and moved on, leaving her behind.

Instead of going to her room, she went back downstairs to seek out Rils Markir. He lived in the officer's wing on the east side, since he was in east forces. She knocked on the wrong door first, but the student in that room directed her where to go.

Rils answered the door, shirtless, yawning. "Well, well, Banyan, I have to say, I don't really want Odion to kill me, so I'll have to decline this little seduction attempt—"

"Don't flatter yourself," she said.

He grinned at her. "Fine, then. Why are you here?"

"You're still doing the prank?"

"Are you kidding? After Gelso?"

"We *have* to do the prank," she said.

"All right, all right, prank's back on," said Rils. "But that ship, what if it's crawling with ice monsters?"

"Next time, we go down there with bows and arrows and swords," said Banyan. "Next time, we are prepared."

"Got it," said Rils. "Actually, I'm in. I wouldn't mind seeing one myself. Like to know what we're up against, you know."

"I do know," she said.

"Tomorrow?" said Rils.

"Meet you at the south entrance," she said. "Third bell after noon."

"I'll be there."

# CHAPTER FIFTEEN

ODION WAS IN Slate's room now, and he was supposed to be getting ready for bed, but he was simply standing there. He didn't know what to do with himself, actually. His heart was thudding away in his chest again, like everything he did around Slate made him nervous.

He hated that.

He despised his own weakness.

Usually, he wasn't weak, that was the thing, and anything that made him weak was something he tried to conquer.

But the thing about Slate was it had always been different with him. Slate wasn't someone he conquered. Slate conquered him. Except, oddly, even though Slate was so easily dominant sexually, he was vulnerable emotionally, romantically. He confused Odion, truthfully. But then, Odion confused himself when it came to Slate.

Growing up, Odion had always known that there was a possibility that he would be sexually intimate with a man, and he'd thought of this with a sort of resignation, not curiosity, not anticipation. He'd always assumed this meant that his preferences lay with women — the way he understood most men's did — and that this aberration because of the dragon heat would simply be something he endured.

Maybe it had all started out that way, but Odion didn't know what it was now.

He definitely didn't think of his time with Slate as something he'd endured.

And the time with the three of them?

Well, Odion thought about that more than was strictly necessary. He'd occasionally, in the few moments he had to himself, which were very few now that he and Banyan had been living together, thought about Slate and Banyan together and touched himself. He couldn't do that often, of course. For one thing, he was usually doing it in bed, while Banyan was sleeping next to him—either in the morning or in the midst of the night. He always felt guilty, as if there were some rule that he was supposed to save every single one of his erections for her, that he wasn't meant to use them for his own private pleasure at all.

He also felt shame thinking about Slate when he was with her, and he refused to allow himself to do that. He'd wipe his mind clear and fill it only with the sights and sounds and feel of Banyan, his Banyan, his mate.

She was perfect.

He was in love with her.

And she was enough.

He did not need this other man in his life. He definitely should not be aroused by the idea of another man fucking his mate. It was perverse and disgusting, and he despised himself for that as well.

"Still dressed?"

Odion whirled.

Slate was coming through the door, yanking his vest over his head. He tossed it on a chair in the room and pulled his shirt over his head, revealing his light-green sculpted chest.

Odion looked away. His cock twitched at the sight of it though. *Traitor*, thought Odion at his crotch.

But then sexual attraction didn't always coincide with rational thought or with emotional truth. Odion could find anything attractive, regardless of whether he actually wanted to have sex with it or not. He tugged on his own vest, fuming.

"I do something that made you angry, Odion?"

"No," said Odion, pulling off his own shirt. When he looked up, Slate was only clad in his smallclothes, and he was sliding into the bed.

Odion looked away.

"Hey," said Slate, "at inns in Aleen, it's very common to pay half-price and share a bed with a stranger. It happens all the time. That's all this is. Sleep."

"I know," said Odion. His hands rested on the buttons of his trousers as he regarded Slate. "You going to watch me take these off?"

Slate smirked. Then he rolled over onto his side, giving Odion his back. "Nope."

Odion shoved off his pants and scrambled into the other side of the bed.

Slate turned down the oil lamp on the side of the bed. "Night."

"Night," said Odion. He rolled onto his side too, his back to Slate.

Odion breathed and listened to the sound of Slate's breath. He thought about how intimate it was to hear another person's breathing. He thought about how they were in the same bed and they were only wearing their smalls. He thought about the first time that he had been in heat and how Slate had been firm but compassionate. *You need this, and it'll be better. You'll see. Show me your cock, and stop thinking about it.*

Time passed.

Slate rolled onto his back.

Odion rolled onto his back.

Slate turned, looking at him on the pillow. "Why'd they sent you to me?"

"I'm demoted," said Odion. "They wanted to humiliate both of us, I guess, and…"

"Yeah, but *does* this humiliate you?"

"I mean… I've haven't been under someone's command like this since being in a bask out on Fort Tillian, when we were attacked," said Odion. "So, it's a step down, I guess."

"Yeah, but it's me," said Slate. "If they wanted to make it

really uncomfortable for you—"

"They think you're very angry about your dragon losing her mate. That you'll take that out on me."

"They do?" said Slate.

"Well, the colonel said he seemed to understand that... that..."

"I'm not *not* angry," said Slate.

"No, I know."

"But we all knew that was going to happen," said Slate. "It was the plan. So, how angry could I really be? I was expecting it."

Silence.

Slate started to speak again. "It feels like this is a punishment for me. You being here, so close, in my bed, and I have to—"

"I don't have to be in your fucking bed!"

"Well, I could make you sleep on the floor, I guess. That what you want?"

"Not really," muttered Odion.

"I didn't do anything wrong," said Slate gruffly. "I'm the one who's been alone out here."

Odion rolled onto his side again, but this time facing Slate. "She told me..."

"What did she tell you?"

"She said if we go into heat, that she doesn't mind."

Slate let out a breath. "But otherwise? Off limits, right?"

Odion didn't say anything.

"Odion?"

"We didn't have much time to talk," said Odion. "But I think so. I don't think she'd like it."

Slate scoffed.

"What?"

"I don't think you understand her very well, that's all."

"Look, she liked us all together when we were in heat, yeah, but everyone likes things in heat. And then everyone comes out of the heat, and... and..."

"Everyone still likes them," finished Slate. "You ever regretted anything that felt good while you were in heat?"

"There are things I'd do in heat that I wouldn't do normally."

"Like what?"

"Like you," said Odion, and then he rolled over again, giving Slate his back.

"Yeah," said Slate. "Yeah. Me too." But his voice was dull. He rolled over also.

It was quiet again, then, quiet for the rest of the night.

But Odion lay awake for a very long time.


BANYAN, RILS, AND an army of students descended on the ship the following day, all with weapons. Because there were so many of them, they had to sneak out in shifts, darting across the grounds in groups of one or two, scurrying on board the ship with hopefully no one the wiser.

But there were no more ice monsters on the ship.

They searched every nook and cranny and found nothing.

In the bottom of the ship, they all gathered, holding lanterns, and talked about how they would move the ship and when.

They would gather their dragons in three nights. Some of the students would need to sneak into the dining hall to open the wide windows. They'd fly the thing up there and the prank would be complete.

It was all decided.

Banyan felt light for the first time in a long time, laughing here with the other students.

When she got back to her quarters, Atohi wasn't pleased.

So, Banyan told her about the prank. Atohi wouldn't have known. She'd just been promoted, after all, and had been in the glider corps. She said Atohi could help if she wanted.

Atohi surveyed her. "You're not even a little worried I'd rat you all out to the teachers?"

"Nope," said Banyan.

Atohi laughed.

Banyan laughed.

"Here at South Ridge Academy, we establish early on that the teachers are the enemy," said Atohi in a lilting voice.

Banyan doubled over, laughing so hard that she was clutching her midsection.

"I'll help," said Atohi.

That afternoon, they had a skirmish. It was with another new bask, which Banyan was pleased to see was headed up by Raini Windborne, who used to serve under Banyan in her bask in the glider corps.

As with last time, Banyan stayed to the back of the battle, just observing.

This was an interesting skirmish, because Raini had been fighting the same chaotic glider battles as Bask Thirty-two. Of course, her newly promoted soldiers barely knew their way around their dragons, nor did they know how to use their weapons.

In this, due to the little bit of practice they'd done with the bows and arrows, Bask Thirty-two had a bit of an edge on Bask Thirty-three.

But because Raini had been trained by Banyan, she'd already divided her bask into groups. She relied on the students with an aptitude for shooting, and she got them into position while the rest of the dragons were meeting in the middle of the arena in a chaotic free-for-all.

Then, from both sides of the arena, hiding behind various structures, came a rain of arrows, Raini's shooters, who destroyed them in a matter of minutes.

Banyan felt sad that her bask had lost, but proud of Raini in the way that she thought a parent must feel about her child or something. Raini was brilliant, and she'd only gotten more so in the ensuing time period.

And here was the truth of the matter.

Banyan needed Raini in the fight against the Frost. If they were truly preparing for a battle here in the school, she needed to be thinking about how she might use her. She needed to be thinking about how she would structure a fight in the school, how she would defend it.

When was the Frost coming?

Did anyone know?

That evening, when she and Atohi were sneaking out to meet their dragons for the prank, she decided to broach a topic with her new commander. (They couldn't go off the landing tower if they wanted to remain secretive, so they had to go and meet the dragons in the woods.) As they walked amongst the trees, Banyan said to her, "I have something I want to run by you."

"All right," said Atohi.

"It's about the skirmishes. I know I said I'd help you win, but I want to do something different, and it'll probably mean that we lose whatever edge we might have had."

"Why do you want to do something different?" said Atohi.

Banyan explained about the Frost, and about what she was thinking, and about preparations.

"What do the skirmishes matter?" said Atohi. "Do it. We all need to be thinking about that, anyway. That's the reason we're here, in the end. That's the reason I was given to the Quorum when I was four years old. To protect the Trinal Kingdoms from threats."

"I'm glad you see it that way," said Banyan.

"I'd have to be idiotic to see it any other way," said Atohi.

"Well, not all of the commanders will see it that way," said Banyan. "Some of them have been fighting skirmishes for three years, and they've been working really hard to beat the games. They won't like it if we strip it all away, and everything they've been planning for is exposed as unimportant. It will make them feel unimportant."

"You'll explain it, though, and they'll understand," said Atohi.

Banyan wasn't certain that Atohi was right, but she hoped she was.

The prank went off without a hitch.

Well, there was a little bit of breakage when they tried to get the dragons to lift the ship. The bottom part of the ship was left behind in the mud, wood splintered, but most of the ship remained intact.

Then they had to break off one of the masts to get it through the window. It was loud, and they were certain someone would come into the dining hall and stop them, but no one did.

Finally, they left, the entire dining hall filled with a huge shipwreck, all of them congratulating each other and laughing.

Banyan asked every one of the bask leaders—the lieutenants and capitans—to meet her out in the woods afterward, and they all agreed.

It was quite late then, and the light in the east was growing. No one was tired, though. They were too exhilarated from the prank itself.

She decided to talk to them about the fact that they all thought the Frost was going to attack the school. She licked her lips. "I'm sure everyone has heard the rumors about the ice monsters, that they are transformed riders."

Everyone got serious all of the sudden. They gazed at her with wide and worried eyes, silent, waiting.

She licked her lips again. "They know everything about the way the Quorum is organized. They were all trained here. They know this is the hub of our resistance. They know, if they take the school down, they take down the Quorum. So, we're convinced they are coming here to attack."

A ripple went through the gathered students, not a vocal one, but she could see them all reacting, their expressions tightening, their postures changing.

"We don't know when," said Banyan. "They can't travel away from the peaks for too long, we don't think. They need the ice monster dragons to breathe out cold air and create a cold enough environment. We don't know how many dragons they have, or—well, there's a lot we don't know. And the Quorum keeps its knowledge close to its chest. But it's going to be down to *us*." She looked out at the other students. "The way they're behaving, moving up people who are first years into the dragon corps? It could be this year."

"There's only a month left of this year," spoke up Raini, shaking her head. "We won't be ready."

"Let's hope it's not this year," said Banyan. "But one thing I know is that we're not ready. And another thing I know is that fighting each other isn't going to get us ready. The Quorum is pitting us against each other, but we are going to fight *together* against the Frost. We will be one army. And we have the advantage of knowing the battlefield. It will be here. I have a proposition, and some of you may not like it."

"What?" said Rils.

"I propose that we ignore the skirmishes for their purposes and start using that time to figure out how to fight the Frost. I have a strategy that I've been using to win, and I'm willing to share it with all of you, so that we can all get better. Also, I'd like to form different ranks within the basks, move all of our best shooters into one place, for instance. We'll use some of the skirmishes as practice time, not as different fighting basks but as one united army."

"What's the strategy?" spoke up someone.

They all laughed.

"You're saying, 'Fuck the skirmishes?'" someone else called out.

"I know some of you have been working for years to win these things. I know you've drilled configurations and made plans and that whatever I'm telling you right now means to throw away all of that, and I know that must feel—"

"Like a revelation," said someone. "The Frost is the reason we're here."

"I don't want to be an ice monster," said Atohi. "That's not how I go out."

"What's the strategy?" said someone else.

"Well, it's sort of obvious," said Banyan. "But it's basically this. The Quorum takes us, breaks us, and tries to turn us all into the same soldier with the same skills. I propose that we observe our soldiers, determine what they're already good at, and have them specialize in only that. We don't try to break 'bad habits' we treat them as 'style.' We work around weaknesses; we don't try to correct them. And we create divisions within the army. We have long distance shooters and short distance shooters. We have fast fliers. We have groups that work entirely to create distractions. We each have very specific jobs, and we become experts at what we're good at."

"What are you good at?" said Rils.

"She's good at *this*," said Raini.

"I think it's brilliant," said Carn Milx. "Even if we only reorganize that way between ourselves, it will mean our skirmishes will be better at honing us to work this way, because we'll improve just from coming up against basks who are worthy of us."

"True," said Banyan.

"The teachers won't like it," said Atohi.

"Someone was just telling me how everyone knows the teachers are the enemy," said Banyan.

Everyone let out a wry and knowing laugh, a bitter laugh.

"We'll vote," spoke up Rils. "All in favor of following Banyan's ideas?"

It was a chorus of unanimous "ayes."


BANYAN NEARLY SLEPT through the prank being revealed. She didn't get out of bed until the third bell, and she had to dress quickly and run all the way down the stairs to get to the dining hall, where the undercadets had already been trying to eat breakfast around the ship, and the staff was running around trying to figure out how to get it out of the dining hall.

Colonel Rabi caught her eye and gave her a mock salute, smiling at her in that way of his that she hated, that fatherly way.

Fuck Colonel Rabi.

He didn't get to pretend that he had some positive

influence over her life, not after everything he'd done to traumatize her thus far.

But the prank brought that same level of lightness to the entire school. It made them all feel as if they were actually simply students and the most important thing was the year-end flag war and that everyone was very concerned with the skirmishes.

It made it easy to pretend they were not soldiers on the brink of war.

It was good.

But the skirmishes changed the following week, due to Banyan's influence.

At first, it was just as had been suggested, with all of the basks leaning heavily into specialization. The specialization had worked very well before because Banyan's bask had been the only one doing it.

Even when she and Odion had been commanding separate glider basks, they'd both been pretending to give configuration orders because Odion had been convinced that the Quorum would put a stop to Banyan's strategy if they figured out what it was.

She wasn't sure they wouldn't try to do it now, but even if they did, they were an entire army against the administration. If they all refused to fight the skirmishes, what was the Quorum going to do?

At any rate, problems began to appear nearly immediately. Now that everyone realized that there were specialized shooters, the first thing they did was try to take *out* the shooters. This meant that the basks began to attempt to hide their shooters, sometimes not even having them enter on dragons, but having them sneak into the arena and take positions behind various bits of cover. This worked until they shot an arrow, giving away their positions, in which case it was a free-for-all.

It was as Banyan had realized before, of course, that half of a winning strategy was surprise or audacity. Once everyone knew what the strategy was, it made things much more difficult.

But this was what would happen during the real war. The Frost knew all their strategies, because the Frost knew everything the riders knew. The only way that Banyan could protect this strategy was to make sure that no one was turned by the Frost, and she could not guarantee that.

Anyway, specialization wasn't the radical strategy she'd used, was it?

No, she remembered now that she had wanted her baskmembers to make their own decisions. The strategy was not to have a strategy, but to allow the soldiers to strategize on their own, on the battlefield.

She passed this information on to the leaders of the basks. She got back the predictable amount of flak, though Raini said that she'd been doing this all along, of course. She remembered.

And then, the skirmishes took on a chaotic flavor that had hitherto been unseen.

The problem with this strategy, Banyan realized, when she saw it employed on a wide scale, was that no one was working together. Sure, they all had the objective in mind of getting the flags off the other team and winning the skirmish. So, they at least had the same goal. But they were all trying to get there in different ways.

This meant that sometimes they got in each other's way.

Literally.

*Idiot,* she thought to herself, *I'm an idiot.*

This was the point of configurations and leadership, and she'd had to tear it all down to see it, and why couldn't she have thought of that theoretically? But clearly, someone needed to be looking at the big picture and making sure that people weren't interfering with their own team members. Someone had to stop the friendly fire from taking them down before they even got going.

So, it couldn't be a free-for-all, then. It couldn't be everyone for themselves.

Before she could even suggest this to the other teams, however, Rils Markir's bask came out with his team members divided into three distinct teams, each headed up by one bask member. They worked utterly independently, but they were dynamic, responding to threats that Rils himself couldn't even see because he was too busy dealing with attack that blinded him from watching everything.

This was the way to do it, then.

Small, dynamic groups.

However, how to keep the strategies from colliding?

She asked Rils, and he pointed out that the dragons in his bask could all communicate mind-to-mind. So his riders were checking in with their dragons who were talking to each other, which meant they had eyes all over the entire arena.

Banyan asked Erach if he could communicate with the dragons in her bask, but he said no. They were a lone-dragon bask, and they weren't close enough to preserve that sort of mind-to-mind link.

*Back to the drawing board,* Banyan thought. She needed to solve this problem, especially because she strongly suspected that the Frost had some kind of deep interconnected kind of ability to think together. They all shared the same purpose. They were all subsumed into some bigger Family, as Deke had called them.

*Individuality is our strength,* she thought.

She knew it was the case.

But how?

Right around this point, she was cornered by Dove, who had been keeping her abreast on Gelso's progress. Gelso had been improving every week, getting better and better. His fever was gone. He showed no more signs of having the Frost sickness. Dove thought it was very, very likely he was cured.

But when she came to find Banyan, she told her that Gelso had disappeared.

"They moved him," said Dove.

"Where?"

"Well, I don't know, do I?"

"Do they keep records?"

"He's scrubbed from all the records. No mention of him,"

said Dove.

Banyan didn't know what to make of this. She asked Dove what she thought it meant.

Dove didn't know either. "Either he transformed and they had to kill him or they took him somewhere else for observation."

"But we don't know which," muttered Banyan.

Dove shook her head.

"Fuck," said Banyan. She didn't like these sorts of loose ends.

Weeks passed with no more information from Dove, and the basks tried all sorts of different ideas, and the arena became more and more chaotic as the time went on.

The year-end flag war was coming, and the skirmishes should be honing in on winners and losers. The two winning forces (organized in four—east, west, north, and south) would fight each other, absorbing the two losing forces as their allies. Then half of the dragon corps would fight the other half of the dragon corps in a large-ranging battle that would be won when one side captured the other's flag.

This flag was different than the small flags that were affixed to them during the skirmishes. This flag would be large and emblazoned with the name of the forces, and it was required to be hidden somewhere within the perimeters set out for the game play.

But with the skirmishes in such a state of flux, no one was winning anything.

Banyan got called to Colonel Rabi's office, which didn't surprise her.

"You've done something to the skirmishes," said the colonel. "The rest of the Quorum isn't pleased, but I have defended you, saying I'm sure you're doing *something*. I have to admit, however, I can't quite figure out what it is. At first, I thought you were creating some kind of class structure within the basks, assigning certain riders to certain tasks—shooting or flying or distraction or the like. But then, it seemed as if all that went out the window? So did you try something different? Or is this another prank?"

She eyed the colonel, wondering if she should bargain a bit with him, or if it would tip her hand. "You want answers from me, I see."

"Oh, you want something from me? What? Should I bring Odion back? Is that what you want?"

She hadn't even thought to ask for such a thing. She wondered what was wrong with her that she hadn't.

It wasn't that she didn't miss Odion.

She did.

Mostly, it hit her at night in bed, when she was alone, and she remembered what it had been to be with him for all those nights together, all those weeks of time when they'd been happy, when they'd had that room with its bath and when they'd been ruling the entire dragon arena, winning every skirmish.

Winning was no longer her goal.

She rarely won anymore.

But she was learning things, at least she hoped she was.

She simply wasn't sure she was drawing any conclusions anymore. She felt too confused about everything.

Anyway, at night, alone, she missed him. She thought of touching him. She thought of the way he made her quiver and sigh. She thought of his lips, his clever fingers, his scaled cock, his…

She thought about Slate sometimes too.

Sometimes she thought about Slate and Odion out there together, and that hurt.

But less because she felt angry at Odion for being with him.

More because she felt left out.

"Would you bring Odion back?" she said.

The colonel smiled at her. "That's not what you were going to ask. What do you want?"

"Did Gelso turn?"

The colonel raised his eyebrows. "Ah, of course. Well, everyone turns after they get a bite, Banyan. I thought you knew this."

"Yes, but his fever."

"You know about that, too." The colonel shook his head at her. "You're more resourceful than we give you credit, I must say." He gave her a little smile. "If I tell you this, you'll tell me what you're up to."

She nodded.

"He's alive. He hasn't turned."

"Where is he?"

"Did I agree to answer unlimited questions? I don't think I did. Your turn, Rider First Class Thriceborn."

She sighed heavily. "I just think these skirmishes aren't making us into what we need to be, sir."

"Which is what?"

"One army," she said. "One army that works together. Because we won't be fighting each other when the Frost attacks the school, will we?"

"We can't know if the Frost will attack here. No one knows what the Frost is planning."

"It wants dragons. Dragons help it spread. This is the place to get a lot of dragons."

"True," said the colonel. "We think it's likely it does come here eventually."

"When?"

"I'm beginning to feel as if you're getting more out of me than I'm getting out of you," said the colonel. "How does what you're doing in the arena turn you into one army?"

"Well, we're just trying different strategies," she said. "It's more about seeing how they work than it is about actually beating each other. None of us care about the standings anymore. None of us care about the year-end flag war. Everyone's worried about the Frost."

The colonel sighed heavily. "Right. I see what you're saying." He furrowed his brow, thinking deeply. He didn't look up at her. "Dismissed, soldier." He gestured absently toward the door.

Banyan left, walking through the halls, wondering how it could be possible she'd only been here a year.

She felt as if she'd lived twenty years at this school.

## CHAPTER SIXTEEN

ODION AND SLATE didn't touch, then, and it was both easy and hard.

Easy because they never talked about it and never acknowledged it and there was no pressure from Slate to do anything of that nature.

And hard because Odion began to realize how much he wanted to. And that felt wrong in a number of ways, mostly because it betrayed Banyan. He didn't understand how he could want Banyan and also want Slate.

That wasn't the way people worked, was it?

People were meant to be paired off, two by two. People couldn't love two other people at once, could they?

Or, he supposed they could, but he thought it could never be equal love. A person would always have a favorite.

*Banyan's my favorite,* he thought to himself.

She had to be. She was female and his mate and brilliant. She was a better soldier than Odion was. She was special and singular and exceptional.

What was Slate except…

Well.

Slate was Slate.

His first.

And Slate knew him in some way that no one else did.

And Slate could be…

But he didn't want to think about Slate that way.

Odion immediately cast about for something else to distract himself with, and he decided that should be the Frost.

They already knew that there were ice monsters further up the mountain.

Though it was typical for watchtowers to send riders up the mountain routinely, to look around and check the perimeters, that sort of thing, Slate didn't. He said that was the way watchtowers fell, and Odion thought he was exactly right.

So, no patrols, not a single one.

There were three villages in the vicinity of the watchtower, and these were checked upon by air only—dragons flying overhead—once every two weeks. They all went together to do these checks, because Slate thought that splitting up was a great way for the Frost to infiltrate the bask.

Once it had done so, it knew *everything*. Slate wanted to keep their secrets actual secrets.

This was a good strategy defensively, but Odion wanted to take the offense.

"We should attack it," he said to Slate. "Has anyone ever tried to attack, or have we just spent all our time with our tails between our legs, running from it?"

"It's the fucking Frost," said Slate. "There are eight of us. We're not attacking."

"But I'm Odion Naxim."

"Exactly why I'm not getting you killed. No one would forgive me for that. They'd kill me for getting you killed."

"I won't get killed," said Odion.

"No," said Slate.

"Please?" said Odion.

"No," said Slate. "I'm in charge, and you're here to learn to follow orders, so no."

Odion went into the mountains anyway.

He and Mirra flew around the top of the mountain, and he wasn't sure what he was looking for. At first, he thought maybe they'd have fires or encampments. Then he realized they didn't need fire, and he wasn't sure if they really needed to eat.

They must eat, right? Everything had to eat.

But it didn't seem as if the Frost *did* eat. Just... spread.

That didn't make sense, he supposed. Maybe the Frost was eating its hosts. But maybe it was just a long, slow consumption, and the Frost hoped to spread many, many times before it used up the body it inhabited.

After several weeks, though, Odion finally found something. It was a hunting cabin, something ancient. The roof had caved in. But they were there. They sat in groups, small circles, chatting with each other as the snow fell on their eyelashes and foreheads, smiling like they weren't monsters at all. There were three ice dragons and seventeen former riders.

He and Mirra flew, out of sight, watching for hours.

It chilled Odion, watching them do that. They seemed normal.

Eventually, he flew off, not wanting them to spot him.

He came back that night, after darkness fell, to find them lying out on the ground, sleeping in the snow, faces dusted with fresh flakes, all of them breathing together, in the same rhythm.

Over the coming days, he watched them and they stayed put in their encampment. Eventually, he told Slate about it.

Slate didn't want to come up and see the Frost camp. "Are you insane? I told you not to do this. You disobeyed orders."

"How are you going to punish me?" Odion was a little too insouciant.

Slate's reptilian eyes flashed. "Don't flirt with me, Odion."

"I'm not..." Odion cleared his throat. "Just come. They're all asleep at night."

Slate came. Maybe because he was curious. Maybe because he wanted to fight the Frost. Maybe because Odion begged. Odion couldn't know.

Slate saw them, all asleep like that.

And then, when Odion began making the plan for the attack, Slate didn't tell him not to make the plan.

They planned and planned.

Weeks went by, and they worked on different ideas, different ways to get away, different ways to be sure it all went off without a hitch.

They checked on the camp, over and over, just to be sure that everything was as it had been.

And then, finally, one night, they struck.

Eight dragons, eight riders.

They took out the three ice dragons first, all of their eight dragons concentrating fire on the three ice dragons, who woke up and tried to put out the blaze, but whose wings were already burning. The ice dragons were outnumbered, and they were smoldering puddles of water, unable to move, unable to fly, and unable to fight back.

The seventeen rider-monsters were motivating at that point. They shot arrows, some of which hit the human riders, but most of which glanced off the dragon scales that they hit. And without any way for the ice monsters to ride into the air on dragon backs and engage with Odion's bask, they were severely handicapped.

There were a few wounds on Odion's side—one rider with an arrow in her thigh and another with one in his shoulder. But no casualties.

And together, Odion and the others chased down each and everyone of the ice monsters and burned them to death, even as they shrieked.

The air smelled like burnt clothes and burnt meat, and the bodies were smoking, charred skeletons.

It was a clear victory.

But that night, when Odion tried to sleep, he thought of the way they had laughed and talked, and the way they sounded just like people when they screamed as they burned to death.

It made him feel ill.

"Offense," murmured Slate in the darkness. "Of course you're braver than the rest of us, and of course it pays off.

We should go looking for another encampment. We should share what we know with the other watchtowers."

Should they?

Odion rolled over into Slate's arms, pressing his face into the other man's armpit.

Slate was stunned. He jolted back for a second, and Odion was sure the other man was going to reject him, but then Slate relaxed, and his arm tightened around Odion, pulling him into his arms.

Odion pressed his face into the other man's flesh.

"Hey," said Slate. "This doesn't seem like some kind of celebratory overture."

"This isn't an overture."

"All right." Slate's arms stayed just as tight around him.

Silence.

Elemental forces, it felt good to be close to someone, to be *touching* someone else.

"What's wrong, Odion?"

"Do we live lives where things are right?" demanded Odion. "Or is it just denial and sacrifice and following strict orders and being forced here and yanked there and—" His voice cut off when Slate's hand landed on the back of his head.

Slate stroked his hair, gentle. "That's not what this is about."

"What if they're not monsters?"

"What?"

"Slate, I told you that they talked and laughed and they seemed just like people, didn't I?"

"You did," said Slate. "But you only have to look at them to see that there's something wrong with them."

Odion groaned.

"This is what we're here to do, you know. We're soldiers and we're here to fight the Frost."

"We're murderers, you mean," said Odion.

"If someone is trying to murder you first, you're defending yourself. It's different."

"Is it?"

"Yes. It's a matter of intention. We didn't *ask* the Frost to start trying to turn us. The Frost began this, not us. If we retaliate, well, they asked for it."

Odion could see this was true, but it didn't really change the way he felt, not entirely. "What if…?" He lifted his head to look at Slate. "What if we could negotiate?"

"How would we do that?"

"I don't know, but that's how the Dragon War ended, with negotiations. It was mutually assured destruction, so they all decided to stop killing each other and now we live together in peace."

Slate chuckled. "Peace in Hazai, sure. But in Aleen, our cities have never quite recovered. The capital city Rillin, it's all rubble. I once went there with a group of my friends. We must have been fifteen, sixteen. We climbed all through the scorched remains. We wandered through what used to be the library there, all of the scrolls and books with singed, unreadable pages, all of that knowledge burned to the *ground.*"

"W-well," said Odion quietly. "Aleen started the war."

"Is that what they teach you in Hazai?"

"Didn't you?"

"No, we didn't." Slate was sitting up now, leaning against the wall where the bed was arranged.

"Well, the first attack was—"

"We had to do something, because Hazai had taken over half of our port cities and any attempts to get them to leave had been met with no response whatsoever. *Your country was the aggressor,*" said Slate, and he sounded truly angry.

Odion swallowed, looking up at Slate. "I… I have no excuses for Hazai, or the Quorum. We all know what sort of leadership that is." Hazai used to be ruled by a royal family, like the other kingdoms, but for generations now, its "kingdom" had really been the purview of the Quorum, a military dictatorship. "I don't doubt what you say. I'm sorry."

"Negotiations didn't work then," said Slate. "We had to fight. No one would listen to us else. After all, we are just the small little green pointy-eared Aleenans. Everyone thinks of us as backwards and living in trees and doing vine magic, and—"

"That's not how I think of Aleenans," said Odion, sitting up, too.

Slate sagged into the wall. "I'm sorry. It's not you." He let out a strangled laugh. "Honestly, I didn't realize I cared. I haven't even been back to Aleen in years now. I don't go. Last time I did, I felt so out of place there, with my family, I realized there was only one place I'd ever belong and that was here. With the dragons, with the riders, at the Academy."

"I feel that way too," said Odion. "They took me from my family when I was four years old. I barely remember them."

"You have it worse," said Slate, giving him a sympathetic look. "I always forget that."

Odion sighed. "What sort of brilliant soldier could I really be, Slate, if I'm this affected by watching the enemy die?"

"The best kind," said Slate, scooting down and putting his arms around Odion again. "The kind who will not risk casualties lightly and who will only hurt as much as necessary. The kind who won't become a monster himself."

Odion turned, facing the man. He wanted… but he shouldn't… "Kiss me," he whispered.

Slate rubbed his fingers over Odion's eyebrow, searching the other man's expression. Then he carefully lined up their faces and put his mouth on Odion's, and it was like sugar and whimsy and softness and pleasure.

Odion clung to the other man.

All they did was kiss.


OUTSIDE ODION'S AND Slate's watchtower, a figure approached. She was wrapped in furs and warm robes, but she did not need them, because she had not felt cold in some time. She had stood close to a fire, however, to warm her skin, to make the supple curves of her breasts feel heated. Now, she would have to stay in the shadows, however, because otherwise someone might notice the gray-ish color of her skin, which was leached of all other color. She had tucked her long white strands of hair away, hiding them.

She had trekked a long way, summoned because of the agonizing deaths of her brothers and sisters. She had been sent by the Family, here to exact a kind of revenge, she supposed.

She had some knowledge of the watchtowers, not because she had ever been to one, but because she'd been told by others, those who'd been riders.

She had never been a rider.

She had been a girl in a village in Hazai. She remembered that life, but she didn't miss it. She remembered that she had wished so hard, wished with every fiber of her being, that Givre Mixel would look at her, would want her, would love her. But he'd only had eyes for another girl in the village, a prettier girl. She remembered that—the competition, the anger, the feeling of rejection…

None of that in the Family.

Anyway, it had all been pain, that life. Only pain.

Now, she was part of something. She didn't have to hurt. And she knew that if she died, the purpose lived on, because she was an extension of the Family, and she was only one being, but that all of them worked together for the spread, the bite, the purpose.

She knew that the windows along this side of the watchtower were bedrooms, and she began throwing stones at one of them. She only hoped she'd get someone's attention, and it would be better if it was a male someone, but she could work with a female too. She knew from the riders that sometimes the females even *wanted* the other females, although in her village, that would have been an abomination.

The window opened, and it was a man.

"Help me," she breathed up at him.

He looked her over. "What are you doing out there?"

"Please? It's very cold."

"Of course," said the man, and he hurried down the stairs to throw open the door and urge her inside.

But she beckoned instead. "This way. With me," she said.

"What is it?" he said, furrowing his brow.

"I need you to come with me," she said, making her voice sound panicked. "Please, it's… when you see it…"

He hesitated. "Let me see your face."

Well, they knew, then. For some time, the enemy had been ignorant of the truth of them out here, thinking them all mindless beasts. But that advantage was crumbling.

She rushed at him, seizing his hand. "Please," she said, voice breaking, and she didn't wait. She pulled his hand up to her mouth and opened her jaw and *bit*.

# CHAPTER SEVENTEEN

AT BREAKFAST AT the Academy that morning, none of the teachers were present. There was a scroll sitting out on a table, and the undercadets had already read it.

Banyan picked it up and scanned it.

It said that the teachers were not insensible to the fact that this had been a trying year. The year-end flag war had been moved up, and as soon as it concluded, the school would conclude. It could be weeks early, depending on how quickly the war could be won. The letter also said that the school had spent too much of its time making the students fight against each other. *But you are one army, one army that must work together against the Frost, which you all know is coming. So, in the year-end flag war, you will be one army. We, the teachers, have hidden our flag somewhere. Once you find it, we all go home for the year.*

This was what came of that conversation with Rabi, obviously.

The letter detailed the perimeters of the game. The flag could be hidden anywhere in the school or within a three mile radius around the school. There were geographical boundary marks. One was the river to the east, and others were various hills and trees and rock outcroppings that were all known to the students.

Typically speaking, there were two flag wars—one for the glider corps and one for the dragon corps. They'd be on opposite sides of the grounds. But this year, all of it had been combined.

Teachers against students.

Well, it was certainly on point for the school.

Outside the window, a dragon flew by. It was one of the teachers on his dragon.

Of course, they were out there protecting their own flag.

Banyan went back to the letter.

*Obviously, we will be looking for your flag as well. If we find it, we go back to studies until the term is out. You have until the fifth bell to hide it. We will be watching. We think this is more than fair since you outnumber us by quite a great degree.*

There was the flag, folded up, next to the scroll.

Banyan picked it up. She turned to look at the gathered students in the dining hall. They were all standing at their tables, silent, because that was the way that they had been taught to enter this place. It was always thus. They came in, ate as quickly as possible, and then left.

They usually only had about fifteen minutes here to eat. It was all decided by bell.

The fifth bell?

"We need to hide this," said Banyan. "The fifth bell will be soon."

All of the students simply stared at her.

Where to hide it?

Banyan looked out at all of the students, trying to think if she'd ever known of anyone who was good at hiding things. She had to admit that it wasn't really part of the skirmishes and they didn't play a lot of games like hide and seek in the school.

Till, a man in her bask, was very fast. He could sprint quickly. It would have to do. "Till!" she called, waving the flag.

He hurried over. "Yes?"

"Get this as far as you can before the bell."

"But where should I hide it?" said Till.

"It doesn't matter," said Banyan. "Just as long as it's hidden and no one sees you doing it." In fact, a random hiding spot was probably better than something that had significance. It would be much harder to guess.

Till took the flag and left.

Banyan surveyed the rest of the students. "Well," she said. "Finish your breakfasts. Then we're going flag hunting!"

"UIN'S MISSING," SAID Slate. "Bed covers pushed aside like he climbed out of bed and hurried out of there. Window's open."

"He climbed out of the window?"

"That would be crazy, right?" said Slate.

Odion pushed past Slate to go into Uin's room. It was just as Slate said. Odion walked over to the window and looked down. He shook his head. "No way. There's no way to climb. He'd have to have jumped. If he had, he'd have broken something."

"His dragon could have been here," said Slate. "He could have climbed out onto his dragon's back."

Odion considered. "Well, I guess—"

"Except there's his dragon." Slate pointed and there, indeed, flying in the air, was Uin's dragon, circling overhead in a pattern that indicated the dragon was worried.

"Can anyone's dragon communicate with Uin's?" said Odion.

"No, they're not in a bask," said Slate. "We're all lone dragons out here." He tapped his chin. "So, he didn't go out the window."

"But he opened it," said Odion. "So, he saw something out there, on the ground, and then he went downstairs, outside, and—" He grimaced. "The Frost."

"What?" said Slate.

"It does this. It probably sent a girl or something. A pretty girl. It probably seduced him and now he's going to come back, *turned*, and he has a key to the door, and he'll attack us in the night while we're sleeping and this is revenge."

Slate furrowed his brow. "This is quite a leap, Odion."

"I'm not wrong," Odion growled. "Tell everyone we're leaving."

"We can't leave the watchtower. Our orders—"

"We will not let these riders or these dragons fall to the Frost," said Odion. "So, we go."

"But they'll just send us back."

"They won't," said Odion. "I'll convince them."

"You're not convincing me, and I actually like you, so I don't see how."

Odion sighed heavily. He regarded Slate. "Did I tell you about Deke Midgurd?"

"Deke who?"

"I guess I haven't told you anything."

"We haven't been talking, no. And I still don't know why you got sent to me. Why were you demoted?"

Odion sighed again. "All right, well, I'm not hiding it or anything, I just didn't feel like getting into it, I guess. But let me explain about Deke." So, he did.

Slate furrowed his brow as he listened. The more Odion talked, the deeper the furrow got in his brow.

"And Banyan also told me that she'd heard from one of the scholars at the school about one of the patients with the Frost sickness, who was bitten by a woman who seduced him," said Odion. "It's one of its tactics, all right? This is how it works."

"Right," said Slate. "Right. I suppose it does make sense. But we still can't simply leave. It'll be desertion. We'll be court-martialed. We'll all be demoted, and—"

"Let's just go to Rabi," said Odion. "He'll listen."

"Will he." Slate leveled a bland look.

Odion groaned. "I think he will."

"He's not head of the army, Odion, he's only the head of the *school*."

"He's in the Quorum. He's high level. He has influence. He's *fucking* General Frax."

"All right, well, if we do this, I accept full responsibility for the bask," said Slate. "You tell him I ordered them out and that they had no choice but to obey. They're not to be labeled with desertion."

"Sure," said Odion. "As for why I got demoted, it's sort of related."

"How? That Deke person is dead and there was no consequence for that?"

"It's related because of the Frost is all. It's related because someone else got a bite. Banyan and I were trying to find out more about it, and we hid him, and they weren't pleased with us."

"You hid an ice monster?"

"He hadn't turned," said Odion. "We theorize that if the bitten person is in the cold, the change happens quicker."

"So, Uin? He's been taken up the mountain?"

"Probably," said Odion. "I guess I hadn't thought about that." He rubbed his chin. "Huh, why doesn't the Frost just bite people in a bask and wait? It would take two weeks for them to transform, and no one would even know." He considered. However, he supposed that people always knew they were infected with the Frost sickness because of the telltale numbness in one's hands and feet that tended to present itself.

It was very distinctive. It wasn't a tingling sort of numbness, like pins and needles, but more entirely unfeeling, and it made doing things like using one's hand to pick things up very difficult. "I guess people always know they're infected with the Frost sickness, though."

"Yeah, sometimes people try to hide it, but they aren't successful," said Slate.

"Apparently, though," said Odion, "the Quorum says, when a normal person gets it—someone not bonded to a dragon—they do just turn into a monster. But the riders, when we get it, we can still talk. The Quorum thought that a person was absorbed, like, their thoughts and memories? But I don't think it's that, not exactly. I think, the reason they know things is because they tell each other. It's just *talking*."

"Well, that would be good," said Slate. "They'd just be

like people."

"Yes," said Odion, nodding, feeling his stomach twist. "Exactly like people." And it turned out that the one thing he was really good at was slaughtering people. Burning them alive. "Look, Slate, we're leaving."

"We're leaving," said Slate grimly.

They left.


BANYAN WAS IN the library, looking at a map of the school that was printed in one of the books. It was old, probably twenty years outdated, but it was better than nothing.

She had the heads of all the basks—dragon corps and glider corps—crowded around the table where she was looking at the book. "So, what do we think about splitting up and each searching various areas?" She looked up at the gathered faces.

No one said anything. They all just waited expectantly.

"Is that an order?" Rils finally said with a grin. "Maybe you should divide us up, Rider First Class Thriceborn."

"It's not an order, it's a question," said Banyan. "I want your advice. I don't want to be the only person thinking about this. Does anyone have a better idea?"

They all simply blinked at her.

Banyan was sort of amazed at how the removal of the teachers from the school had so little influence on anything. The bells were still tolling, and the students were still following them for the most part. They weren't going to classes, but they had showed up at the right bells for lunch, had come in and sat down in silence, just the way they typically did.

Individuality might be their strength, but routine was what kept them in motion. Most of them weren't used to thinking either. They were all very used to having someone else do the thinking for them.

And these were the bask leaders.

She rubbed her forehead. "It's not a particularly innovative idea. Someone's got to have some other thought about how to look for the flag besides divide and conquer."

"I've got something," said Atohi.

Banyan gestured to her. "Lieutenant, by all means."

"We capture Major Yorns and tell him that we have captured his wife, Capitan Yorns, and that if he doesn't tell us where the flag is, we'll hurt her."

Banyan's eyes widened. "Well, that's extreme." She considered. "Possibly effective."

"Nah," said Raini. "I doubt Yorns knows where the flag is."

"They're the only mated couple of the teachers," said Atohi, shrugging.

"Well," Banyan said in a thoughtful voice, "that opens up an entirely different avenue of attack than I was thinking of. If we think of the flag's location as essentially intelligence, then we don't have to find it as much as we have to get someone to tell us where it is." She sat back in her chair. "Who wants to be in charge of that?" She gestured at Atohi. "How about you?"

"Me?" said Atohi.

"Yes, I want you to handpick a team to send out as spies to try to get close to the teachers and listen in. Maybe we infiltrate somehow. Maybe someone pretends to be injured and tries to get to the teachers that way. I don't think we should threaten or torture anyone. It *is* just a game."

"I don't know anything about any of that," said Atohi.

"If you don't want it, does someone else?"

"It seems like it should be you," said Rils to Banyan.

"I can't do everything," she said.

"Well, I can take over organizing looking in the school," said Rils. "We'll have dragon corps search the building and glider corps search outside."

"And we have to consider the fact that they haven't hidden at it all," said Banyan. "They could just have it in their main camp, which means that to get it, we'd have to attack."

"Would they do that, though?" said Raini. "We outnumber them ten to one."

"That's why I need intelligence," said Banyan. "But I guess I can run intelligence. Raini, then I want you to be the head of offense."

"A-all right," said Raini, looking surprised.

"You'll be great," said Banyan. "If I'm heading up intelligence, I think I want the undercadets, don't I? Anyone who hasn't been accelerated is going to be more useful for my purposes. So, I guess I'll leave you to it." She got up.

They all looked at her, puzzled, worried.

"What?" she said.

"You're Banyan Thriceborn," said Atohi. "And you're leaving us in charge?"

"I don't want *anyone* to be in charge." Banyan threw up her hands and stalked out of the room.

She was heading up the stairs to find the undercadets, who had all gathered in the north tower, in the room where the focus training was usually conducted, when someone came running down the stairs.

"Rider Thriceborn, I was coming to find you!" she called, well, practically wailed. "It's Odion Naxim."

Banyan froze. "What about Odion?"

"He's here."

## CHAPTER EIGHTEEN

SHE LOOKED THE same, but Odion had forgotten how much he liked looking at her, how she was pretty and yet stern, how her beauty made him want to look at her from all angles, how she intrigued him, how she seemed so strong and so intense and so, well, freckled. He was just grinning at her.

Slate was talking. "You have to know where the teachers are."

"No, they all left, and we see them flying around outside the windows on their dragons on occasion, but we don't know," said Banyan, gesturing with both of her hands. "I'm telling you, this is the year-end flag war, and they're the enemy. We don't even know where their camp is, but I'm trying to put together a team of spies to go and find out what we can about them."

"Spies?" said Slate. "Great God Tan, you're all taking the flag war far more seriously than anyone ever has."

"I just want it over," said Banyan.

Odion reached for her.

She came over and put her hand in his, still talking to Slate. "They told us that if we beat them, we get to go home early, and everyone could stand a break. Everyone is worn thin at this point. The terror of it, it's getting to us all."

Odion put her knuckles to his lips.

She started, a stain of blush splashing across her cheeks

and forehead. She tugged her hand back, shy, smiling. "Odion," she scolded in a voice that sounded soft, not the way she'd been talking at all.

"We need to talk to Rabi," said Slate. "But if he's not here, we'll talk to someone else in the Quorum."

"No," said Banyan, "they all left. The teachers and every other member of the Quorum or the army who lives here. No one is in this place except the students and cleaning and cooking staff."

"Weird," said Odion. "Why would they do this? Why change the flag war?"

"I think it was my fault," said Banyan. "I might have said something to the colonel. Maybe I gave him the idea. What do you need to tell him?"

"We attacked and killed a nest of ice monsters," said Slate.

"Nest?" said Odion. "That's what we're calling it?"

"What else would you like to call it?" said Slate. "A swarm? A horde?"

Odion shook his head. "Those are worse."

"Anyway, they decided to retaliate," said Slate. "So we left before they could. It's a strategic retreat, not that I think the Quorum is going to see it that way. I strongly suspect they order us right back out there after stripping us of our ranks and sending us to three hours of focus training."

"How'd they retaliate?" said Banyan.

"Well, Uin was missing. His window was open."

"They sent someone to seduce him out," said Banyan.

"Exactly," said Odion.

"From that?" said Slate. "She hears that, and she jumps to the same conclusion as you? Really?" He shook his head at them. "Both of you, you're weird, you know that?"

Odion laughed.

Banyan lifted her chin at him. "Weird, huh?" She was grinning.

Slate's voice dropped in pitch. "Very weird."

"Well, look, Major Nightwing," she said, folding her arms over her chest, "the minute me and my weird spy group figures out where Colonel Rabi is, I'll let you know. Until then, unless you're placing yourself under my jurisdiction—"

"I understand you've been demoted to rider first class," said Slate.

Banyan rolled her eyes.

"Yeah, I'm not taking orders from you," said Slate.

"I think we're done here," said Banyan.

"Because you think the *game* you're playing is more important than fighting the actual Frost," said Slate.

"You just told me you strategically retreated from the Frost," said Banyan.

Odion smirked.

Slate shook his head at her. "You know something?"

"What?"

"I'm beginning to think I might like you after all," said Slate. He shrugged at her and then loped off up the stairs, heading for the top of the landing tower.

Banyan was gazing after him, lips parted. "He's…"

"Yeah," said Odion, nodding. "I should go after him."

"Do you have to?"

Odion considered. "If I stay, won't you just ignore me while you try to beat Rabi at whatever this game is?"

"I mean, yeah, but we could hold hands," said Banyan.

He laughed. "I'm going."

"Without one kiss? How long has it been? Are we mated or—" He interrupted her by kissing her hard, pulling her into his arms.

She clutched at him, frantic, hands everywhere, tongue moving rapidly against his, a little noise in the back of her throat. And then she pushed him away and ran a hand through her hair. She was blushing again.

He liked it when she blushed.


BANYAN SENT OUT riders first, to fly over the area and

look for an encampment, just in case the teachers had decided to all cluster together in some obvious spot. They didn't find it, but they did find the enemy flag.

It was high in a tree, wrapped around the trunk. If a dragon flew up there, they would not be able to get to it because the branches were too long. It wouldn't be possible to reach in and get it. However, there was no point in trying to climb up either, because the branches up there were too fragile to be stood upon. It was right there, but they couldn't get it.

Banyan spent the entire afternoon and evening trying to get the flag.

Nothing worked.

She sent some of her undercadets back to the school to spread the word and ask if anyone was good at climbing trees.

No one came back.

The dinner bell cut cold and clear into the air and all the students with her got antsy.

"Well," she said, "I'm not your superior officer. You have no orders. Do as you like."

This made them all look very nervous. They shifted on their feet and looked at each other indecisively.

"You could go and get dinner, of course," said Banyan, "but the flag is right here, and if we can get it, then it's over. We *win*."

They looked at her, wide-eyed, anxiety all over them.

"I'm not telling you what to do!" She threw up her hands.

They just stared at her.

Slowly, while her back was turned, more and more of them sneaked away, back to the school, back to the warmth and light and the dinner bell. She stayed out here. She knew that the rules of the year-end flag game said nothing about moving the flag. The teachers could come and take it away. If she didn't stay here and bear witness, they could take it while no one was looking.

Luckily, someone sent out a small woman named Ginia, who came with a sling that she fashioned around the tree trunk. Using it, she could sit back against it and use her feet, and she could scale the tree easily.

The flag was in their hands in a half hour.

But they still didn't know where the teachers were, so Banyan took the flag inside and draped it out over the south tower. Of course, it was dark, and she didn't know if anyone saw. She stayed up there with it until someone came up to tell her that Colonel Rabi was downstairs in his office, waiting for her.

He was merry. "That was abundantly quick, Banyan," he said.

"Well, that was an abundantly stupid place to put your flag," she said.

"We did think it would be harder for you to get it down," he said, grinning at her. "We had a devil of a time getting it up there, let me tell you."

She surveyed him, feeling let down, actually. She'd thought this might be more of a challenge, fighting the teachers. That was it? That was the year-end flag war? "Odion and Slate are here."

"Well, that's against orders," said the colonel. "Can't imagine that will go well for them."

"They say it's a strategic retreat from the Frost," said Banyan. "They also say they took out a nest of ice monsters."

"Took out a nest?" The colonel was surprised. "I'm fairly sure that was *also* against orders. Do they want to be court-martialed? Is that it?"

Banyan shrugged.

"Well, leave that to me," said the colonel. "You're finished with the school year. You can go and visit your family now. We'll see you back here for the next term, which will be in three and a half months. Enjoy your break."

"That's it?" said Banyan. "What about Odion?"

"Well, I suspect he'll be graduating."

"I'm not graduating?"

"It was only your first year at the school."

"Yes, but—"

"You're dismissed, soldier."

"What about Odion and me? Are we allowed to see each other? What are you playing at now? First, you were trying to shove us together, now you seem to want to tear us apart, and—"

"Rider First Class Thriceborn, you seem to think we are scheming on a level higher than we could possibly scheme. There is no conspiracy to keep you from your mate. If you wish to see him, see him. Now, you're dismissed."

When Banyan got back to her room, all of her things were gone. She groaned, glaring at the empty bed. She really wished they would stop moving all her things without her.

It turned out that everything she owned had been loaded onto a pack that was strapped onto a harness on Erach. She was to leave, she was told. Head home. Have a nice break. Off with her.

She went looking for Odion instead.

But he was talking to the colonel, so she waited in the hallway outside the colonel's office until Odion and Slate came out.

They both broke into smiles at the sight of her.

And she felt confused, she had to admit, because *look* at them. Odion's brown skin; Slate's light green skin. Their eyes, so exotic and intense. Their lean, strong bodies encased in their tailored uniforms.

And both of them smiling at her like that.

It was confusing to say the least. A dizzying kind of confusion that she didn't entirely want to end, but confusing nonetheless.

She fell into step with them as they walked through the hallways. "Well, what happened to you two? Are you court-martialed?"

"I have to report to my immediate superior, Corporal Malloway," said Slate. "There might be some kind of punishment, but probably not a court martial. I think they're going to have me take the bask out to burn up more nests, honestly. The colonel asked a lot of questions about that. I think they want to observe how that happens."

"And I've been given two weeks leave before I have to

report for my official first assignment as a full-fledged dragon rider," said Odion.

"So, you did graduate," said Banyan. She couldn't help but burst out with, "What am I supposed to do? The colonel told me to go on break with my family for three and a half *months*. I couldn't *possibly*."

"Maybe you should," said Odion. "We'll all be back together at the school when the Frost attacks, after all. You should have some time being normal before that happens."

"I'm not normal," said Banyan. "And the only thing I've ever wanted is to fight the Frost. You two get to go out and do it, and I'm supposed to go *home*?"

Both of them eyed her.

Slate nudged Odion's shoulder with his own shoulder. "Tell your girl you don't want her to leave, idiot."

Odion shot a glance at Slate and then turned back to Banyan. He shook his head. "Slate, you don't understand about her. She doesn't need me in that way."

*What?* Banyan's lips parted. She couldn't find her voice.

Slate's voice was deep and melodious. "Yes, she does." He moved forward, away from Odion and advanced on her. He stopped, inches away, and she had to crane her head up to meet his eyes. He looked her up and down, giving her an easy grin. "Stay."

Her mouth was dry. "I'm not going anywhere," she decided. Her voice wasn't steady. "Slate, when do you report to your superior?"

"Tomorrow morning," said Odion, approaching. Now, he was shoulder-to-shoulder with Slate again, and he was grinning at her and then grinning at him.

"So, we have the rest of today," said Banyan.

"Let's do something together, the three of us," said Slate.

Banyan let out a little breath and looked at Odion, who was still grinning at Slate.

Slate snorted. "You two, really. You're just begging for someone to order you around."

"No we're not," said Banyan.

"Definitely not," said Odion. He took Banyan's hand and

pulled her in against his body. He slung an arm around her.

"So, uh, what are we doing, then?"

Slate laughed softly, shaking his head. "Oh, *I'm* supposed to decide?"

"You just said you wanted to order us around," teased Odion.

"That's not what I said," said Slate, lifting his shoulders, waggling his eyebrows at the both of them. "I didn't say anything about what I want. No one asks that."

"I'm asking," said Banyan. "What do you want?"

Slate blew out a huff of air. He shoved both of his hands into his pockets and turned, looking around. "That's a lot, isn't it? What about you, princess? What do you want?"

"I'm not a princess."

"Don't like it when I call you that?" Slate fixed her with a look. "What are you going to do about that?"

Odion tightened his grip around her shoulders and kissed her temple. His voice was gravelly. "Well, I know what I want."

"You do?" said Banyan, looking at him.

"Let's go pay for a room," said Odion. "With one bed, and you two can wrestle out who gets to call who princess—"

"You want that?" said Banyan, surprised.

Odion let go of her, holding up both hands. "Sorry. Never mind. It seemed like there was... you two were... but if you're not—"

"No, I am," she said. "I just thought *you* weren't."

"Oh, *I* am," said Odion, nodding.

Slate snorted. "Let's go, both of you. You're pathetic is what you are."

"Pathetic?" said Banyan, stiffening.

Slate moved closer. "Pathetic," he breathed in her ear. "Very, very pathetic and you need someone to take a strong hand with you and teach you better." He glanced at Odion. "Both of you."

A wicked grin split Odion's face.

Banyan felt a rush of something hot and wild go through

her.

"I guess I got time to take you both over my knee, one after the other," said Slate, slinging an arm around her and then one around Odion. "Let's go pay for a room somewhere. Yes?"

"Yes," Banyan felt herself saying, before she could really think it through.

Odion's smile deepened. "Yes," he said.

# CHAPTER NINETEEN

SLATE SHUT THE door behind them and Banyan stood in the middle of the room, looking at the bed, and then at Odion, and then back at Slate. Her heart was beating wildly, and she could feel it at her temples and at her wrists, and this was crazy, and she wasn't even going through a dragon heat, and what was happening?

She should talk to Odion. She and Odion needed to have a discussion about—

"So, look," said Slate, "this doesn't have to be complicated. We can just be blowing off steam, yeah?" He turned to Banyan. "Truth is, I've been lying next to your boy here without putting a finger on him for months, and it's been making me crazy. So, I could stand a release too. Just once more. Work all this out of my system, I guess. This'll be like, uh, goodbye?" He raised his eyebrows questioningly at her. "Yeah?"

"Goodbye," she repeated. "That's what you want?"

"I think so," said Slate, nodding. "I mean, if I hadn't been having these wild and embarrassing little fantasies about the two of you, maybe—"

"Me too," Banyan was saying before she could stop herself.

"Really?" said Odion, who was grinning at her. "Really?"

"Sorry," she whispered.

"No, no," said Odion. "I just didn't think you'd ever

agree to this again."

"You're not... I mean, you're not jealous?" she said.

"I'm as jealous as the elemental opposition of ice and fire, but the jealousy makes me hot," said Odion. "So, uh, so... it's fine."

"You two should both stop talking," said Slate. "Unless you want out of this, in which case you should say something now, before this carriage gets on the road."

"I don't want out of it," Banyan said, and then felt horrified she'd actually said that out loud. She scooted closer to Odion. "What do you mean by jealous?"

"Shouldn't be jealous," said Slate. "Shouldn't, because you two are mated, and I'm not mated to either of you anymore, and whatever I was, it was just some little dalliance for the two of you to work through together on the path to your happily ever after, so I don't see why there's *any* reason to be jealous."

Odion laughed. He went over and sat down on the bed and ran a hand over his face. "We going to talk or fuck?"

"That was exactly my point," said Slate.

Banyan surveyed them both. "Maybe we *should* talk."

Slate stretched his neck. "Look, you don't like something, how about you just say, I don't know, *glider*. That's an unlikely word to say during sex, right? So, you say that, and everything stops."

"That's not what I'm worried about," said Banyan, but now she might be worried about it. "You anticipate doing things I don't like?"

"I don't know, it's different when you're in heat," said Slate.

"Exactly," said Banyan.

Odion rubbed his chin. "Actually, Slate, you and I have never done this when we weren't in heat."

"Oh, believe me, I'm aware. But this is just goodbye, so it doesn't *mean* anything, and—" He groaned. He nodded at Odion. "Undress. Take everything off, and then undress Banyan."

Banyan twisted her hands together. "Do you want it to

mean something? You and Odion, you guys have this—" She broke off. "You really haven't been touching each other? But Odion, I told you—"

"You said if a heat happened," said Odion. "It didn't."

"Yeah, but I meant that it would be all right if you..." She spread her hands. "If it's Slate, it's different." She was sort of just now realizing this. Maybe she hadn't wanted to admit it to herself. Or maybe she was only saying it because it had been a long time, and she was in a heightened state of arousal, and certain things seemed fine that maybe didn't always seem fine.

And Slate was so... handsome, after all.

"Are we talking or are we doing this?" said Slate.

"Well, maybe if we talk, it'll make things easier," said Banyan.

Slate scratched the back of his head. "Hey, princess, I get my orders in the morning, and they probably send me out to the Ice Mountains, and I probably get turned into an ice monster, and it probably doesn't really fucking matter what I want or whether it means anything or not. You two are going to win this war. I'm just some soldier. I don't matter. So, take it *off*, princess. Show us your tits, huh?"

"You're just calling me princess because it annoys me," she said. She turned around and gave Slate her back. "Unlace my vest?"

Slate stepped forward and started on her laces.

"That's not true," Odion said from the bed.

"Shut your mouth, pretty boy," said Slate darkly.

"I mean it, you matter," said Odion. "You definitely matter, and there's no way you get turned into an ice monster—"

"If I turn, I want to be killed," said Banyan. "Odion wants to be set free."

"That is not what I said," said Odion. "I said, if you turned, I'd just let you bite me, and that nothing would be important anymore, that we could just—"

"Join the Frost?" said Banyan horrified.

Odion got up. "Let's definitely stop talking." He seized

the bottom of Banyan's vest and yanked it up over her head.

Banyan raised her arms to help. Then she lowered them and tugged off her shirt. She was bare beneath. She still wasn't used to the scales on her nipples, but they no longer surprised her when she saw herself without clothes. She turned, shaking her breasts at Slate. "There. Happy?"

"Very," said Slate thickly. "Hello there."

Odion was kissing her, one hand cupping one of her breasts and she fell into that, a deep pool of sweet sensation, one of her hands winding up to cup the back of his neck.

Then, she felt the hot wetness of Slate's mouth on her other nipple and she moaned.

Slate kissed his way up her body, over her neck, to just below her earlobe. "I want to watch you get fucked, princess. I want to watch him take you."

She shivered, reaching for Slate, moaning into Odion's mouth.

Odion broke the kiss, eyeing Slate. "That's what you want? Seriously? Why bother with all of this, if it's just some voyeuristic thing to watch—"

"You just want to watch me fucking her," said Slate witheringly.

Banyan pushed on Odion's chest. "I want to watch you two fucking."

They both turned and looked at her, surprised.

"Yeah, princess?" said Slate, grinning.

"There are a number of interesting ways we could probably all fit together, you know," said Odion.

"Thought them all through, huh, pretty boy?" Slate reached for Odion.

"Maybe," breathed Odion, going closer to Slate.

"Kiss," whispered Banyan.

Slate gave her a wicked look. "You, princess, full of surprises."

And then Slate and Odion's mouths were on each other, and the two men were in each other's arms, and she couldn't look away from that. They were both so beautiful and so male and so enticing, and watching them touch each other, it made her body feel tight and bothered and flushed.

She stood there, lips parted, thighs pressed together, staring at it.

Until Odion's hand shot out and he pulled her in and kissed her and then shoved her at Slate, whose mouth found hers, and they both tasted the same, since they'd been kissing. They tasted like each other.

She tugged at their vests. "Off."

Both of them started reaching back to work at their laces. She helped.

In minutes, all three of them were shirtless, and that was wondrous. They lay on the bed, tangled up, pressing their bare skin into each other, kissing, both of the men finding her nipples now and again, either with their fingers or mouths.

It felt good, and she was aroused, but she thought what she liked most about it right then was simply touch. And being able to be vulnerable, half-naked in the arms of other half-naked people, and no fear of attack, no pressure of anything to think about or worry about, nothing but this moment.

And then Odion was tugging off her trousers, and she was being pushed back up on the bed, and she suddenly had two men's faces between her thighs, and they seemed to be in some sort of competition to get their tongues on her pussy.

She giggled, liking it, writhing, laughing, moaning.

It felt good.

Of course, it was never going to make her come. She needed concentrated similar movement. Circles or up and down or side to side, and all in the same place and over and over again without interruption. She thought about telling them that, but they seemed to be having so much fun shoving each other out of the way and kissing each other occasionally in between kissing her, she just... she couldn't.

Slate suddenly rocked back, looking up at her. "She's not in heat."

"I'm not," she said, holding his gaze.

"Not going to be that easy to get her off," said Slate, crawling up the bed. "Lick her the way she likes it, Odion. Did she teach you that?"

Odion raised his head from between Banyan's thighs. "Yeah. She did."

"So, lick her, then," said Slate, imperious. He put his mouth to one of Banyan's nipples. He put his fingers on the other one. He held her gaze as he suckled her.

Banyan swallowed and surrendered.

Well.

Tried.

Now, it was all about her. Both of them concentrating on her. And she wasn't sure why it wasn't working, why she still felt so nervous, why she wanted to escape this and fall into a fantasy—a fantasy *about* the men on her, no less.

*They're right here. Why do you need that?* she thought at herself.

"Hey." Slate's voice.

She looked at him.

He kissed the hardened peak of her nipple. "Talk to me about what you're thinking right now."

She shook her head hard. "N-no."

"No?" Slate was delighted by that. "Is it really dirty and embarrassing, princess?"

"It's—" She swallowed. "It'll... I don't want..."

Odion's tongue dragged itself over her clitoris.

She moaned. "I can't come if I don't *fantasize*."

"Fantasize about what?" said Slate, smiling at her.

"No, it's about... well, when I was with Odion, and I was thinking about both of you, I felt guilty, but now you're both here, and I don't see why I can't—"

"Shh." Slate put a finger on her lips. "You sound worried, princess."

Odion lifted his head. "So, you've been fantasizing about Slate when we've been together? Really?" He wasn't upset by this. He sounded pleased.

"Just to come," she said, looking down at him. "Not the whole time. Just... to get there, it's as though I need to concentrate but *not* concentrate, and it helps to... I wish I didn't."

"What would you fantasize?" said Slate, kissing her nipple again. "Odion wants to know, don't you?"

Banyan cringed. She was embarrassed, but Slate had this way of making embarrassment arousing somehow. She shut her eyes, and she relaxed into it, embracing all of it. "I don't know. Usually the two of you together."

"Watching us?" said Odion into her sex, giving her another lick.

"Watching us... kiss?" said Slate.

"Yeah," she said. "And... and other things, like touching each other's..." She couldn't, she couldn't say— "Cocks." The word made her clench. She groaned.

Odion's tongue went faster against her clit.

"O-or..." She was getting closer. "Or, um, sucking them. Sucking on each other." Her voice was breathy as Odion's mouth went frantic against her.

She threw back her head, panting.

"Good, princess?" said Slate.

It was good, but she couldn't talk. She was concentrating on an image in her head of Odion's mouth fastened around Slate's cock, and Slate's eyes shut, and—

"Say it, princess," ordered Slate in a voice that was firm and velvet.

"Good," she managed.

"You picturing that now?" murmured Slate, making an idle, shivery circle around her hard nipple.

"Yes," she said.

"Who's sucking who?" said Slate. "Or are we both doing it at the same time?"

Her eyes opened wide. "How would that even...?"

Slate laughed. "Great God Tan, we'll have to *show* you, won't we? Get her *off*, Odion, we have *things* to do."

She bit down on her lip. She was hovering in that near-orgasm space, where it was all close, but where it was tentative, where it might happen, but it could all fall apart at any second also. She shut her eyes again, thinking about

Odion sucking Slate, thinking about Slate lazily telling Odion to do it harder or faster, and she suddenly fell off into deeper pleasure, and she immediately knew the orgasm was now an inevitability.

She gasped. "Fuck."

"Yeah?" said Slate. He pinched her nipple.

She cried out, cresting.

"Yeah," said Slate. "Just like that, then, just there, princess."

"Oh, Agnis above," she muttered, and the world folded in on itself and then exploded in goodness as she clenched and clenched. It was too much. She had to shove Odion away, slamming a hand against her mound to push out all the last little twitches.

"Fuck, fuck, fuck, she's so sexy when she comes," breathed Slate.

"She's beautiful," said Odion.

She opened her eyes to find them both staring at her, and she liked this, could easily get addicted to this, to two men worshipfully watching her find her pleasure.

"Hey," said Slate. "Welcome back."

She snickered at him. "I've been right here."

"You know what I mean." He was smiling at her. "Look, I want you to do whatever it takes to come. I don't care how you get there. If you want to fantasize about Colonel Rabi mounting General Frax—"

"Eew!" she said.

Slate laughed. "Just… do it. Because I like watching you fall apart, so I could give a flying fuck what it takes."

"Totally," said Odion. He rubbed her leg. "You can tell me things, you know."

Why was it so easy to tell *Slate* things?

"I know," she whispered.

"On your back," said Slate to Odion.

"Huh?" said Odion.

"Yeah, we're going to show her how we can suck each other at the same time."

"Maybe I want to be on top." Odion raised a lavender

eyebrow.

"On your back," said Slate.

"You know, this ordering-me-around thing?" said Odion, getting on his back and undoing his trousers. "I think you think it's that I like being told what to do, when it's really that you just get off on—"

"I'm going to shove my cock in that mouth and shut you up here in a second," said Slate.

Odion's entire body shook with laughter. He shoved his trousers down and Banyan sat up at the first sight of the nubs on his scaled cock. She hugged her knees to her chest. Oh.

But then Slate was naked too, and his green cock had the starburst pattern of scales around the head, and it was mesmerizing, and he was arranging himself over Odion, and it seemed obvious to her now. Of course that would be how it worked. Of course it was easier on a bed.

Then both men had each other in their mouths and she let out a delighted laugh.

Which made both of them groan.

She looked from one place they were joined to the other and then back and again and she liked it. Both of them looked good with their mouths full, and the sight of their shafts appearing and disappearing made her freshly climaxed pussy jump.

They didn't last very long, and she was a little disappointed about that.

"Been too long," said Odion as he threw himself back on the bed.

"Little embarrassing how quick that was," agreed Slate, wedging himself in next to Odion, so that Odion was in the middle and the other two were pressed into him on both sides.

"Quick nap," said Odion, shutting his eyes.

Slate laughed.

Odion laughed, too, and then… fell asleep. Just like that.

Banyan looked over the expanse of his brown chest at Slate, whose eyes were open and gazing at her.

"You're not sleepy?" she said to him.

"Not particularly," said Slate.

Odion moaned in his sleep between them.

"If we talk too loud, we'll wake him up," she whispered.

"Serves him right," said Slate, but he was also whispering.

And then they were both looking at Odion's soft cock, lying against his belly.

And then back into each other's eyes.

Banyan swallowed. "This… what are we doing?"

"Goodbye, remember?" he said.

"Yeah, that's why you're giving me instructions on how it's all right to fantasize when I come," she muttered. "Because we're never doing this again."

Slate winced. He settled down next to Odion and stared at the ceiling. "You got me, princess. I'm, uh, I get attached. Always have. Even just from heat. I don't know what it is, but I fuck someone and they feel like…"

"Like what?"

"Like they're mine."

She sat up to look down at him.

"I don't mean that in a weird, possessive way."

"I think you do," she said. "Well, a possessive way, maybe not a weird way."

He shook his head. "I wouldn't dream of thinking of trying to stake a claim."

"Maybe it's just because we were mated," she said. "I mean, you remember how it felt."

"And now, you're mated to him."

"I read a thing once about a male dragon mating more than one female at once."

Slate's eyebrows shot up.

She lay back down.

It was his turn to sit up and look down at her. "What are you saying?"

"Nothing," she muttered. "Literally saying absolutely nothing."

He eyed her. "All right, princess, I'll level with you."

"You're never going to stop calling me that, are you?"

"You really hate it?"

She sighed. The truth was, she did not actually hate it.

"I fall kind of hard," said Slate. "And no one ever…" He groaned. "It's always kind of one sided. Lenia—she was… I had a thing with her, but I don't know that she had a thing back. And then there's this—with you two. Where I'm just the *definition* of a third wheel. And I do mean it as goodbye, because this will fuck me up if I do it again. I should have made this a clean break a long time ago. If you and I hadn't gotten accidentally mated, I would have. I'm not a complete idiot, you know."

"I don't think you're an idiot," she said. "I shouldn't have said that…" She massaged the bridge of her nose. "He said he was jealous, so I didn't mean to…"

Slate sighed heavily and lay back down.

She didn't say anything.

He didn't say anything.

## CHAPTER TWENTY

ODION AWOKE TO find Slate gone.

Banyan was curled into him, snoring gently. He sat up, confused, because he'd been pretty sure that had just been the opening act, and that they'd have more to do. All they'd done was oral, for fuck's sake. He hadn't meant to fall asleep, but he'd come too hard. It had been a while since he'd come at all, admittedly.

He'd been relegated to jacking off in the middle of the night when he was sure that Slate was asleep. Lots of times, he tried to stay awake long enough to be assured of such a thing, but failed, fell asleep, and his balls never got emptied. So, actual orgasms had been few and far between over the past few months. This one had been hard and intense. He didn't always fall asleep after coming, but with an orgasm that powerful, yeah.

He looked around the room and saw that Slate was not gone, but was just across the room, sitting at a table in front of an empty fireplace. He had a scroll that he was currently rolling up as he looked across the room at Odion. "Uh, hey," said Slate. "I was, uh, I was leaving a note."

"You're leaving?"

"I feel like…" Slate was dressed. He got up and shoved his hands in his pockets. "You told her you were jealous."

"Yeah, but I didn't mean like that." Odion got out of bed and stepped into his trousers.

"How did you mean?" said Slate.

"Just... you know... that shit you do with me, it gets me all worked up," said Odion. "I like the idea of her liking your cock better than mine. I like being... I don't know." He lowered his head, embarrassed. "I don't even get it, honestly. It's so fucked."

"Well, I like it in reverse, so it's convenient, anyway," said Slate.

Odion approached the other rider. "Yeah, but that makes sense, because it's about you dominating me, right, and everyone gets a charge out of that."

"Do they?" said Slate. "Is that the most pleasurable thing? Dominance?"

Odion halted, staring at Slate.

"To me, it's about how it intertwines," said Slate, putting his fingers together. "Like, I might dominate you, but it's only because — at that point — you own me. I wouldn't bother taking the time to order you around if I hadn't already..."

"Already what?"

"I was going to say something fucked up and untrue, like 'fallen in love.' But we both know it's just sex." Slate shrugged. "We all agreed to this when we were horny, and now we've all had an orgasm and the smoke has cleared and..." He shrugged. "I think I should go."

"I don't think that," said Odion.

"It's scary to be owned," said Slate tightly.

"I don't own you," said Odion.

"You don't *want* to own me," said Slate.

"I just think you should fucking belong to yourself is all," said Odion. "And I'll belong to myself, and Banyan can own herself, and—"

"You know what I mean."

"I'm not sure if I do."

"I talked to her," said Slate.

"Oh," said Odion, hanging his head. "She told you to go."

Slate sighed. "No, she didn't. But you two don't talk to each other."

"How could we? We've been separated for months."

"Well, your first chance, you put me in the middle of it, so that you can't talk," said Slate. "I don't think you want to talk. You had months to work through whatever it was that happened with us in the heat, and you apparently never did."

"Work through it how?"

"Like, decide what it was. Was it a thing you guys like to do together? Was it a one-time thing that happened that you both regret? Did it matter that it was me? There are a number of fucking things you could have worked through."

Odion shifted on his feet. "It's just awkward to talk about."

"Right, fine. This is why I'm leaving. I can't... with this." Slate gestured at him, at her. "I'm older than both of you."

"By two or three years," said Odion. "You act like we're children—"

"You act like children."

"No, we don't."

"Look, it's not like you were a fucking virgin when I touched you or something—"

"I was," said Odion. "I thought you knew that."

Slate swallowed. He rubbed his upper lip. "Shit," he muttered. A long pause. "She, uh, were you *her* first?"

"No," said Odion, glaring at him. "And that's how I know the jealousy thing with you is fine. Because *that's* jealousy. Anyway, he's dead."

"That Deke guy," said Slate, nodding. "Of course."

"Don't go," said Odion. "I think maybe we all three need to talk."

"It's going to be dawn here soon."

Odion looked outside the window, looked at the position of the moon. "Yeah, looks like not for five or so hours, actually."

"I'm just going to walk," said Slate. "Maybe fly with Yilia. I need some space to clear my head."

"What if she wants you and I want you?" said Odion. "What if none of us want this to be goodbye?"

"You're mated," said Slate. "This will never be... I'll

always… no."

Odion sighed. "Maybe I get that, actually."

"Look, this is your story," said Slate. "It's about the two of you. The two super intelligent, super talented, most innovative soldiers ever seen. You fall in love, you bond mated dragons, you save the Trinal Kingdoms. There's no place for me in this story."

"What if we want to make a place for you?"

"Well, you can't," said Slate. "Some things can't be…" He closed the distance between them and seized Odion by the shoulder. "Fuck, do you have any idea how absolutely beautiful you are?"

Odion's lips parted.

"I… Great God Tan." Slate kissed him, a harsh kiss, a quick kiss. And then he let go and dove for the door.

"Wait," said Odion.

Slate did not wait.


"I CAN'T BELIEVE he said that," said Banyan, who was wrapped up in the bed sheet, huddled up against the wall. She considered. "No, I can believe it. It actually sounds just like him. But I wish he wouldn't have said it."

"Really?" said Odion, who was sitting on the foot of the bed, only wearing his trousers, chest bare. "He's not wrong that we never talked."

"Well, I like him," said Banyan. "I know you like him."

"Yeah, but… people always have a favorite, right?" said Odion. "And I like you more than I like him."

"Oh," she said.

Odion grimaced. "I see, then. You like him more than you like me."

"No," she said quickly.. "I just don't… I don't know if I *do* have a favorite."

"No?"

"We're mated," she said. "And you're… you're Odion

Naxim."

He chuckled.

"No, seriously, I never... the first time I saw you, it was like you were instrumental in making me a woman," she said.

"What?" He shook his head at her in disbelief. "What?"

"I never felt attraction like that before. So... so... you'll always be..." She groaned, dragging her hands over her face. "But it's like I couldn't compare the two of you. I love you, because you're you, and I feel what I feel for him because he's him, and it's not even the same thing. It's just different."

"You don't love him?"

"Can I be really honest?"

"Please."

"It doesn't hurt you if I say I think I could love him?"

He shook his head. "Not if..." He swallowed. "If that meant you'd let me love him."

"I don't want it to be like that with us, Odion." She eyed him. "I don't want us to need permission from each other. I don't want us to limit each other."

His mouth quirked into a smile. "I should have realized you'd be this way."

"What way?"

"Just... adventurous. You're always ready for whatever comes," he said. "Well, good. Because I don't want it that way either. But, you know, I think he does."

"What?"

"He said all that shit about being 'owned,' right? I think he might want us to get permission from him."

She giggled. "I might not mind that from him."

"Well, I gotta say, that doesn't entirely make sense to me."

"He's... he's not like us, Odion." Banyan crawled across the bed. "Maybe that's why we need him. You said it to me, you remember? When you were trying to convince me to be with Deke. That we don't love like that. Because we're too consumed with this other passion, which is the Frost, which

185

is the war, which is... I don't even know what it is, but it always comes first. He'd, however, anchor us."

Odion let out a breath, nodding. "I know exactly what you mean."

"Well, we need to go after him," said Banyan. "Except I guess he's with the corporal now, and he's probably getting orders, and you only have two weeks, and I... what am I doing with myself?"

Odion kissed her, pulling her down into his lap. "Princess, go home to your family."

"Wait, when did you start calling me this?"

Odion grinned at her. "Suits you."

"Does not." She eyed him. "Should I call you pretty boy?"

Odion just laughed. "You call me anything you want, princess."

She shoved him.

He held her all the tighter. "I mean it. Go home. I want you to have that."

"There's nothing to have," she said. "That's not my home. The Academy—"

"Not a home," he countered. "But I get it. I understand. I don't feel comfortable going back to my family either."

"We're mated," she said. "So, I think I should be able to come along on your assignment. I know it's unprecedented—there's never been a mated pair where one of the pair is still a student and the other isn't. But at least for the break? Can we try to make it happen?"

He nodded. "Sure. But we'll go home first, to your home, and we'll at least visit. Just for a day or two, all right? And then we spend your whole break together if we can."

"Yes, please," she said. "And maybe we can ask to be stationed with Slate. If we're asking for things."

"Worst that can happen is that they say no," said Odion.


MALLOWAY WAS ODION'S direct superior, also, and he

said he needed to check on Odion's requests. So, Odion left his meeting and went and found Banyan, who'd been wandering around the empty halls of the school.

"It's so weird here with everyone gone." She was whispering.

It *was* strange, but Odion was used to it. Most years, he hadn't gone home. He hadn't always stayed here, either, however. Usually, the Quorum found something else for him to do, like last year, going and judging tournaments.

They went up to the landing tower and their dragons circled overhead.

Banyan wanted to know if he'd found out anything about Slate. He said that Malloway wouldn't tell him yet, but that he'd requested to be stationed with Slate again. "It'd be an odd arrangement, a mated pair with a bask that isn't theirs." But everything was strange these days. He could hardly remember what things were supposed to be like. He looked out into the distance at the icy peaks of the mountains on the horizon.

"I'll ask Erach if he can find Yilia," said Banyan.

"Good thought," said Odion. "How's he taking that, by the way?"

"He's been antsy," said Banyan. "He didn't like the way I was running the skirmishes, that's for sure."

"What were you doing with the skirmishes?"

She sighed and then launched into a long explanation, which Odion listened to, thinking on his own about it. "I think you're missing the point," he said when she was done.

"What do you mean?"

"You're thinking that it should be, uh, egalitarian, and it's not that. Or, it sort of is, but you're missing why you're brilliant, and I've always seen it. It's not that you let people be in charge, it's that you see them."

"See them? What are you talking about?"

"Most people don't see other soldiers as individuals," said Odion. "I don't." He touched his chest. "I see the battles, the strategies, the strengths and weaknesses of the whole. You see soldiers' individual strengths. When I first saw you fight, at the tournament, this is what I was trying to explain to Gilvrist. You used Deke because he was the best at aiming. You used the other soldiers because they were the best at what they did. That's what makes you a good leader. You see the individual, but you can't expect them to put all that together on their own. You have to be the leader and make the plans. You just... you don't treat each soldier as interchangeable, that's all."

She let out a breath. "Well, it seems I'm good at seeing everyone's strengths except my own."

He chuckled.

"Why'd you go on the offensive with the Frost? Why'd you disobey orders?"

"Honestly? Because I was trying to distract myself from Slate."

She laughed. "So, it was about sex."

"When I'm around Slate, everything's about sex."

She threw back her head and really laughed.

He put his arm around her. "Anything from Erach?"

"Give me a minute." She waited. And then she nodded.

Odion felt something from Mirra, though, a jolt of anxiety, of jealousy. "Shit."

"What?"

"It's Mirra."

"Oh, she doesn't want to be supplanted by Yilia," said Banyan.

"She's just young and insecure," said Odion.

"Why'd they mate her to you?"

"I think it was another of their challenges," said Odion. "They did that a lot. Handicapped me to see if I could rise above it. But now, Mirra and I are bonded, and I can't imagine being bonded to another dragon."

"That's your strength," she said. "Turning weaknesses into strengths."

"You think?" he said.

She nodded.

"Look, you go to Slate," he said. "Tell him what we talked about. See what he says? I'll stay with Mirra, keep her calm, soothe her as best I can. We both know that the mating is going to hold, at least until the Frost is defeated. After that, well…"

"I mentioned something to Slate," she said. "I read about it in a book. It was about a male dragon mating two females."

"You mean Erach could mate them both?" said Odion wonderingly. "Like a rooster with more than one hen."

She nodded. "Yeah. It's not common for dragons, but it's apparently done. I should have read more about it, but I was distracted at the time."

"Where did you find this book?"

"In the library here."

"So, what if I go look into that, and you go find Slate?"

"What about Mirra?"

"I'll soothe her first." He grinned at Banyan. "You feel it, right? Like the three of us, it's something."

She nodded. "I do."

"Go convince him," said Odion.

"I'll try."

Their dragons alighted.

They climbed aboard and took to the air.

Odion rode with Mirra, allowing her to flood him with all the images of fear and loss that she was thinking. Of course she was worried, he realized. She'd lost her bask too young. She hadn't been ready to lose her parents. Now, Erach—though he was her mate—was her only family. Since Erach was older, it was easy to see how she was conflating it all. She had lost her family too young, and her sense of security was shaken. Odion soothed her through the bond. He assured her that they were together forever, that nothing could ever break their connection.

It helped her.

When she dropped him back off, she was in a much better mood.

He went down to the library. No one was in there. Much of the time, the library was staffed by student scholars, and they'd left for the break as well. He used the scrolls in the front of the room to look up the subject of dragon mating, and he finally found a few books.

He piled them on the tables in the library, adjusted the light on the oil lamp there, and began paging through.

At first he didn't find anything. He searched the indexes and the table of contents. He flipped through and read the headings of each of the chapters.

But finally, when he was going through the third of the books he found, there it was. He read a paragraph that explained that male dragons had been observed, on occasion, to mate more than one female dragon. It tended to happen in times when there was an imbalance in the ratio of males to females, when females outnumbered men. Before the riders had interfered with the dragons' society, this used to be more common, because of various dragon territorial skirmishes. Dragons tended—like many animal groups—to send their males into danger more frequently than their females. Many creatures seemed to instinctively protect their women, their wombs.

Of course, the bonding effectively wiped that out of the human dragon riders, so it didn't matter. And because of the way the bonding worked on the dragons, now their females fought too, and their children, too.

Not the smallest, youngest children, of course. No dragon was made to fight or bond until they were full grown. But the dragons still treated their full-grown children like children for many years. And it was these basks that the riders took into war.

At any rate, a male mating two female dragons was possible, but the book didn't know how it was accomplished, exactly.

Mating itself was easily understood but typically speaking, if a dragon mated another female, it broke his original bond. The writer of the book didn't know how one bond was maintained while the other was being formed. He speculated that it was impossible, actually.

*It's quite likely that dragons can only have one mating bond, and so this arrangement results in the bond switching back and forth between the females involved. The male dragon is sometimes mated to one, and then, when he engages in copulation with the other, the mating bond changes to her.*

Odion squinted at the text, not liking that at all. That would mean that his bond with Banyan would switch on and off too. She'd sometimes be his mate, sometimes Slate's mate. Was that what he wanted?

He didn't, of course. He wanted her to always be his mate. But he had to admit he wouldn't really mind if she was sometimes Slate's mate. Better still, however, would be if there could be some kind of three-way bond, all of them feeling each other.

For Mirra, losing and regaining the mating bond over and over would not be pleasant either. He thought that might traumatize his dragon. He didn't want that to happen.

He reached for the next book, but he didn't find any information in that one.

And then that was it, the sum total of the knowledge in the South Ridge Academy library. Odion sighed heavily.

"Just once," he murmured, "I'd like something in the world to work out for me without finding out that the cost of it makes me question if it's even worth it."

## CHAPTER TWENTY-ONE

ERACH'S ABILITY TO find Yilia was a little eerie. Banyan had to admit that the connection she had with Erach wasn't as strong as it had been when he was bonded to Yilia. Now, when she directed him to find her, it strengthened, and she realized that the dragon had pulled away from her on purpose. He resented her.

This hurt.

Erach sent to her through the bond pictures of them flying over the frozen mountainside, pouring down fire all over the ice monsters.

She realized he was telling her that he was with her because he wanted to stop the Frost. He considered her a necessary sacrifice. Leaving Yilia, mating Mirra, another sacrifice. He wasn't particularly pleased about it, however. He endured it.

She felt guilty, especially that she hadn't seen this. She'd been so concerned with all the other aspects of her life, she had ignored Erach and ignored his feelings.

*And to think,* she thought, *I thought that my dragon was special.*

He was special, but she wasn't treating him like a special dragon. She was treating him like a mare she could saddle and order around for skirmishes in the arena.

She sent an apology through the bond.

Erach was gruff in return, seemingly unprepared for her

regret.

But then, there was Yilia, and they were diving down into the trees, where the dragon was sunning herself on a long, smooth rock next to a waterfall—white water everywhere— and there was Slate, swimming beneath them in a pool of clear and sparkling water.

Erach swooped down, letting Banyan scramble off his back on the bank next to the pool of water. Then he took off after Yilia, who had taken to the air at the sight of Erach.

Slate waded out of the water. He was entirely naked, because *of course* he'd be naked, and Banyan shifted on her feet as he climbed up out of the water and casually used a towel to rub at the droplets of water on his muscled stomach and thick thighs.

She tried not to look at his penis, but it was just there, and it was kind of perking up, getting more erect as if her gaze was teasing it stiff. She looked down at the ground, clasping her hands behind her back. "Did you get your orders?"

"Yeah, I did," said Slate.

"Do I get to know what they are?"

"Why are you here, princess? Does Odion know you're here?"

"Yes, he knows. He wanted to stay and try to soothe Mirra and he said I should talk to you. He and I talked. We, um, we…" Now, here she was, and she didn't know how to even say it. She lifted her gaze, but at that point Slate was rubbing his towel over the scales that surrounded his genitals. Almost everyone seemed to have the scales there, replacing their pubic hair. She gaped, her mouth dry.

His cock was now very erect. He gestured with the towel. "You want to help me dry off or something?"

She let out a little noise and scurried over, taking the towel out of his hand. "Maybe."

He snatched the towel back, holding it between them, right over his crotch. "Sorry, I'm just… you're…" He let out a little laugh. "I was right. The Quorum is outlining this offensive strategy, and we're going to be scouting out camps of ice monsters and burning them out. We won't be settled anywhere. We'll camp as we advance. They want us to take back Bastia Mountain. I leave tonight."

"Tonight," she said.

"Tonight," he confirmed.

"Well, Odion is requesting to be placed with you, and I'm requesting to be placed with him."

"What?" said Slate.

"We talked," she said. "We want you."

Slate's fist tightened on the towel. "No, you don't."

"We do," she said. "Both of us. I left him going to look up dragons mating two females in the library."

Slate's eyebrows lifted. "Seriously?"

She nodded.

He ran a hand through his hair, shaking his head. "I wasn't expecting that."

"Do you want us, too?"

He looked up at her, his expression nearly shy. He gave her a half smile.

"Do you want me?" she said. "I know you said you didn't really like me, and I sort of stole Odion from you and—"

"I want you," he said. "I don't know how something like that works, though, with three people? Does that work?"

"We're not like other people," she said. "We're not going to have a normal relationship."

His smile widened. "The Quorum won't like it."

She shrugged. "The Quorum should be used to things like this. In heat—"

"Well, that's heat." Slate lifted a shoulder. "But if we really were all mated to each other, well, they couldn't ignore that." He stopped then, a far-off look in his eyes. "Sorry," he said. "It's Yilia. She picked up on what I was saying. She's, um, she's not particularly happy with Erach."

"I can only imagine," said Banyan. "But Erach really loves her. He cares about Mirra, but it's not the same. He wouldn't have done it if he'd had a choice. I forced it—the Quorum forced us to force it."

"No, I know," said Slate. "But Yilia, she doesn't want to be mated to Erach at all right now. And if she was going to be, I don't think she'd be pleased at the idea of sharing him."

Banyan winced. "Right, I can't think any of the dragons will like it. It'd be a strain for Erach. He knows that he favors Yilia, and he'd be very aware of the pain that was causing Mirra, which he wouldn't want to do. It would be messy."

"Good for us, bad for the dragons," said Slate. "But let's go see what Odion's figured out."

She nodded.

They flew back, and Erach was sending amused thoughts at her through the bond at the prospect. He wasn't actually opposed, she didn't think. She knew how he felt. Two men for her? Two females for Erach? She clutched him as the wind blew her hair away from her face and giggled into the breeze.

But it was clear that Erach didn't know how to do it. He sent images through the bond (graphic images which made her a little uncomfortable) of his mating with the other dragons. She got what he was trying to say. When he'd bonded with Mirra, he'd still been in love with Yilia, and the bond had broken. How could he preserve the bond with Mirra and add the bond with Yilia? He didn't know if he could have more than one at a time.

Odion's news wasn't heartening. He met them at the landing tower and he explained to them what he'd found out in the library as he was climbing onto Mirra's back. Then, all three of them took to the air together.

The three dragons flew together, and Banyan brought up the rear. She didn't know where they were heading.

As they flew, Erach seemed to process what Odion had explained. He sent pictures through the bond of his going back and forth between Yilia and Mirra, of a bond that went back and forth. Banyan sent back confirmation that was the theory. She knew Odion hadn't liked it, but she didn't know if she minded. She would have time with each of them, and she could make it work. She supposed it would be nice if Odion and Slate could be bonded together, however.

Eventually, the dragons landed in a clearing in the woods. There was a very huge flat rock that got the sun, and the dragons all trooped over there after letting off their human riders. They stretched out on the rock, sunning themselves, basking in the warmth.

"When are you leaving?" Odion said to Slate.

"Tonight," said Slate.

"Of course they're shipping you off right away," said Odion. "But maybe we'll join you in a couple weeks. We're going to Noch to see Banyan's family first."

"We don't have to," said Banyan, shaking her head at him.

"Nowhere else to go," said Odion with a shrug.

Slate looked out at the dragons. "They won't assign you with me."

"They might," said Odion. "After all, if you're really going out there on the offensive, that was my idea, and maybe I should be part of implementing it."

"I think they want you to stay safe and have more ideas, Odion," said Slate. "I don't think they want you on the front lines. I, on the other hand, am totally expendable."

"Don't say that," said Banyan.

"They're definitely not going to let you both go out there," said Slate.

"They might," said Banyan. "I'm getting an idea, actually."

"Are you?" said Odion, smirking at her.

"You going to share?" said Slate.

"The scholars, when people have the Frost disease, they give them something towards the end. It supposedly puts them to sleep, but apparently, it's deadly. Except that you can't kill an ice monster unless you destroy the brain. But it knocks them out, anyway. So, maybe we could tip our arrows in it, and shoot the ice dragons. If they don't wake up, I think one fire-breathing dragon could take out an entire nest of ice monsters."

"One dragon," said Slate quietly.

"Of course, you get the idea to have people work independently," said Odion.

"I don't know if that's why I got the idea," she said. "But

maybe we could just end it. It would mean a concerted effort, though, I think, everyone striking at once. If the Frost knows we're coming, it'll defend itself. But if we found all the camps and struck all at once, we could end this thing during the school break. It could just be over." The words came out of her, and she was stunned at having said them out loud.

She waited for Odion or Slate to disagree, to point out something she wasn't thinking of, but they both only nodded.

"So," said Odion, grinning, "we go to them and we say, 'We have the way to defeat the Frost,' and we'll give it to you only if you agree to let us be assigned together."

Banyan grinned back.

Slate rolled his eyes. "They're not going to cave to your stupid demands."

Odion shrugged. "They might."

"They treat you differently than they treat the rest of us," said Slate, shaking his head at them. "Both of you."

"Well, now you're with us," said Banyan. "So, they'll treat you that way, too."

"Am I, though?" said Slate, looking back and forth between them. "If we could really end the war with the Frost now, before the new school term, then... what happens to us?"

"Then we could just be together," said Banyan. But she felt a rush of something hot and panicky rising in her spine at the thought of that. She'd come here to avoid being a wife, to avoid being mundane. If there was no danger, what would she do? What would *Odion* do?

"You'd have to go back to school," said Odion. "I wonder if they'd make you do three years?"

"They couldn't," she said, shaking her head. "I'm a rider already. They couldn't send me back to the glider arena!"

"Maybe it'd be nice," said Odion. "You could just be a student."

"I want to be with you," said Banyan. "We're talking about trying to mate all of us, all three of us — "

"Yeah, but then your life is decided," said Odion. "And you might not want that."

"Maybe what you mean is that *you* don't want that," said Slate, his voice gentle as he regarded Odion.

"No," said Odion. "I want to be a rider. It's all I've ever even considered being."

"They took you when you were four years old, right?" said Banyan. "You've never had a choice."

"There's no choice now," said Odion.

"Well, we'll get you one," said Banyan. "When we do this, when we destroy the Frost, we'll get you a choice." She nodded. "Odion gets a choice. And Slate, you get consideration, and a voice. And I get…" What did she want? She shook her head. "We're getting ahead of ourselves. Let's just focus on eradicating the Frost. That's enough to think about, right?"

Both of the men smirked at her. "It's enough."

"Do we go to Malloway?" said Banyan. "He doesn't seem to have the authority."

"Well, we can't go to Rabi," said Odion. "But he doesn't have the authority either."

"You can't just go and demand an audience with a senior member of the dragon rider army," said Slate.

"General Frax," said Banyan.

"General Frax," agreed Odion.

"She's not going to even see us," said Slate.


"ODION?" SAID COLONEL Rabi. He was at the door of the quarters he shared with the general, which was in the Academy, up in the reaches of the west tower. "Banyan? I thought I told you to leave."

"We need to talk to General Frax," said Odion.

The colonel shook his head. "No. Out of the question."

"Ask her," said Banyan. "We know she's in there with you."

The colonel slammed the door in their faces. Two minutes later, he opened it back up. "She says no," he said.

"She'll want to hear this," said Odion. "Banyan figured it out."

"Figured what out?" said the colonel.

"How to end the war and defeat the Frost," said Odion.

The door shut again, hard. There was a longer period of time now, voices within, and then it reopened, and the colonel stepped out of the way.

General Frax came out into the hallway. "We'll go to my office." She looked them over. "Why is he here?" She pointed at Slate.

"He's with us," said Banyan.

The general nodded slowly. "Hmm." She moved through them and walked down the hallway. They all had no choice but to follow.

The general's office was in the portion of the school that was used for the administration and scholars, not the portion for the students. It was huge, with wide windows that overlooked the sparking river below. In the distance, the peaks of the mountains stood tall and menacing on the horizon. The general sat down at her desk, the window at her back, and surveyed them.

Banyan wondered why you'd have an office like this, with a view like that, and put your back to it.

Colonel Rabi stepped in behind his mate as she settled into her seat. He put his hand on her shoulder.

Banyan, Odion, and Slate faced them both.

Odion spoke. "We have some requirements that need to be met before we tell you our strategy."

The general looked up at the colonel, not pleased. "This is your doing. You made him this way."

The colonel leveled his gaze at Odion. "You're a soldier in this army. You'll tell us, or you'll be punished."

"That's not how you want to play this," said Odion. "We have a strategy that could wipe out the Frost before the next school term. We know that you're assuming the Frost is coming to attack the school, and that it will get there because it destroys and absorbs our entire army as it advances. We have a strategy that saves lives and protects potential students. You're going to waste time trying to torture it out of me instead of giving us a few very reasonable requests?"

"Torture, really?" the general rolled her eyes.

"He's very dramatic," agreed Colonel Rabi.

"Listen, we've already generated a strategy," said the general. "We're sending soldiers out right now. You." She nodded at Slate. "I don't see why you're not involved in implementing that strategy."

"It's not going to work," said Slate. "It's too staggered. We take one mountain, and the Frost regroups and figures out how to fight against us."

"All the Frost needs to do is turn one soldier and it will know our strategy," said Banyan. "Which is why we need to—"

"Banyan," said Odion tightly.

She flinched. Well, the general had nearly tricked the strategy out of her, hadn't she? She gave the woman a nod of respect. General Frax was as good at mind games as her mate.

"Maybe we want that," said the general. "Maybe we want the Frost to be afraid. Maybe we think that if we let the Frost realize that it can't win—"

"It doesn't care about winning," said Banyan. "It's just trying to reproduce. This is instinctive behavior for the Frost. It'd be like trying to convince humans not to have sex. You can try, but it doesn't work. There are always children being brought to the cloisters in Noch, after all, women claiming they belong to the men there who've taken vows of celibacy that they can't follow. The Frost reproduces by spreading, and it will keep doing that as long as it lives. We can't reason with it. We can't frighten it. The only we can do is extinguish it."

General Frax gave her a look that bespoke respect. "Matthew, *this* one. You were right about her."

The colonel was giving her that fatherly look again.

Banyan sneered at him.

He looked even more proud.

"All right, all right," said the general, with a shrug. "What is it you want?"

"We want to work together," said Odion. "The three of us. We want to explore the option of all three of our dragons mating. And we don't want to be separated."

"After this is over," said Banyan, "we want a say in where we're assigned. If the war is over, we don't want to be flung to the whims of the Quorum. We want some agency over our futures."

"Done," said the general, with a shrug. "All right, the strategy, then?'

"Done?" repeated Slate.

The general turned on him, blinking eyelids scaled in bright silver.

Slate ducked down his head. "Sir, apologies, sir. It's just that…" He glanced sidelong at Odion and Banyan. "You'd never let anyone else speak to you the way you let them talk to you."

"Yes, it's an oversight on my part," said the colonel. "I'm far too soft on them both. Overly indulgent. And then I come home and tell Marigold about it, and she gets soft by proxy. I fully accept the blame. We don't have any children, you know, but I feel like the students at the school are my—"

"Shut up," snarled Banyan. Because he wasn't any kind of father figure. A father figure didn't look a girl in the eyes the night after she'd stayed up all staring at a barricaded door, thinking her would-be rapist might burst back in at any second, and say to her, *The important thing is that you defended yourself admirably.*

She clenched her hands into fists, feeling her anger simmering inside her.

Colonel Rabi inclined his head. "Oh, all right, all right."

"The strategy?" said the general mildly.

"There's something that's given the patients of the Frost sickness at the end," said Banyan. "It's a poison, but it only makes them sleep for a time. I propose we tip our arrows in and shoot the ice dragons with it."

"First things first," said Odion. "The first phase of the plan is reconnaissance. We go out and discover every single nest of ice monsters. We map them. We do not engage. Otherwise, it's business as usual until we've found each and every one."

"All right," said the general. "And then with the poisoned arrows?"

"Yes, because then, we can take out each nest with only one dragon and rider," said Banyan.

"So," said Odion, "we all strike at once. One night, kill them all."

"And then it's over," said Banyan.

"Well," said the general, stroking her chin. "Seems obvious now that you say it like that." She looked up at the colonel. "Matthew, why didn't we think of it?"

"We're not Banyan Thriceborn," said the colonel affectionately.

The general smirked. "All right, let us talk about it. You're dismissed."

"What about Slate?" said Banyan.

"Major Nightwing is also dismissed," said Colonel Rabi.

"He has orders to leave this evening," said Banyan. "We all want to be together."

"Yes, Major Nightwing's orders have changed," said the colonel. "I'll take care of that." He tilted his head to one side. "Why don't we let you three stay here? One of the rooms with the bathrooms and the larger beds? Take anything empty."

"Thank you, sir," said Slate.

"Don't thank him," said Odion.

"We'll send for you when we're ready to discuss things further," said the general.

## CHAPTER TWENTY-TWO

SLATE LOUNGED AGAINST the shut door in the room, looking around. "I never even headed up a bask in school. I never had access to a room like this. You two act like it's nothing. I think I should hate you both, really."

Odion was lying on the bed, staring at the other man, thinking about how good he looked. "Well, you should just work that hate out then? I mean, I think the colonel basically told us to go find an room and stay busy fucking each other."

"What?" said Banyan, who was also on the bed, but sitting up, legs crossed. "He did not."

Slate surveyed them both. "I guess our little interlude was cut short earlier."

"Yeah, you want to order us around and dominate us and *own* us," Odion teased, winking at Slate.

"I *am* going to put you over my knee, Naxim," said Slate darkly.

"Threaten me with a good time," said Odion.

Slate suddenly strode across the room and pulled Odion up off the bed.

Odion felt his breath come in sharp gasps as he was face-to-face with the other rider, looking directly into Slate's reptilian eyes. They were basically the same height, but Odion was arguably a little broader than Slate. He was Odion Naxim, and Slate was just Slate. He was pretty sure that—in any kind of fight—he'd win. And yet, whatever was making his heart pound right now was the anticipation of just the opposite, of being treated like the loser, being used and punished.

Slate seized him by the neck. "Turn around."

Odion shut his eyes, a tremor going through him. "Can't while you're holding onto me."

Slate shoved him around. He pressed into Odion's back, and Odion felt Slate's erection against his backside. Slate whispered in Odion's ear, "Undo your trousers."

Odion swallowed. He shot a glance at Banyan, who was frozen in the middle of the bed, her bright eyes eager as she drank this in.

"Princess?" said Slate. "You going to touch yourself while you watch your boy get taught a lesson in respect?"

"Oh, shit," whispered Banyan, visibly shivering.

"Undo your trousers," hissed Slate. "Didn't you hear me?"

"I heard you," said Odion, glancing over his shoulder, giving Slate a mischievous look.

Slate's hand landed on one side of Odion's ass cheek through his clothes, hard enough to make a resounding crack through the room.

Odion swore. Fuck, he was hard.

And that had *hurt*.

Slate's hand was there, rubbing him briskly. "Trousers off, pretty boy."

Odion undid them. His cock was peering out of the flap in his smallclothes.

"Look at that," said Slate, running his nose over the line of Odion's jaw. "Someone's excited. You like it when I teach you how to behave?"

Odion groaned.

"Do you?" said Slate. "Your cock likes it."

"Fuck," breathed Odion.

"Push down your trousers and smalls," said Slate. "Show us your bare ass and your hard cock, Odion. Do it now."

Odion didn't even hesitate. He just obeyed. He looked at

Banyan, and she had her hand inside her own trousers. Her gaze was honed in on his erection, and she was biting down on her tongue, which protruded between her teeth. The sight of her made his cock jump.

"There we are." Slate's thick strong palm ran itself over Odion's ass cheeks. Slate cupped him and squeezed him, and dipped a finger into the crease. "You like that, too, don't you?"

Odion just breathed.

"Say it, pretty boy."

"I like it," panted Odion.

"You like it when I touch your ass."

"Yes."

"You like it when I spank it."

"Fuck, Slate, you—"

"You like it when I *fuck* it," Slate said through clenched teeth.

Odion groaned.

Slate's hand landed loudly on Odion's bare flesh. "That what we're going to have to do here, Odion? To get you to behave? And for our princess here, because she wants to watch, she says. You want her to see you bent over and split open and taking me? You want her to watch you submit to me?"

"Oh, fuck, please?" breathed Banyan, who had shoved her shirt and vest out of the way to bare one plump breast with one stiff green-scaled nipple, and Odion watched as she teased and twisted the little hard nub, and he moaned.

Slate spanked him again.

Odion's cock jerked.

Slate rubbed the sting out. "You going to get fucked for our girl, then?"

"Yes, elemental forces, yes," Odion murmured.

Slate reached around and wrapped his palm around Odion's cock. He squeezed.

Odion let out a strangled noise.

Slate kissed Odion's neck, squeezing him gently. "Good, pretty boy, that makes me very happy." He licked the shell of Odion's ear.

Sensation flooded Odion. "Shit," he breathed.

"Princess?" Slate's voice was deep, vibrating through him.

"Yeah?" said Banyan.

"You look in that bedside table drawer. There's always grease there," said Slate. And it was true that Academy rooms tended to be stocked with these sorts of tools to facilitate sexual activity. "Get that out and hand it to me."

"Sure," said Banyan, crawling over to do just that.

Slate spanked Odion again, still squeezing and releasing his cock.

Odion mewled.

Slate kissed his temple. "It's been a while, pretty boy. Missed you."

Odion collapsed back into the other man's chest, offering Slate his lips. Slate claimed them, and they kissed a long, wet, sweet kiss until Banyan was there with the tin of grease.

Then Slate kissed her, just as deeply and thoroughly. "Thank you, princess. Now, I want you to take everything off. Will you do that?"

"Yes," said Banyan, shy, smiling. "May I kiss Odion?"

"Oh, good princess for asking permission." Slate kissed her again. He swatted her ass gently. "No."

"No?" said Banyan with a little laugh, but she settled back on the bed and started taking off her clothes.

Slate stepped on Odion's trousers and smalls, which were pooled around Odion's ankles. "Step out of these so you can spread your legs, hmm?"

Odion did as he was told, and then Slate pushed him down, gently but firmly, so that he had his cheekbone against the bed, ass in the air, legs spread, looking sideways up at naked Banyan.

She gave him a little impish grin that told him she was enjoying this as much as he was. He shut his eyes. He didn't know why he liked this. Maybe he shouldn't. But it was good. And he couldn't wait to watch Slate take charge of Banyan. He wasn't sure what about that would be more arousing — being able to watch Slate or getting to see Banyan surrender or just seeing the both of them together.

Slate's greased fingers were between his ass cheeks, rubbing against him *there*. He shuddered at the sensation. That part was always pleasant. It felt very nice to be teased there, and then it felt, well, less nice to be penetrated, until he got used to it, got stretched, and then it felt good again.

But thinking about the unpleasant part in the middle made him feel a sort of anticipation that made his cock pulse. It was more intense if he was subjecting himself to discomfort. It heightened everything about the act. It made it *more* for everyone involved.

"Relax for me," said Slate, his voice like midnight. "Don't worry, Odion, I'll go slower. We're not in heat."

"A-all right." There was something vulnerable in Odion's voice, but he *was* vulnerable right now. This was likely the most vulnerable expression he could possibly *be* in.

"Shh," said Slate. "I got you." And his finger was worming its way into Odion's body.

Odion tensed, involuntary.

"Breathe, baby," said Slate. "Let me in. Let it happen. You know you want it."

Banyan shifted, biting down harder on her tongue.

Odion turned his attention to her, and Slate suddenly slid all the way in, his entire finger. Odion made a noise.

Banyan let out a cry. "I'm... fuck. I'm going to *come*," she managed.

"You like this, huh, princess?" Slate started finger-fucking Odion's asshole.

Odion let out a series of noisy, harsh breaths.

"*You* like it, pretty boy?"

Odion just breathed.

"Say it." Slate's voice was iron. "Or tell me you need more grease."

"I like it," Odion ground out. He did not really like it. It was uncomfortable, the first stretch. It didn't hurt, not exactly, but it felt *wrong* — things were not meant to go into him *there*.

"More grease," said Slate. And there was more grease, and it did make Slate's finger slide easier, and Odion was nearly used to that when there was another finger, and Odion grunted, and Banyan let out a series of breathy cries and then clamped her thighs together, pressing her fingers against her pussy.

"Did you come, princess?" said Slate.

"Sorry," she said.

"Oh, an apology?" said Slate. "You want a spanking?"

Her eyes lit up.

Slate chuckled. "Bring that ass here, then, princess."

Odion was too busy watching Banyan's breasts bounce as Slate smacked her, listening to her little breathy cries as each blow landed, to mind that Slate had just put another finger in him.

And then, suddenly, no fingers at all. Slate's hands, both of them, on his cheeks, squeezing him, patting him, as he talked to Banyan. "How's your pussy, princess? Too sensitive, or do you think you can lie back there with your legs spread wide and touch yourself for both of us to watch?"

"What if I say it's too sensitive?" said Banyan.

"Too bad," said Slate. "Do it anyway, princess."

She let out a delighted laugh and bounced back, thighs falling open, her scaled sex wide open and on display. She was glistening and wet and her clitoris was swollen and prominent. She started to rub one finger over it.

Odion moaned and put his hand on his achingly hard cock.

"No," said Slate, slapping at him. "None of that."

"Slate, please," said Odion. He wasn't in heat. There was no way he would have an orgasm just from a cock in his ass—it wasn't even likely that would happen when he was in heat, after all, even if it was possible.

"You trust me to take care of you or not?"

Odion sighed.

"Do you?"

"I trust you." Odion stared at Banyan's wet pussy, at her

round breasts. She looked enticing and perfect.

"You want my cock?"

"Yes," breathed Odion.

"I don't believe you, pretty boy." Slate spanked him again, and then stuck a finger in his stretched asshole.

"Fuck," said Odion. "Please, Slate, please, I want your cock."

"Where do you want it?"

"In my asshole, fuck you, *please*."

"I like hearing you beg to be fucked," said Slate, and then he pressed the head of his cock against Odion. "Hold on, let me grease myself up here, and then I'll get all the way in there, pretty boy, fuck you nice and deep and good."

Odion grunted, still staring at Banyan, beautiful, naked Banyan.

It went in slow, and he was stretched, but Slate still felt big.

Odion moaned.

Slate moaned.

Banyan sat up and squeezed one of her nipples and whispered, "Oh, Ignia and Agnis above, *look* at you."

Slate's voice was tattered. "Shit, you feel amazing, Odion. You all right? Am I hurting you?"

"No, no, no pain," said Odion, because there wasn't. Sometimes, in heat, they were both too eager to bother with proper stretching, but this had been enough, and he was fine, and it felt invasive and sweet and wonderful. He just… he wanted… "Please?"

"Mmm?" Slate was steadily and slowly dragging himself in and out.

"My cock, fuck you, Slate, you said you would take care of me—"

"Sorry, pretty boy," said Slate, out of breath, and his greased hand was there, hot and slippery and encasing Odion, and he rubbed him and teased each of Odion's nubs, and his cock worked his ass steadily and rhythmically.

Odion let out something like a sob.

"Good?" said Slate, gentle, hoarse.

"Yes, fuck, yes, so good," said Odion.

"Great God Tan, you're…" Slate was kissing him, kissing his neck and his earlobes and his jawbone. "Odion, Odion, Odion."

Odion turned and found the other man's lips.

"You're beautiful," said Banyan. "You're both *so* beautiful."

"Princess," said Slate, his voice ravaged, his mouth still on Odion's. "You all right there?"

"Beautiful," she whispered.

Odion opened his eyes to see her frantically rubbing her own clit with a sort of fierceness he'd never quite seen from her. "I want… Banyan, come over *here*."

"Oh," said Banyan. "Is it all right, Slate?"

Slate chuckled roughly into Odion's ear. "You're so submissive, both of you. Here you are, the hope for the Trinal Kingdoms, the only way we're going to beat the Frost, and you're at my mercy."

"Fuck you," said Banyan, but she was turned on and breathy. She scooted over, seemingly knowing exactly what Odion wanted. She lined herself up with both of them, and Odion pushed himself up on the bed to make room for her.

"Keep touching yourself," said Slate, as he guided Odion's cock into her body.

She threw back her head and moaned as he breached her.

Fuck, she felt amazing. Odion wanted to seize her hips, but he couldn't. He was bent in half, and he had to use his hands to prop himself up. He couldn't thrust into her, either, at least not until he seemed to find the other aspect of the rhythm that Slate had inside him. Then he could move with the other man, in time with him, letting him set the pace.

"Kiss her," Slate ordered in a garbled voice.

Banyan brought herself up to meet his lips.

Kissing her was like coming home.

Odion groaned against her lips. "Not going to last," he gasped.

"Not yet," breathed Banyan, flopping back down, gazing up at the two of them, rubbing her clit. "Please, not yet?"

That actually made him nearly crest. He had to shut his eyes, go blank, try not to think of anything even remotely sexy, shut it all off, but it was right there, right *there*, ready to overtake him.

"Oh, just fuck me, it's like *both* of you are fucking me," said Banyan. "Please, I'm so close."

"We wait for our princess," said Slate in his ear, firm.

"I am," protested Odion, who was still moving, still fucking Banyan's perfect wet pussy and fucking himself on Slate's hard cock jammed all the way inside him, and somehow, through all of that, keeping himself right here on the fucking edge of this monster orgasm that wanted to wash through him.

"Sorry," said Banyan.

"None of that," said Slate. "You're never sorry for coming. You know I want it. You know I want to watch you fall apart."

"We both do," said Odion in a hoarse voice.

And Banyan bit down on her tongue again and writhed on the bed, her beautiful green-shimmering breasts jiggling enticingly, her freckles winking at him, her face contorted in ecstasy, and he *felt* it.

"Fuck," he breathed.

She clenched on him, and he lost it. He tipped right off into thin air, like a free fall when his glider wouldn't open, and then—the wings went out and he came so hard he thought he was going to die.

And Slate was still *fucking* him, swearing at his back.

And that only seemed to deepen it, Banyan's little sweet twitches on his cock, the battering inside his asshole, surrounded by them both. He let out a little keening cry.

Slate slammed into him and let go, peppering his neck and shoulder with kisses.

Banyan sighed in pleasure.

Odion shut his eyes.

*Perfect.*

# CHAPTER TWENTY-THREE

SHE WAS IN the middle and they were both curled around her. She was facing Slate right now, and Odion was spooning her from behind, but she'd rolled over a few times and done it the other way. She had her fingers on Slate's chest, touching his smooth, light-green skin. His eyes were open in slits and he was smiling at her.

She was very surprised at how much she'd liked watching them have sex. The best part had been watching Odion let go like that. No, the best part had been watching Slate let go. Even though he had been the one calling the shots, there was a point where he seemed to break, where the pleasure overtook him, and she could feel how much he loved Odion coming off of him in waves, and that had been beautiful.

She was glad she'd been involved in the end, but she hadn't needed that. She didn't know why she didn't need it, why simply watching it would have been enough, but she also knew it was true.

"You going to sleep, princess?" whispered Slate.

"Eventually," she said, leaning over to capture Slate's lips with her own.

He kissed her earnestly, softly, letting out a little noise in the back of his throat. He pulled back. "I'm not going to sleep until you do."

"Oh, is it like that?" She giggled. "You make fun of us for

wanting to be dominated in bed, but what's your little domination game all about, hmm? What are you trying to prove, Slate?"

He sighed heavily. "You ordering to me to go to sleep, princess?"

"What would you do if I did?"

He shut his eyes. "I would not sleep." He yawned.

She chuckled. "Don't sleep, then, Slate. Stay awake."

Slate didn't open his eyes. He made a humming noise, and then his breath grew more and more even.

Banyan shut her eyes, too, snuggling back into Odion, who let out a sleepy moan as he tightened his grip on her hip.

She slipped off into a dream, and in her dream, she was climbing through the frozen mountains. She looked to her left and to her right and she was surrounded by ice monsters. They were all walking together, moving in unison. She looked down at her hands and they were colorless.

She was an ice monst—

She woke up, sitting straight up, panting, her heart pounding wildly.

And the door opened.

Colonel Rabi took in her nudity and slammed the door, coughing. Through the door, he called out an apology. "Meet us in Marigold's office in ten minutes."

Next to her, Slate and Odion were stirring.

Odion touched her back. "Hey, you all right? What did he do?"

"It was a dream," she said, lying back down.

"What was it?"

"I…" She shook her head. "Can't even remember anymore. I feel like I barely closed my eyes. How long did we sleep?" It was dark outside now, and she must have slept for hours.

Slate was already out of bed, getting dressed. "We just got orders. Don't you two feel as if you have to follow orders?"

"She's upset," said Odion.

"She can handle it," said Slate.

"I can," said Banyan, getting up and finding her own clothes.

They were back in the general's office in less than ten minutes. She had a map of the Ice Mountains spread out on her desk. She was drinking some bourbon from a glass tumbler. She set it down on the edge of the map and poked it in the middle. "We're putting you here. This will be the headquarters, and we'll send out groups to map the nests of ice monsters. You'll be in charge of that, and of taking all of the intel from everyone to figure out how best to formulate the attack. Then, whenever we do that, you'll be here, sending out signals from the tower—"

"Signals?" said Odion. "We need to be part of the attack."

The general raised her eyebrows. "You can't be in the thick of the front lines and also concentrate on leading."

"But I *need* to do this," said Odion. "The Frost killed my bask."

General Frax just gazed at him.

Odion lowered his gaze. "Right. We'll stay where it's safe and send everyone else out to take the risks."

"I know you were pitching to us some kind of accelerated time line," said the general. "But the truth is that we don't know how many nests they are, nor do we know how many ice monsters there are. It may take much longer than you think."

"We can estimate," said Banyan. "We can look at the sizes of the villages it's taken over and the riders we know it's attacked. We can assume all of those people were turned, and we can get some kind of number."

"All good points, but let's leave the time it will take open. We don't need to rush it," said the general. "Better to do it right than to botch it and leave a few nests behind."

Banyan nodded. The general was right.

"Anything else?" said the general, looking at her. "That we need to be thinking of?"

Banyan felt a little off balance at being asked such an all-encompassing question, but she answered it truthfully. "We need to properly brief every rider in the army," she said.

"They all need to know how the Frost turns them."

"They do," said the general. "We keep things from students, but we've never hidden the bites or the turn—"

"They need to know about seduction," said Banyan. "That's the way the Frost gets the riders. They need to be suspicious of any woman or man who seems amorously interested in them. They shouldn't accept help from strangers. They shouldn't help strangers who ask for it. They should never go somewhere with someone alone." She sighed. "On the other hand, however, we can't tell them what we're planning."

"The riders?" said Odion. He sighed. "Because if any of them are turned, the Frost will know."

"We'll just say it's on a need-to-know basis," said the general.

"No," said Odion, "it's too easy to guess what we're doing. Mapping out the nests? And after Slate and I attacked one? It'll be common knowledge in no time."

"So, we need a plausible lie, then," said Banyan. "Something that everyone will believe and something that will not hurt us if the Frost hears it."

"That's a tall order," said General Frax.

"Let me think about it," said Banyan. She didn't like the idea of lying to the riders, but it was necessary to win.

"I will think about it as well," said the general. "Anything else?"

Banyan considered. "Not that I can think of." She turned to Odion and Slate. "You two?"

"Me?" said Slate, shrugging. "Strategy is not my thing."

Odion licked his lips. "If our behavior the night of the attack is new, it could tip the Frost off. So, I think we should get in the habit of flying all over their territory, all of the time, conspicuously, so that they get used to seeing us, and then—when we attack—they won't be expecting it. It'll also provide a cover for us flying all over to look for nests."

"Good thought," said the general.

"Maybe that could be part of the ruse," said Banyan. "What if we tell our soldiers that we have intel that the Frost is going to attack and we're looking for specific information to use to defend ourselves. They need to look for the nests, but they should also be looking for paths and trails the Frost might use to navigate the snow, that sort of thing?"

"Good, that'd work," said Odion, nodding.

"I like it," said the general. "All right, we'll gather everyone together in two days. We're calling everyone in from the watchtowers at this point. Then we'll regroup here." She pointed at the map again. "We'll use some temporary encampments to keep everyone together."

"Is that wise?" spoke up Slate. "We're abandoning all the watchtowers?"

Colonel Rabi spoke up. "You said, I seem to remember, Major Nightwing, that by staffing those watchtowers, we were simply giving the Frost more fodder."

"I meant that without a strategy, we were being picked off," said Slate. "But the villages, they rely on that protection, and if there's no one there—"

"It won't take long," said Banyan. "We'll map the nests in no time, and the Frost won't have time to attack."

Slate took a deep breath and nodded. "All right, then."

"Two days from now, and I'll want you all present at the debriefing for questions. Odion, seeing you at the head of it will be good for morale," said the general.

"Uh, I don't know about that," said Odion. "I don't think the general opinion of me is respect. They resent me."

"You'd be surprised," said the general. "You too, Banyan."

"Me?" Banyan drew back. "How do they even know about me?"

"There's talk," said the colonel. "We all want this war with the Frost over. If you're involved, the riders will take this seriously. They know you're both the best."

Banyan wasn't sure how to take that.

She also wasn't sure what she was meant to do with herself for the next two days. Mostly, she spent her days flying with Erach. She explained the strategy to him, and he responded with such exuberance, she knew that he was pleased. But—like Odion—he wasn't happy at the idea that they wouldn't be leading the attack.

Banyan herself didn't care. Maybe it was some kind of male thing, and it transcended species. Men wanted to physically get revenge, even if it didn't make any sense for them to be the ones out there fighting?

Whatever the case, neither Erach nor Odion seemed particularly convinced that they wouldn't be part of the actual attack. She could tell that both of them wanted a traditional picture, a surge of dragons heading directly into a surge of ice dragons, fire and ice colliding in the air, a battle, a clash of opposing forces.

This wouldn't be that.

It would be surreptitious. It would be sneaky. It would be done under the cover of darkness. It wouldn't be a battle but a slaughter.

Oddly, it made her think of Javor Derowen. She knew he deserved the way that she'd gone after him, and she didn't feel guilty about it. She also knew the Frost had to be stopped.

But she was uncomfortable when she was forced to face this part of herself.

She remembered Deke, when she'd broken off their romantic relationship, how he'd said that he'd never really known her and that she was nothing but ego. She worried that not only was he right but that what she was best at was actually destroying things.

*No wonder you didn't want to be a mother,* she thought. *You're the opposite of nurturing.*

Ultimately, it didn't matter if her worries were right, though, not if her abilities could end the war with the Frost. She'd use what skills she had for the good of the Trinal Kingdoms, and she wouldn't try to suppress anything.

In the afternoons, she looked in the library for more information on three-way dragon bonds, but there was nothing beyond what Odion had found.

And at night, she, Odion, and Slate tried different ways to fit all of them together. She bent over on her hands and knees and took Slate inside her pussy while she sucked Odion's cock. Slate fucked her while he sucked Odion. Odion fucked her while he sucked Slate.

The boys didn't put it in each other's asses again. She was coming to understand that was a bit of a production, a sort of special-occasion activity that they didn't do every single time. Easier to get off some other way.

As for her orgasms, they were easier, but they weren't entirely coming from outside stimuli. She kept her eyes open to take in what they were doing, but she couldn't help but spur herself on by imagining sexy things, usually in Slate's voice but often in Odion's, too. It didn't feel to her as if it was a betrayal.

In some ways, she simply enjoyed the insertion of another person into the whole thing, because she'd felt so on-the-spot when it was one-on-one, just her and Odion.

But she worried she'd miss it at some point, or that the boys would miss being alone together or that she'd become very curious about what having Slate all to herself might be like.

And — for whatever reason — the idea of Odion and Slate having sex without her there?

It stung.

It hurt.

It made her feel rejected and lonely. She didn't want them to. So, she couldn't ask for such a thing in reverse, she didn't think. It wasn't fair.

Oddly, she'd sort of thought they might do it before. Or even that they had been doing it when Odion was stationed out there under Slate's leadership. Then, the idea of it hadn't bothered her, but now…

Well, maybe it would change over time. For now, they all seemed to be happy to be with each other all together, so hopefully, it could remain that way for the foreseeable future. Hopefully, if or when things changed, she'd be ready to change with it.

Eventually, everyone was there, and she stood with Odion and Slate behind General Frax as she explained the mission to the men and women gathered there. As they'd planned, she did not tell them that they were moving in the offense.

Instead, she said that the offensive move that Odion and Slate had made had angered the Frost, and they had good intelligence that the Frost was planning a widespread retaliation. She said that they would be mapping out all of the Frost's encampments and paths to human villages in anticipation and that they'd be flying over the Frost's territory constantly as a mission to confuse them.

The riders were unsure of this, because many of them hadn't been aware that the Frost was so capable of strategic movement.

The general responded that the Frost absorbed the strategies of the riders who it turned.

But Banyan didn't think this was right anymore. They'd talked about it, and she and Odion thought that what happened was that the Frost was just people, and they retained all their memories and even most of their personalities. It was only that now they were obsessed with spreading the Frost. The reason the Frost could strategize was because it turned dragon riders into the enemy.

But Banyan decided not to quibble with this. It was essentially the same thing in the end, and thinking of the ice monsters as individuals with their intact personalities would only make it harder to kill them all.

But that's what this was.

It was an attack and it was annihilation.

## CHAPTER TWENTY-FOUR

TWO WEEKS IN and everyone was antsy.
 Odion and Erach both wanted to leave and be part of the scouting missions. She fought with her dragon, saying she needed to stay here. Erach sent pictures to her of his flying alone, coming back and giving her information about what he'd found out. She sent him pictures of his taking Odion on his back.
 Erach wasn't pleased.
 Dragons did let other people ride on their backs, of course, and it was even more common amongst mated pairs. So, she wasn't sure what she thought about this, but she was pretty sure Erach didn't like Odion.
 Perfect.
 She convinced Erach with the thought that this would keep his mate safe. However complicated Erach's feelings were for Mirra, he still was extremely protective of her. He liked the idea of her staying out of harm's way and not flying with Odion.
 So, then she had to bring the idea up to Odion, and he wasn't entirely pleased either. "I can take my own dragon. Mirra wants to be part of this, too. It was her family who was killed."
 Since Banyan couldn't communicate with Mirra herself, she supposed she had to trust Odion this was true. She asked Erach, and he communicated a serene and happy

Mirra, but Erach had a vested interest in lying about Mirra's emotional state since he wanted to keep her safe.

Slate was listening in on the conversation with Odion, because he was listening in on everything. He felt useless. He complained that he'd been relegated to being there with them because he was basically being kept out of harm's way because he had sex with them.

Banyan was frustrated that neither of them could understand that leadership was an important part of warfare, and that it involved staying out of danger because dead leadership wasn't nearly as effective as alive leadership. If leaders died, it meant that new leaders had to arise and that changed the chain of events. Keeping a leader alive was good. That was all. It didn't mean they were cowards or unwilling to do the work the other soldiers did.

It only meant that they had different work and this work required that they stay alive.

No matter how she explained this to them, the boys wanted to go do dangerous things.

Finally, she just threw up her hands and sent them all out. Odion on Mirra, Slate on Yilia, Erach on his own. "Fine," she said. "Go, then. Bring us back useful information, please."

But as time passed, it began to be clear that there was an inherent flaw in her plan, one she hadn't thought of.

It was impossible to know if they had all the nests. They couldn't really check everywhere, and even if they could, they couldn't be sure that the nests weren't hiding or moving, or anything like that. They couldn't be sure they weren't counting two nests more than once.

They could not be assured that when they struck, they eradicated the Frost.

Banyan quickly realized this, and decided it didn't matter. They'd have to adjust the strategy. First step would be a massive blow against the Frost. Whatever was left, it would be a mop-up action. They'd have to engage with whatever was left behind in the weeks after the first attack. They might not be sure that the Frost was completely destroyed, but any attack would mean that they could find and destroy the nest.

"It'll be like destroying rats in the grain," she said to General Frax. "They might keep coming back, but now we know how to do it."

General Frax said no. "You promised me a victory, Major Thriceborn." They'd all been promoted at this point. They were all majors. "I want a decisive and clear victory. Go back, look at it again, and come back when you've solved this problem."

There was no way to solve the problem, however. It was impossible.

She talked it over with Odion, and he agreed. They talked about it naked in bed while Slate paced at the foot of the bed saying that they were giving him a headache and he wanted to attack and why couldn't they just attack already?

And Banyan wondered if the general was right and she was too influenced by her boyfriends and her dragon, who all wanted her to attack *now*.

Everyone was antsy.

Banyan was antsy, too.

She had promised an end to the Frost War, and she wanted it over, now, wanted it badly, even though she was beginning to realize that possibly, maybe, this war didn't end.

There was only one way to end the war with the Frost. Exterminate it. Kill an entire species. Was that possible when deep down, within every species, survival was the deepest code, written on its soul? Wouldn't some part of it survive somehow?

She could try to kill it, but she began to think that maybe it wouldn't die.

And then, there was one element of the plan that they never even tested.

The poison-tipped arrows.

The plan hinged on one thing, and one thing only, and that was taking out all the ice dragons.

This was because the ice dragons themselves were the thing that had changed about the Frost itself. Before the

Frost infected dragons, it couldn't spread, and the reason it couldn't spread was because it couldn't control the temperature.

The ice dragons allowed the Frost to invade and bite an entire village because the ice dragons could breathe out ice clouds, which lowered the temperature to below freezing.

The poison worked on people infected with the Frost, but it had never been given to an ice dragon.

Banyan didn't even think to question that.

Instead, she lay on the bed while Slate paced and said things like, "We have direct control of the army. The riders are taking their orders directly from us. I say we move without the general's say-so. What's she going to do once the attack's already happened?"

"We'd be disciplined," said Odion.

"But we'd have won. We'd all be war heroes," said Slate. "She couldn't do anything too bad."

"We won't have won," said Banyan. "The Frost will still be out there. We won't know how much of it we've actually attacked."

"Look, we're watching these encampments, and they're not moving," said Odion to her.

"That doesn't mean there aren't encampments which are moving." Banyan glared at him. They'd been *through* this.

"It could mean that," said Slate. "It's possible that it does mean that."

Banyan had to agree it was possible but not guaranteed. The general wanted a guarantee. A guarantee wasn't going to happen. But then, there were very few guarantees in life.

"Let's just do it," said Odion. "We came out here to do it. We've combed the mountains. We know where they are. Why are we just sitting here?"

And they could only have these sorts of conversations for so many nights in a row before Banyan began to feel swayed.

Wasn't she Banyan Thriceborn?

Hadn't they been saying since the beginning that she and Odion were going to defeat the Frost together?

So, the poisoned tipped arrows were given out, and the riders were dispersed into the darkness. They flew the way they always did, up over the mountains and into the deep, cold, territory of the Frost.

Banyan stood in the tower and watched them go, her heart in her throat. She stayed behind and let Odion and Slate and Erach all go.

She stayed, and then she got the view from Erach's eyes as the poisoned arrows penetrated the ice dragons and they did absolutely nothing.

She watched as Erach watched the ice dragons—there were five of them in that nest—fly into the air and outnumber and overpower the *one single rider* who'd been sent to take out an entire nest of the Frost. They hadn't only sent one rider for each nest, true. The numbers didn't quite work out that badly. But they had broken up the basks and they'd sent two or three riders out for each nest. They'd all be outnumbered, because the Frost had turned village after village and watchtower after watchtower and then the Frost had gone and infected wild dragons who had never bonded with humans, and Banyan and the humans were at a disadvantage. The Frost had grown stronger while they'd grown weaker.

She watched and she realized what she'd just done.

She'd singlehandedly destroyed the entire army of dragon riders. She'd sent them out to die—not just to die—but to be turned.

In one night, she would lose all her forces and her enemy would gain them all.

# CHAPTER TWENTY-FIVE

ODION FELT IT as soon as Erach did, because Mirra got the information from him. And he got from Mirra that his new orders, coming from Banyan, were to change course and warn other riders.

He hesitated, because want he really wanted to do was burn to death some ice monsters.

He thought back to the attack at Fort Tillian, watching the way the dragons and riders had twisted and fallen and died. He remembered Genevieve, lying on the ground, her body twisted in a way that no one's body should twist. She'd fallen off her dragon, but she was still alive. She was groping for her bow and arrows. She was screaming.

And then the ice monster, jaws wide, seizing her, biting her...

Burn them, that's what he wanted to do.

But it was only an instant of hesitation, because he quickly understood what was happening and why they were in trouble.

How could they have forgotten to test the poisoned arrows? How could they have been so idiotic?

Surely, General Frax would say that she would have demanded that happened before they acted. Surely, General Frax would be livid and smug and—

None of that mattered.

Everything was ruined, and it was his own damned fault.

*Banyan wanted to be cautious, and I wanted revenge,* he chided himself as he and Mirra took to the air and flew as fast as they could.

He intercepted a rider. "Stand down," he called to them. "Abort mission. Head back to headquarters. Tell anyone you see on the way. Do you understand?"

"Understood, sir," said the rider, turning around.

Odion got four or five more messages out and then he felt the chill on the air before he saw the ice dragon.

It was coming from the east, and he could barely make out a rider on its back. The rider had a bow and arrows, and they stood out stark and black against the white of the ice monster and the ice dragon.

Odion shot first.

The arrow burrowed itself into the ice monster's chest and nothing happened.

Of course not.

*The head, the head,* he said to himself.

But now an arrow was coming straight at him. It nicked his arm. He brushed it away and shot again. This time, he aimed for the ice dragon's eye.

Hit.

The ice dragon shrieked and swooped down out of the sky.

Odion clutched Mirra and flew on.

It was only moments later that he realized *why* the bow and arrows were so visible and black. Usually an ice monster's weapon would be as ice covered as anything else, but this bow and arrows had been taken from a human dragon rider. The arrow that nicked him must have been tipped in the poison.

His stomach turned over. That poison was deadly. Of course, he'd barely been nicked, so it might not kill him, but his entire body seized in awful pain.

He lost control, toppling off Mirra's back, limbs flailing.

He was in free fall for several moments, ground rushing up, knowing with certainty he was going to die by hitting the ground very, very hard. But then Mirra was there, catching him.

No.

Not Mirra. An ice dragon. The rider on the back of it smiled at him, and he recognized him. It was someone from the Academy, someone who'd graduated ahead of him. The ice monster bared its teeth and they were sharp and glistening like a thousand shards of ice. And then—it *bit*.

## CHAPTER TWENTY-SIX

BANYAN WAS PLEASED to see how many of the riders had actually made it back. She'd gone out and she'd gotten to Slate. Odion had been gotten by Mirra's and Erach's ability to communicate. She'd spread the word to as many as she could and they'd spread the word further, and more than half of them were back.

She apologized to them. "This was my fault," she said. "I never tested the poison on the arrows. It was an oversight from the top. We should never have sent you out there."

Slate was there, shaking his head at her, telling her not to admit blame.

She didn't care. She sent them all off to their tents and quarters—because many of them were in tents in the courtyards here. Once everyone was secure, she went to go and tell General Frax.

General Frax and Colonel Rabi were staying in the bottom floor suite of the same tower where Banyan was staying. They had the whole bottom floor, so Banyan knocked on the door in the hallway, waiting.

There was no answer, and the door was locked. Slate was with her. His eyes were wild and he was sweating and worried.

She yelled out, "General!"
She yelled out, "Marigold!"
She yelled out, "Matthew! Colonel? Anyone?"

She and Slate went outside the tower and walked around and they found a window that had been broken. It was a huge picture window, floor to ceiling, and it was shattered. They walked inside, over the shards of glass, through a sitting room, following the turned-over furniture and broken vases to the nearby bedroom.

Inside, the scene was grim.

Colonel Rabi was holding General Frax's lifeless body in his arms. She had a knife buried in one of her eyesockets. He was sobbing.

Banyan couldn't even find words.

The colonel looked up at them. "They came in the window." He pointed. And then he pointed at two bodies, heads removed, strewn across the floor on the opposite side of the room. They both had white hair. "I killed them, but not before they bit us both." He held up his arm, held up the bite. It wasn't even bleeding. It looked like it was frozen, like there were little crystals of ice forming on the teeth bites.

"No," whispered Banyan, realizing that the general had a bite on her arm, too.

"She was so fast," said the colonel. "She said we didn't know how long we had before it would take control of us and she took up the knives. She gave me one, said she loved me, and then…" The colonel lifted his other hand. There was a knife there. "I know I need to…" He held the knife out to Banyan. "But maybe you…?"

Banyan backed away, shaking her head. "Colonel Rabi, no."

"You want to," said the colonel, giving her a little smile. "I still remember the way you looked at me after Javor went after you. It was my fault. You blame me. Do it. It'll feel good."

Banyan's throat closed up. She backed away. "No," she breathed. "No, no, no."

"Well, where's Odion?" said the colonel. "He killed Javor. Killing me will just tidy it all up."

"He killed Javor?" said Banyan. "Javor's dead?" She looked at Slate for confirmation.

He only shook his head. "I don't know what you're talking about."

Banyan couldn't handle it. She turned and ran, going back through the broken window and running out into the night. Erach, where was Erach?

The dragon was there, alighting in front of her, panic coming through him in long red images. She couldn't understand what it was, but it was something with Mirra, something with the bond, and that was when she realized she couldn't feel Odion.

She scrambled onto Erach's back, and they took to the air.

Erach flew them into the mountains.

The air grew colder and colder and then her dragon swooped down, through the trees. It was just below the altitude where the snows would start, so the air was not freezing, but it was chilly.

Mirra had three arrows in her. She was licking at her right leg.

*Bite*, Erach thought at Banyan, the word very clear.

"No," said Banyan, and then she saw Odion.

He was behind a tree, and there was an ice dragon's head right next to his feet. He was holding a bloody arrow in one hand and a bloody knife in the other. He turned to look at her. "Banyan," he whispered.

"No," she said again. She rushed to him. "No, no, no." And she was looking all over his body for the bite, but it was right there, right there in front of her. Her fingers hovered over it, over the little crystals that were growing, just like the colonel's. "No."

"I'm sorry," whispered Odion. "I killed the…" He pointed at the ice dragon, and then further off, there was an ice monster rider, with an arrow sticking out of his temple. "I don't know why I bothered."

"No," she said again. Tears were streaming down her face.

Odion let out a breath. "All right, well, I want… where's Slate?"

"I didn't… I didn't even…" She turned back to Erach,

trying to tell him to go and get Slate, but Erach was consumed with Mirra, his mind alight with fear and worry, impenetrable to Banyan's communication.

"I just wanted to say goodbye," said Odion. "Does that…? I love him, Banyan, and I hope you don't—"

"Of course," she said. "We'll, um, we'll just have to go back." She ripped off her sleeve and started to bind his bite. "No one has to see it."

"Banyan—"

"There's a cure," she said. "We saw that there was a cure. The fever. Dove says that they have vials of it, and we'll get back to the Academy and we'll… there's a *cure*, Odion."

He only blinked at her. "Do we know that? They took him away. They sent me with Slate. We don't know anything about Gelso."

"We know he didn't turn," she said. "I confirmed it with the colonel."

"When?"

She clenched both of her hands in fists. "Of course, he was trying to get information from me out of the time. Maybe he would have said anything at all to get me to talk to him. Maybe he just wanted to give me false hope. Maybe I can never believe anything out of that man's mouth, and I just had the chance to kill him, and why didn't I do it?"

"Kill him? What?"

Banyan stalked across to Erach. She put her hands on the dragon, and she said, "Let's go. You have to take Odion and me back to the school."

Odion and Erach answered in unison, one aloud, one booming in her brain.

"Not without Mirra."

Banyan let out a cry. She went to examine the young dragon. Mirra had arrows in her. They were deep. There was blood. Banyan was shaking all over. She let out a little cry and she turned to look at Odion and then she couldn't look at Odion.

She couldn't *think*.

It was over, wasn't it? The army, what was left of it? More

than half of the riders had come back, yes, but General Frax was dead and Colonel Rabi was bitten. Who would run the school now that the colonel was gone?

Would there *be* a school?

How many riders had she given to the Frost tonight? How many dragons?

She fell to her knees, gazing up at the dark sky overhead, and she let out a scream.

"Shut *up*." Odion was next to her, on his knees, taking her hands. "Banyan, they are all around us. They will hear you and they will come down out of the ice and they will bite you too."

She whipped her head up to lock gazes with him. "Maybe that would be fine."

"Are you insane?"

"We'll be together. Isn't that what you said?" She shrugged. "You said, if I got bitten, you'd let me bite you, and then nothing would matter."

"You have Slate now."

"General Frax is dead," she said. "Colonel Rabi is bitten."

He pulled his hands out of hers. "Really?"

"Almost half the riders fell tonight. They'll all turn. Unless I could cure them... cure them all..." She shook her head. "We need to go." She got up and turned to face Erach. "We'll come back for Mirra, but you have to take Odion and me to the Academy."

"No," said Odion.

She turned back to him. "No? What are you saying?"

"It's not responsible, Banyan." He was getting to his feet. "I probably have time, but what if I'm like Deke? What if I turn fast and I'm trying to bite people?"

"You have time. He was in the cold, and if you're—"

"This is just a theory, Banyan, like the poison arrows. We've never tested it. And this cure of yours—"

"I have to try, Odion."

"No," said Odion. "You have to kill me."

## CHAPTER TWENTY-SEVEN

THERE WAS A rustling sound in the trees.

Banyan turned, her senses on high alert, her whole body tense and ready.

A dragon's snout came through first, but she recognized it.

"Yilia," she cried out. She took off running for the dragon and for Slate, who came right behind his dragon.

Slate caught her in his arms. "Princess, you just ran off—"

"It's Odion," she interrupted. "He's bitten."

Slate let go of her. He staggered to the side.

And Odion was there, catching him.

At first, Slate clutched Odion close, but then Slate fought him off. He shoved Odion. He raised both of his hands and let out a high-pitched agonized noise.

"They'll *hear* you," said Odion.

Slate shook his head. He looked at Banyan, and then back at Odion. He let out noisy, labored breaths. "Where?" he said finally. "I don't see a bite anywhere."

"Banyan tried to cover it up because she has this crazy idea—"

"It's not a crazy idea if it works," said Banyan. "There might be a cure, Slate."

"What?" Slate turned to Odion. "Is that true?"

"No," said Odion. "No, it's just... it's wishful thinking. She's—"

"It's not wishful thinking," said Banyan. "The reason we were separated, the reason he was sent to you and away from me was because we kept someone with a bite hidden for observation to see if he turned, and that person got a fever, and he never turned."

"What?" said Slate.

"The fever burned it out of him, see?" said Banyan. "It's slowed down, the Frost sickness, if there's no cold, and it's killed if it's burned. The fever, it's too hot. It kills it. And we don't have much time, because Dove said that if the transformation is complete, it won't work."

"That was all speculation, Banyan," said Odion. "Whatever she said, she couldn't have known."

"Well, we still have to try," said Slate in a hoarse voice.

"Thank you," said Banyan. "Put him on your dragon, would you? Take him out of here now. And Erach and I, we'll try to think of what we can do for Mirra—"

"I'm not leaving Mirra," snapped Odion.

Slate seized the other man behind the neck and pulled him close, so close that their foreheads were touching. "Odion," he breathed. "We have to try. I will force you and don't think I won't."

Odion struggled.

But Slate didn't let go.

And Odion was crying, tears leaking out of his eyes and he went limp, collapsing into Slate's chest.

Slate cradled him. He looked over Odion's head at Banyan. "Where do I take him?"

"Dove's not there," said Banyan. "She's Hazain, though, where would she be during the school break? Where do scholar students go?"

"Sometimes to their families. Do we need her?"

"I…" Banyan didn't know. "She said they keep vials with the sicknesses in them. We have to give him a fever."

"How?" said Slate.

"I don't know," said Banyan. "We need a scholar, I suppose. Maybe someone in the school. We'll just have to force them to help us."

Slate thought about this. "All right. I can do that."

"Good," said Banyan. And then there was a sharp, stinging pain in her shoulder. She reached back and—

An arrow?

Without thinking, she tugged it out.

Blood rushed out.

And as she turned, she could see them coming down the mountain. There were many of them, rows and rows. At least a hundred, maybe more. They were all armed with arrows, and their white hair and white skin gleamed in the moonlight. Overhead, above them, were ten ice dragons, flying in circles overhead.

"Surrender Naxim, and we let you go free," called a man in the front, shaking his bow at them.

"Odion Naxim is part of the Family now," cried another.

"We need him for the purpose!" yelled someone else.

"He's ours. He is our leader, the one who will deliver us from the depths of icy cold into the light of the sun," said a man with colorless dragon scales over one eye. "Surrender Odion Naxim or die."

"Or join us," said someone else.

Banyan couldn't think, couldn't even process this, but of course it made sense. Of course the Frost wanted Odion, because he was brilliant, and of course, the members of the Academy who'd been turned into ice monsters would remember and—

She reached out with the bond, for Erach, sending him images of fire. *The Frost, Erach, isn't this why you bonded me?*

Erach's attention came to her, startled. He'd been so wrapped up in Mirra, he hadn't even noticed the approach of the ice monsters, and this horrified him. He let out a roar, blowing flame into the night sky.

And all ten of the circling ice dragons breathed out their icy breath and doused it.

Odion looked up into the air at the smoke dissipating against the tree branches. He looked at the rows of ice monsters. "Kill me."

"No," said Banyan. She gestured with the arrow that had

struck her, the one that she'd plucked out of her own skin. "No."

Odion snatched it out of her hands and made to stab himself in the eye with it.

Banyan stopped him, tackling him into the ground, taking the arrow from him and hurling it off.

The ice monsters advanced.

Odion shoved her off, his voice gruff. "Banyan, don't be an idiot. They can't die. We'd have to cut off each of their heads. Kill me and they give up."

"Do they give up?" said Slate softly, gazing at the coming white-skinned creatures with dull eyes. "Or do they take Banyan as their consolation prize?"

Odion went still.

"Odion, no," said Banyan. "They haven't even heard of me yet. There's not enough of them turned to remember that I exist."

Odion got to his feet. "They've heard of you."

"Slate," said Banyan.

Odion raised his voice, addressing the approaching ice monsters. "Me? You take me, and you leave them. You leave Banyan?"

"Stop him, Slate," said Banyan.

"We will honor your bargain," said the the scaley-eyed man, holding up his arms to halt the army of ice monsters. "Come to us."

Slate wrapped an arm around Odion's neck.

Odion was too quick. He dropped into a crouch, drove an elbow into Slate's shin, and then, standing, swept Slate's feet out from under him. Slate fell down, sprawling.

Odion stalked away, throwing over his shoulder, "I love you, Slate, but you've never been a match for me in any kind of fight."

Banyan hurled herself after him. "*I'm* a match for you."

Odion turned away and kept walking.

She jumped onto his back. He tossed her off like she was nothing. She collided with a tree trunk, gasping.

"You're always going to be a girl, Banyan," said Odion.

"You're brilliant, but you don't have a lot of upper muscle strength."

She got to her feet and started after him again.

"Yilia!" cried Slate.

But Yilia's fire was doused, just like Erach's had been.

And Odion was among the ice monsters now. The ice monsters closed ranks around Odion and began to retreat.

Banyan got to her feet. She could run after them now, again, but Odion was right. They were vastly outnumbered and they didn't stand a chance against them. She screamed, "Odion, you can't do this for me."

Odion's voice carried back to her, though she couldn't see him. "I know you never wanted to be one of them."

"But... Odion..."

Slate grabbed her, whispering in her ear. "He's going to try to find a way to kill himself, first chance he gets."

She sagged into him. "No."

Slate pulled her close. "We wait until they're out of sight, and then I take Yilia."

She nodded, looking up at him. "Yes," she breathed.

He nodded back.

"Get him back?" she said.

"Definitely," growled Slate.


EXCEPT HE DIDN'T.

He went away after the ice monsters, and the ice dragons disappeared from the sky, and he was gone a long time.

Long enough for Banyan to think it all through seventeen times, and to come up with seventeen different ways she could have ended it all.

She had a dragon who breathed *fire*.

Admittedly, Erach was distraught and preoccupied with Mirra, so he hadn't been paying any attention. But maybe... Maybe they shouldn't have just *given up* when the fire was doused.

They were outnumbered, yes, but they had *fire*. Maybe if she'd started trying to shoot the ice dragons, or if they'd taken the fight to the air. Even if they'd just poured flame into the approaching ranks of ice monsters, that would have been something. If they'd burned at least half of them before they gave up, that would have meant they tried.

But no.

She'd seen Odion bitten, and suddenly, she was *stupid*.

She fell down to the ground in a heap of sobs, and Erach didn't come to her to comfort her. She felt something through the bond, and she thought it might have been resentment.

She wanted to die.

She had failed everyone, and without Odion...

A lot of time passed. Enough time for Mirra to succumb to her bite and begin to twist and scream and then freeze, stock still, and she and Erach huddled together and watched the dragon's pink scales turn colorless and white, as if she were covered in ice.

Banyan didn't understand. Why was Mirra turning so quickly? Did the dragons simply behave differently?

She buried her face in Erach's scales and he breathed out huffs of smoke, and Mirra eventually flew away into the bone-colored sky of dawn.

They could have killed Mirra, of course, but Erach couldn't bear it, and Banyan was in no position to force it.

Only then did Slate return, haggard, his expression hollow. "Couldn't find them," he said. "Yilia and I searched all over. I don't know where they took him."

"Maybe a cavern or underground or something," said Banyan, remembering Deke saying he'd been taken into a cavern. "We'll try again. We won't give up."

"It's too late, Banyan," said Slate, and his voice was full of disdain.

She knew he was right, but she shook her head. "It's not too late."

They went back to the encampment. Turned out half of the riders who'd come back the night before had bites but had been too terrified to know what to do. None of them had turned yet, though some of the dragons had.

Colonel Rabi was nowhere to be found, and Banyan found Corporal Malloway, who gaped at her with a stunned and terrified expression on his face. He was in no shape to take over the forces, and he seemed to be the highest ranked member of the army she could find.

She and Slate took charge in a sort of interim manner. They made everyone go back to the school, and Banyan went out in Hazain and asked questions about Dove. It turned out Dove lived in the village nearby the Academy, and she wasn't too hard to find. Dove was happy enough to come back to the school.

All of the riders with bites were sequestered in one room, and Banyan insisted Dove be in charge of their treatment, and they were all given the fever.

There were twenty of them.

Thirteen survived.

Seven turned.

The difference turned out to be the poison arrows. Some of them had been shot with them, and the poison had killed them.

"That's the turn," said Dove. "It's death. They can't live in the ice, after all, Banyan. They're dead. They're frozen."

"But they're not dead," Banyan raged, even as she looked at the seven heads with their white hair and their colorless eyes and their pasty skin. They'd all been beheaded after the turn. Too dangerous.

"They're dead, and the Frost is the only thing animating their brains and their nervous systems," said Dove. "That's why they only die when you get their brains."

"But that doesn't make sense!" Odion. The arrow. The one he'd used to kill the ice monster, where had he gotten that arrow and wasn't it one of the poison arrows and —?

It didn't matter.

It was the turn.

The *turn* was death.

Deke had explained it. He'd talked about the pain, being

unable to move, everything agonizing even as he was frozen stiff. He'd died and frozen and come back. Odion had certainly turned by now.

The fever, it wouldn't cure him.

He was gone.

She didn't want to believe it.


THE QUORUM WAS made up of ten people, two of which had been General Frax and Colonel Rabi. That should have left eight, but the night of the attacks, the Frost had come down in droves, invading their towers, invading villages. The broken windows and the attacks on the general and the colonel had not been isolated.

Four members of the Quorum lived.

They convened and decided to suspend any punishment for Banyan and Slate until after the war was over. They said that she needed to win it for them if she didn't want to be hanged for war crimes.

"You know how many deaths are on your head," said General Wilt. He hadn't been a general before, but he'd been promoted. Banyan wasn't sure by whom. Maybe by himself. Wilt was younger than Rabi had been. He was half-Hazain, half-Aleenan. His skin was brown, but his hair was not purple. It was bright, bright blue. His ears pointed like an Aleenan too. "You know what you've done, and your penance must be to serve the Quorum and serve the Trinal Kingdoms."

Banyan bowed her head and agreed.

"We'll be working closely together, then," said the general. "We've long thought the final battle would be fought at the South Ridge Academy. Now, it seems it will be our one remaining stronghold. We will call back all the students, and you will lead them, Colonel Thriceborn."

Colonel? She was currently a major. He'd just skipped her up two rankings.

Some things didn't change, like being promoted and feeling like it was really punishment.

"I'll be running the school in Colonel Rabi's place," said the general.

Perfect.

"The minute your dragon goes into heat, Colonel Nightwing," said the general, "I expect you two to be a mated pair."

Slate stiffened next to her. They weren't... they hadn't...

Not so much as kissed.

Maybe it had always been about Odion, in the end. Both of them had wanted *Odion*.

"Yes, sir," said Slate.

"Yes, sir," she said.

"You were mated before, were you not? You do share a bed currently?" The general glared at them.

"We will do as the Quorum demands," said Slate.

"We serve the Trinal Kingdoms," said Banyan.

Well. At least they had the same rank now. That put them on equal footing.

# CHAPTER TWENTY-EIGHT

ODION MOVED THROUGH the hallways quietly.

*Looks smaller,* he thought. He hadn't been away from the school for that long, he didn't think. It had hardly been a month. But everything was different now.

He stopped in office of the dorm mammi. No one was there. He was glad. He didn't want to talk to anyone else. He looked at the ledger there. Ah, that was their room. Too bad. They didn't have one with a bath anymore. He'd give them his sympathies, he supposed.

Maybe he could even use it to help convince them. It wasn't much, but it was something to start with.

*They haven't even given you a bath.* He smirked. Well, the Quorum had never treated any of them well, though. That was the funny thing. He'd been devoted to the Quorum, too. But he hadn't understood devotion before being welcomed into the Family. He hadn't understood purpose or drive or anything else.

He wanted to share it with them, that was the truth of it. The bite. It was the best thing that had ever happened to him.

He barely got into the room before Banyan had him pinned to the door, sword to his neck. Slate climbed out of bed more slowly. He stood behind Banyan and gaped at him.

"Banyan," said Odion. "Can you not with that?"

"Are you going to bite me?" she said, her voice breaking.

"I swear, I won't," said Odion. "Not until you ask me to."

She scoffed. "As if I'd do that."

"I have to try, princess," he said.

She jammed the tip of the sword into his neck. "Don't call me that."

Slate stepped forward and seized her arm, tugging her backwards. He swallowed hard, the knob in his throat bobbing visibly. "Banyan. It's *him*."

"I told you this," she said to Slate, sword tip dragging against the floor. "I told you it's not like we thought before. They're still themselves."

Slate stared at him. "It's you."

Odion smiled at him. "It's me. How are you, Slate? Miss me?"

Slate's face twitched.

Odion wanted to touch him. He wanted to touch them both. They were so warm and alive, and he felt something surge in him that surprised him. It wasn't the purpose, and he wasn't sure he wanted to turn them.

This, his new existence, it was cold all the time.

He swallowed, furrowing his now-colorless brow, and looked down at his shoes.

"Come with me," said Banyan. "We'll hide you, and Dove can try. I know it didn't work before, not on the other ones that had turned all the way, who had… *died*, but maybe, with you, maybe…" Tears started to stream down her face. Her voice was thick. "You've always been special, Odion."

"Try…?" He met her gaze. "Try what?"

"To cure you," said Banyan.

"Ah." He chuckled softly. He glanced at Slate. "I won't be able to get in this easily next time, I don't think. You'll have thought it all through, shored up all the little spots that the students would have known about. This will change everything. I suppose I knew that when I came. I knew you wouldn't come with me, either of you. But I had to try. I had to ask." He looked first at Slate and then at Banyan. "Join me. Together, we can conquer all the Trinal Kingdoms and turn everyone. And it's not like you think it is. I'm not dead. I'm very much alive."

"The *Frost* is alive," said Banyan. "The Frost is animating your body."

"It's not like that," he said. "It's not like what we thought. It's nice."

"That's what Deke said," she said with a little shrug. "And I killed him anyway. But I can't kill you, Odion, I *can't*."

Odion reached out and took her hand. "Banyan. Please?"

She snatched her hand away and wiped at the tears which were still flowing down her cheeks.

Odion reached for Slate.

Slate backed away, wary.

"I sort of knew it would go this way." Odion folded his arms over his chest. "I could have just sneaked in here and bitten you both." Why hadn't he done that? This was now his game, in so many ways. He was the great and celebrated Odion Naxim and every member of the Family had ceded to his brilliance immediately. Yes, he must lead them all. Yes, he would take charge of the war. Yes, he would command them as they spread.

*If I wanted to fulfill the purpose, I'd have bitten them already.*

"You wouldn't have managed it," said Slate tightly.

"No," said Banyan.

"Maybe I want this," he said, stepping closer to Banyan, raising his eyebrows. "Maybe you want it, too. Deep down, you and me? We were made for this."

"What are you talking about?" She was still crying.

"This is what we've been preparing for all this time, love." He reached out and cupped her face with one hand. "A war, and isn't war better against a worthy opponent?"

She jerked back. "You're leading the Frost now."

He gave her a little bow. "Everything is a battle."

"And I always win," she said, her voice hard.

"Well, we'll see about that."

"I've always been better than you," she said, baring her teeth at him. "We both know that."

"Do we know that?" said Odion. He tilted back his chin. "Tell me you're not just a little bit excited at the chance to find out."

Banyan swallowed. She didn't answer.

Slate let out a low, harsh laugh. "*This* is you two? This?"

Banyan glanced at him. "Help me. We'll get him to Dove—"

"There's no cure at this stage, Banyan," said Slate.

"We can't kill him," she said. "We both love him."

"*I* love him," said Slate. "You…" He glared at Odion. "You two, I don't know what you have, but whatever it is, whatever twisted little game of war and sex you two are playing…"

He didn't finish.

The words just trailed off into the darkness of the wee hours of the morning, and they all gazed at each other.

Odion stepped closer to Slate, who held his ground, nostrils flaring. Odion touched the other man's jaw, a feathery caress. "I love you, too. For finding my vulnerability and exposing it. For making it pleasure. For owning me."

"I don't own—"

"And I love Banyan," interrupted Odion. "For challenging me. For rooting out all of my areas of excellence, even the brutal ones. For sharpening me, like a whetstone. For letting me do it to her, too." He turned to look at her. "We've never been good for each other, princess, not exactly, but we've been what the other craves, and we both know it."

"I should kill you." Her voice shook.

"You won't." He kissed her.

She shoved him off.

He tried to kiss Slate, but Slate put a hand in the middle of his chest and pushed, his face twisting.

"Let the games begin, then," he said.

"It's not a game, though," said Banyan. "Not anymore."

"Let the *war* begin," said Odion.

Slate's voice was strangled. "You came here to taunt us?"

Banyan just glared at him.

"Or is this the way you two flirt?" said Slate.

Odion opened the door. "When you're ready for my bite, when you're ready to surrender, you just let me know. I *am* going to win. The Family will win. There are more of us, and we don't have nearly as many weaknesses as you, and we're, well, *better* than you humans. Morally. Strategically. In every way." But he couldn't deny something about their warmth was tantalizing. The feel of his lips against their skin, the way it heated him...

He threw himself out into the hallway and retreated.

He worried someone would come after him on the way out of the building, but no one did.

So, it was just the colonel waiting for him on the back of one of the ice dragons. Odion waved up at him.

"You're back alone," said the colonel.

"But I *am* back," said Odion, climbing onto Mirra's back. The bond was gone, now, of course, but in a way, they were all bonded in the Family. "I told you she wouldn't kill me."

"I told you she wouldn't come with you," said the colonel. "You had the chance to end it all, just now, but you didn't."

Odion just laughed.

"Sometimes I wonder what it is I turned you into, Odion," said the colonel.

"Sometimes, Colonel Rabi," said Odion, "I think you take far too much credit for accomplishing anything at all."

The colonel only laughed.

The two flew off towards the ice-tipped mountains.

Odion had been built for war, trained for it since he was a small boy. If it was war the Quorum wanted, Odion would give it to them.